RUGGED COWBOY

HOPE ETERNAL RANCH ROMANCE, BOOK 3

ELANA JOHNSON

CHAPTER ONE

Dallas Dreyer breathed a silent sigh of relief as he saw the city limits sign for Sweet Water Falls. He'd been driving for hours, and he was so ready to be out of the car.

At the same time, the temperature gauge on the dashboard told him not to get out of the car unless he wanted to be instantly incinerated. How Nate could get married in weather like this, Dallas didn't understand.

Why Nate wanted to get married at all eluded Dallas. Bitterness gathered on the back of his tongue, and it was new and hard to deal with.

He'd had no idea Martha was so unsure about their marriage. She'd been coming to River Bay for over two years—every week—and she'd brought the kids many times.

Her departure from their life had surprised him. Shocked him, actually. Rendered him speechless.

He could clearly remember when he'd gotten the news, and that he'd sat on the bottom bunk where he'd been sleeping for twenty-seven months and just stared.

Even when Slate had come to tell him it was time for dinner. Even when Luke had gotten him a special pass for an extra hour in the library without anyone there, Dallas had just stared at it.

He didn't know what life would be like on the outside as it was. And without Martha? Dallas didn't know how to function.

She'd been in Louisiana for the past three months, and her sister had been taking care of his two children. Martha had left them behind too, and Dallas honestly didn't comprehend her behavior.

He'd been released five days ago, and Amy had been kind enough to come pick him up. She'd brought Thomas and Remmy with her, and Dallas had held his children tightly for several minutes right on the sidewalk outside the River Bay Federal Correctional Facility.

He glanced to Remmy, his six-year-old asleep in the backseat of the used sedan his brother-in-law had helped him purchase.

Dallas had money from before his time in prison, but not a whole lot. Enough to buy new clothes and this car and food and gas for the trip to Sweet Water Falls.

He'd stayed with Amy and Brent for a couple days to

get the essentials in order, and then he'd set his app to direct him to Hope Eternal Ranch.

He would not miss Nate's wedding. The man had done more for Dallas than anyone else on Earth—save Martha. But now that she was gone, Dallas's only fall-back was Nathaniel Mulbury.

Ted Burrows was at the ranch too, and Dallas couldn't wait to see his friends. The pull to them was all he had left, and he'd embraced it. After they'd come for Family Weekend and treated him exactly like one of their brothers...Dallas got choked up just thinking about it.

"Turn right in a quarter mile," said the cool female voice of his navigation app. Dallas started to slow down, and his son lifted his head from his game machine.

"Almost there, bud," Dallas said, surprised at how chipper his voice came out.

Thomas nodded and powered down the game. Dallas felt like he didn't know his ten-year-old. He'd missed all of his eighth and ninth year on the planet, and though Dallas had seen his son start to grow in his permanent front teeth and he'd gotten emails with attachments of the boy's art, it was completely different than being with the child day in and day out.

Dallas had never considered the fact that he might be a single parent one day. Martha had been the perfect surgeon's wife, and she'd charmed hospital administrators, kept the house tidy and the bills paid, and the children in appropriate, wholesome activities. Dallas had loved coming home to her and the kids, and until the lawsuit that had diverted his life onto another path, he'd been blissfully unaware of any of the things he was currently dealing with.

He made the right turn, and the road started to wind out of town. Dallas glanced at his new phone, the weight of it heavy in his mind. He'd used smart phones before of course; he'd only been in prison for thirty months. But he'd gotten used to short, clipped calls, only at appropriate times. To make a call whenever he wanted, for however long he wanted was a bit novel to him.

"Just a couple more miles," he said more to reassure himself than Thomas.

And just a couple more miles and a few more minutes down the road, Dallas made the right turn onto the road that had Hope Eternal Ranch at the end of it.

The road turned from asphalt to dirt, and the sedan bumped over the new surface. He crossed a bridge, passed the trees, and the ranch spread in front of him.

A massive house sat just beyond a small patch of grass, which had a fence separating it from a large gravel pad, where Dallas pulled to a stop.

He peered out of the windshield, taking in the house that was really two houses—one on each side of a three-car garage. Nate and Ted had told him all about it, and Dallas could see the appeal of it.

And then Ted was walking toward him, a giant smile

on his bearded face. Dallas started laughing and said, "Come on, guys. Let's get out."

He got out of the car and met Ted at the opening of the fence. The other man had four inches on Dallas, and at least fifty pounds. He really was like a big teddy bear, and Dallas clapped him heartily on the back as they embraced.

"Look at you," Ted said, and that was all. Dallas didn't need more; he knew what Ted meant.

Look at him outside the fences of River Bay. Look at him in regular clothes. Look at him, a single dad to two kids.

Those kids came up beside him, Remmy clutching her blanket, though it was far too hot to cart that around for long, and rubbing her eyes.

"Guys," he said. "This is Ted Burrows. Do you remember him?"

"Yes," Thomas said at the same time Remmy said, "No," and shrank into Dallas's side.

He put his palm on her back and gave her a quick squeeze.

"He's one of my best friends," Dallas said. "Ted, these are my kids, Thomas and Remmy."

Ted crouched down, his smile bright and genuine. "Hey, guys. I've got something for you in the West Wing. It involves chocolate. You want to come see what it is?"

Remmy edged away from Dallas, and Ted straightened as he took her hand. Thomas looked up at Dallas, and he nodded. "I'm coming in too."

Thomas went ahead of him, and Ted chatted with Remmy about her blanket and the character on her T-shirt.

"Oh, our clothes." Dallas turned back to the car to get the small suitcase he'd brought with their dress clothes for the wedding. "I'll catch up. I'm grabbing our clothes."

He retrieved the bag and turned to follow Ted, but they'd disappeared. A flash of panic hit Dallas, and he worked to tamp it back. He hadn't been alone for so long, and he didn't like the feeling of not knowing exactly where to go.

The panic itself was new, and Dallas loathed it. He'd never had a confidence problem or been plagued with anxiety or other mental illnesses. But his incarceration had changed a lot more than the status of his marriage and the age of his children.

He walked down the driveway toward the wide garages, and Nate came out of a doorway, clearly looking for Dallas.

Relief rushed through him, and to his great surprise, tears pricked his eyes. "Nate," he said, and Nate's face burst into a grin.

"You made it." He came down the few steps and engulfed Dallas in a hug. They embraced for several long moments, neither of them saying anything.

"Come on in," Nate finally said, falling back. "There's food, and you can change."

"The big day," Dallas said.

"Yeah, in a couple of hours," Nate said, ducking his head so the big, black cowboy hat he wore hid his face.

Dallas studied his friend—the man who'd literally saved his life on the inside. There was something so different about him, and yet so familiar.

"I like the hat," he said, and Nate glanced up. He reached up and touched the cowboy hat as if he didn't even know he was wearing it.

"It's useful," Nate said.

"And you like it," Dallas said, because he may not have seen Nate for a while, but he knew the man didn't do anything he didn't like for very long. At least not by choice. Now that they were out, they could all choose.

"I like it," Nate admitted. "Come meet Ginger." He led the way up the steps and into the house, which had blessedly cool air conditioning.

Dallas immediately looked around for his children, and he didn't have to look far. They sat at the bar with two other kids, one of whom Dallas recognized. Connor, Nate's son. The other was a dark-haired girl who looked to be close to Thomas's age, and he assumed that was Ted's fiancée's daughter.

Dallas couldn't remember her name, though, and he paused as he took in the enormity of the kitchen.

An auburn-haired woman turned toward them, a

warm smile on her face. She came over to Nate, and he took her hand in his. "Ginger, this is Dallas Dreyer."

"One of your boys," she said, extending her hand toward Dallas.

"I'm actually the same age as Nate," Dallas said. "But it's so nice to meet you." And he was one of Nate's boys. Nate had created a family inside River Bay, and Dallas had been lucky to be included in it.

He smiled, which was also not his default for the past couple of years. But the gesture sat nicely on his face, and he watched his kids as they stuck chocolate kisses into cookie dough.

It felt like such a normal thing to do. A normal place to be. He liked the energy in the house, and he needed somewhere like this to settle down.

He wasn't sure where he'd go after the wedding. He had the house in the suburbs of Houston, but he wasn't sure he could just go back there.

The man he'd been the last time he'd left that house didn't exist anymore. He didn't want to interact with any of those neighbors. He didn't want to go into the bedroom he'd once shared with Martha.

So he'd sell that house and find somewhere else to build a life. He'd lost his medical license, so he couldn't go back to that career.

He wanted to be a mechanic, open his own shop, and take care of his kids.

He let Nate sweep him into the kitchen for a sandwich, where he met Ted's significant other, Emma Clemson.

The girl was definitely her daughter, as they looked so much alike, and Emma introduced the girl as Missy.

Dallas met a couple of other women and cowboys, and then everyone started talking about getting ready for the wedding.

"You can use this bedroom," Ginger said, taking him down a hall to a room with a queen bed in it. "Ted said he'd come get you guys when he goes out to the tents."

"Thanks," Dallas said, herding his kids into the room with him. The door closed behind him, and he just wanted to lie down for a bit. Close his eyes and just see if the world was the same when he woke up.

Instead, he hefted the suitcase onto the bed and opened it. "All right, Tommy," he said. "Here's your suit."

"It's way too hot to wear a suit," his son complained.

"Yes, it is," Dallas agreed. "But Nate said they have misters and fans out in the tents, so it'll be okay." He had to believe that, because if he didn't, he wouldn't be able to get himself to leave the house.

The West Wing, he told himself. Apparently, all of the women lived in the house on this side, and all of the cowboys lived in what Nate had called the Annex, the house on the other side of the garages.

After they returned from their honeymoon, Nate and Ginger were going to move into a cabin in the corner of the yard, which was apparently next door to where Emma lived with her daughter.

Dallas found that odd. Ginger owned this house and this ranch. Seemed to him that the other women living in the West Wing should have to find somewhere else to live so she and Nate could live here. But he hadn't said anything. He didn't know the situation, and if prison had taught him one thing, it had taught him to reserve judgment on things he knew nothing about.

He pulled Remmy's dress out of the suitcase and told her to get changed. He then stepped out of his khaki shorts and T-shirt and started buttoning himself into the suit he'd bought off the rack at a cheap department store.

He couldn't remember the last time he'd worn something off the rack, and it was simply another testament of how different his life was now.

With everyone changed, Dallas told Thomas to go brush his teeth, and he pulled a hair bag out of the suitcase. Amy had put it together for him, and it had a brush, two combs, a bunch of hair ties and bows, and a spray bottle so Dallas could do his daughter's hair.

He'd done it twice now, and he still felt like Edward Scissorhands when he touched his daughter's fine hair to try to make it into something beautiful.

"Ponytail?" he asked her. "That'll keep your hair off your neck, and you'll be cooler."

"Can you do two ponies?" she asked.

"Pigtails, sure," he said, because he'd done those

yesterday. Well, he'd done half of the hairdo. Amy had demonstrated how to do the first one, and he'd attempted to copy her on the second one. He'd only had to try twice before he got it tight enough.

Today, he sprayed and parted her hair, then began smoothing the hair on half of her head into a pigtail that sat just above her ear. The right side was easier than the left, and he secured that one on the first try.

The other side took a couple of tries, but he eventually persevered, and he grinned at Remmy. "All ready."

"Thanks, Daddy." She threw her arms around his neck, and Dallas's heart swelled to three times its normal size.

"Love you, bug," he said, calling on the familiar nickname from years ago.

"Love you too, Daddy."

He was so grateful she did, and he hoped she wouldn't have too many memories of his absence in her life. He adored her high-pitched, Texas-twang voice, and he threaded his fingers through hers.

"Let's go wait for Ted out in the kitchen."

Thomas was out there, wiping down the counter, and Dallas paused to look at him. When had he become responsible enough to clean up without being asked? Dallas barely did that.

"Thanks for doing that," Dallas said, not sure how to relate to his son.

"There's a bunch of chocolate on the floor right there,"

he said, and Dallas went to the sink and got another washrag. He wetted it down and moved over to the floor where sure enough, chocolate had been tracked toward the door he'd entered from the garage.

He didn't want to kneel down in his suit, so he bent over and started scrubbing the dried chocolate. After several minutes and several trips to the sink to rewet the washcloth, he got the floor clean.

"There."

He stood up and looked at his hard work, a sense of pride moving through him. He'd felt like this after stitching up the arteries leading to a heart too, and after getting all the parts in the exact right spot to rebuild a motorcycle engine.

"I'm so late," a woman said, and Dallas turned toward a tall, dark-haired woman he hadn't seen in the brief time he'd eaten a sandwich earlier. "Excuse me."

She ran toward him, her cowgirl boots making loud, slapping noises on the floor. He backed up, an alarm sounding in his head.

"The floor is—"

She yelped as she slipped, and time slowed into terrible bursts of motion. The woman flailed her arms.

"Wet," Dallas finished.

He reached for her.

She grabbed onto his forearm.

But she was going down.

He blinked, and he was bending over, her hand still gripping his arm in a painful way.

She groaned, her eyes staring straight up as she was now flat on her back on the floor.

"I'm so sorry," he said. "Are you okay?"

She blinked a couple of times, and a brand-new fire entered those dark eyes. Dallas felt sure he was about to be burned, and he actually found himself welcoming it.

CHAPTER TWO

Pain radiated through Jessica Morales's body, and while she wanted to get up, she couldn't. She was used to going and going and going, and she was strong.

But her back was in control at the moment, and she was not moving.

Anger flowed through her like river rapids, and she stared into the light gray eyes of a man she'd never seen before. "What were you doing?" she demanded.

"There was chocolate on the floor," he said, kneeling beside her. "Can you sit up?"

"I think so." She groaned again, wishing she wasn't in the presence of a handsome man with such a noise coming out of her mouth. Her back spasmed, and she stilled.

"I don't have time for this," she said. "I have to get out to the stables and get the horses ready."

"I'll help you," he said, putting his hand on the back of her elbow.

"Who are you?" she asked.

"Dallas Dreyer," he said. "I'm a friend of Nate's."

"If I don't get those horses ready, the wedding will be ruined." Another flash of impatience hit her. "Help me up. You'll have to come help me. Do you know anything about horses?"

"Not really," he said, practically lifting her off her feet.

"Great," she muttered. She took in his appearance, and he wore a cheap suit. At least it was clean. His hair was cut short and spiked in the front, and if he stayed outside for longer than twenty minutes without a hat, he'd be fried under this intense sun.

She didn't care. Or maybe she did.

Jess wasn't entirely sure what was running through her body. Attraction? Could that be true?

"Dad?"

"Let's go," Dallas said. "You'll have to lead us to the stables though." He looked at Jess. "We don't know where they are."

A boy that stood to his shoulder came to his side, as well as a little girl. Jess hadn't even seen them in her haste to get out to the stables.

These were brand new cowgirl boots that she'd bought specifically for the wedding, and they had no traction on the bottom. A wet floor had taken her down, and humiliation started to rise from the soles of her feet.

She left the West Wing, already too hot so that when she took in a lung full of the September air, she almost passed out from heat exhaustion.

"What's your name?" Dallas asked, and Jess realized all of her good sense had fled the moment she'd slipped on the floor. Maybe she'd hit her head too hard. As if on cue, the back of her skull sent a dull ache toward the front.

"Oh, uh, Jessica," she said. "Morales."

"These are my kids," he said. "Thomas and Remmy."

"Daddy, I can't keep up," the little girl said, and Dallas slowed down.

Jess did not. She really had to get Marshmallow Crème and Texas Tyrant saddled and decorated for the wedding. Nate and Ginger weren't doing anything very traditionally, including the casual lunch they'd had *before* the wedding, and they were riding horses down the aisle instead of having Ginger's father walk her toward a waiting Nate.

Jess had done horseback weddings before, and she knew how to braid manes and tails, weave in flowers, and balance crowns on the horse's heads to make them a beautiful addition to the ceremony.

She'd gone to town to get the flowers, and she'd missed most of the lunch. Thankfully, the flowers waited for her in a cooler in the stables, and she just needed to get there.

She'd bathed Marshmallow and Tyrant that morning, and they still waited in the wash bay.

"Hey," she said to them, always better able to relate to horses than people. Her disastrous relationship with Spencer proved that. And the brief relationship she'd tried with a man named Preston before that. And the boyfriend she'd had before that? They'd only dated for a week before everything fell apart.

Jess frowned at the track her mind took. She'd never dwelt much on the barren wasteland that was her love life. She didn't like acknowledging and facing her failures, and the fact was, she'd failed with every man she'd ever tried to get close to.

"I think there's something broken inside me," she whispered to the cream-colored horse. Marshmallow Crème had beautiful, long lashes and a supremely calm demeanor. Jess had loved her from birth, and she'd raised her the past three years for just this moment when she would carry Ginger down the aisle toward her happily-ever-after.

"All right," Dallas said, stepping to her side. "Tell us what to do."

Annoyance sang through Jess, but she had barked at him to help her. "If you'll grab that cooler, I'll start braiding." She looked at him, which bordered on dangerous. He was extremely good-looking, and though Jess had just bowed out of a relationship with Spencer a couple of weeks ago, she wondered if she could ask Dallas to dinner.

He has two kids, she reminded herself as she turned

Marshmallow around. Not that she didn't want children. But she barely knew how to take care of herself, and she'd never had a relationship for longer than two months. So the thought of getting to know Dallas and two children was so far outside of her realm of reality.

She tethered Marshmallow and moved back to her tail.

"What are you going to do?" Remmy asked, and Jess smiled down at the little girl.

"I'm going to braid her tail," she said, starting to part the hair. "And we're going to weave in ribbons and flowers. She's going to carry the bride for the wedding."

It was all so romantic, and Jess longed for a horseback wedding of her own. She'd have to figure out how to have a boyfriend for longer than a couple of months, though.

So it was probably hopeless to even think about something like riding a horse toward her anxious groom.

She focused on her work and asked Remmy for the flowers when she needed them. Dallas fed them to his daughter, and she didn't go more than a few feet from Jess's side.

Jess eventually relaxed, and she'd dressed both horses in record time with the help of Dallas and his kids.

"All right." She reached up and wiped the back of her hand across her forehead. "It's hot."

Something was definitely wrong in the stables, and Jess had just realized it. "The air conditioning isn't working."

"You air condition the stables?" Dallas asked.

"Yes," Jess said. "They're temperature controlled, because it can get so hot here." She sighed and turned around. "I need to check it."

"I'm really handy with machines," Dallas said. "I'll come with you." He started to say something to his children, and Jess took a few steps away to wait for him.

"They're going to wait here," Dallas said. "Lead on."

Jess took him down the aisle to a locked door and fitted her key into it. "This is the control room." The door swung open, and a burnt, mechanical smell met her nose immediately.

"Oh, something's burned up," he said, stepping past her. He went straight to the air conditioner and started fiddling with the front panel. A moment later, it came off, and Dallas coughed.

"Do you have any tools?"

"There's a toolbox on the shelf there," she said, pointing.

Dallas followed her finger and found it, pulling it down with authority. He came alive as he rooted through the box and emerged with a wrench.

Jess sure did like watching him, as he had a lot of confidence now when he hadn't before. He moved with precision, and only five minutes and a couple of grunts later, he swung the whole front of the air conditioner open.

"Yep, you've got a belt here that's come off and burned

up." He looked at her. "I don't suppose you have spare belts?"

"I have no idea," Jess said.

"Do you have a ranch mechanic?" he asked. "Maybe someone we can call?"

"No," Jess said, though Ginger had talked about hiring someone to maintain their equipment. "I'll call Ginger."

She really didn't want to, but Ginger loved the horses as if they were her own offspring. She wouldn't be happy they didn't have the temperature controls they were used to.

"I'll look on the shelves," Dallas said, and Jess took a few steps away to make the call.

"What's wrong?" Ginger asked when she picked up Jess's call.

"How do you know something's wrong?"

"You said you'd see me with the horses unless there was a problem." In the background, Jess heard Ginger's sisters bickering about something to do with Ginger's hair.

"The air conditioner in the stables burnt out a belt," she said. "Dallas has it open and he can fix it, if we have another belt."

"Dallas?"

"Yeah." Jess continued to walk down the aisle, but she lowered her voice anyway. "He seems to know exactly what he's doing with it." He'd been a natural with a wrench in his hand, and Jess wished she didn't find that quite so attractive.

"I know Nick bought spare parts," Ginger said. "I'd look on the shelf."

"He's doing that," Jess said.

"He's really mechanical?"

"Seems to be," Jess said, shrugging though her friend couldn't see her.

"Are we still on schedule?"

"The horses are ready," Jess confirmed. "I've got ten minutes, right?"

"If I don't kill Sierra," Ginger whispered, probably because her sister was hovering and wanting to change something Ginger didn't want changed. "The sooner, the better."

Jess laughed and said, "I'll do my best." She turned back toward the mechanical room just as Dallas poked his head out of the doorway.

"Got it," he said. "You want to see?"

"You found a belt?"

"Yep," he said. "And fixed it." He wiped his hands on a towel that was probably dirtier than his skin.

"And fixed it?" Jess didn't believe that, but as she walked into the room, the air conditioner kicked on with a resounding click.

She met Dallas's eyes, and with that smile on his face, a charge filled the air surrounding them that left Jess's bones vibrating and desire filling her.

"Thank you," she said. "Will you please help me get the horses over to Nate and Ginger?"

"You bet," Dallas said, and they went to retrieve Marshmallow Crème, Texas Tyrant, and his kids.

Ten minutes later, Jess delivered the horses to the preparation tent, and helped Ginger into the saddle. She went around Marshmallow and pulled out the train so it lay exactly right.

Nate sat in the saddle by then, and he looked tall and regal and absolutely amazing in his tuxedo and deep black cowboy hat.

Jess's emotions clogged her throat again, and she nodded to Ginger. "Give us two minutes to find a seat, and then you're set."

"Thank you, Jess," Ginger said, smiling. She seemed softer today, and Jess was glad. Ginger had so much to be in charge of around the ranch, twenty-four-seven. She had to wear the stern expression and ask the hard questions.

But not today.

Jess hurried into the main tent, where thankfully, the misters and fans had the temperature at a tolerable level. Hannah and Michelle had saved her a seat in the front row, and she heard Dallas's footsteps behind her as Ted had saved him and his kids seats there too.

So she sat down next to Hannah with a whispered, "She's beautiful," and her skin tingled as Dallas sat right beside her and drew his daughter onto his knee.

She glanced at him, that electricity between them still crackling. She wondered if he could feel it too. Spencer had, and they'd tried going out several times. He'd even tried to kiss her—and it hadn't been horrible.

It just hadn't been memorable. By then, the snap, crackle, and pop between them had fled.

Jess had no reason to think this attraction between her and Dallas would last longer than it took for Ginger and Nate to say, "I do," so she faced the front, determined not to make a fool of herself again.

CHAPTER THREE

Dallas wasn't sure why his heart was bumping quite so violently in his chest. Maybe it was because the last half an hour had been a lesson in how to rush through things to be on time. Maybe it was because he'd picked up a wrench and done something useful for someone else for the first time in a long time.

He got to work on cars in River Bay, but he didn't know who they belonged to. His time in the mechanic bay was limited, mostly to when he taught his weekly classes to other inmates.

Maybe it was the magnificent sight of Nate atop a gorgeous, gray horse, his hand clasped in Ginger's as her creamy white horse pranced perfectly beside the gray one.

The crowd stood and Dallas slipped Remmy into his arms as he joined everyone on his feet. His legs ached, and his back twinged with pain, reminding him of his first major interaction with Nathaniel Mulbury.

He'd saved him from a gang fight. Broken it right up as if Nate wore the badge of the warden. Dallas hadn't seen anything like it, but the other men—even the rougher ones —respected Nate. So when his face had hovered above Dallas's and asked, *Are you going to lay there all night?* Dallas immediately wanted to get to his feet.

He hadn't been able to, and Nate leaned closer, his mouth hardly moving as he whispered. *Don't let them see you like this. I'll help you stand up.* He'd put his hand out, and Dallas had used the man's strength to help him do everything after that.

Stand. Walk inside. Get cleaned up. Get his bunk and trunk set up. All of it. He hadn't left Nate and Ted's shadow for longer than it took to shower and use the bathroom for the first three months of his prison term.

After that, the leader of the gang who'd beaten him got released, and everything in Dallas's life had improved. Apparently, the guy's sister had been impacted in the medical malpractice suit that had ultimately landed Dallas at River Bay.

He'd been married, with a family. Some men lost all of that when they went to prison, and Dallas had counted himself as one of the lucky ones whose wife stuck to his side, brought the kids to see him, and held everything together while she kept her head high.

In the end, though, he had lost everything the day

Martha had filed for divorce, dropped the children at her sister's, and fled Texas.

Nate and Ginger arrived at the altar, which had seemed so big to Dallas when he'd first sat down. But now, it made sense. The pastor climbed a few steps and stood at their level, his face smiling and beaming first at them, and then out at the crowd.

Even Texas couldn't ruin this wedding with her wickedly hot temperatures, still breezes, or buzzing insects. Inside the tent, the fans and misters had managed to keep things relatively cool, and Dallas glanced at Jess as everyone started settling back into their seats.

Maybe his pulse had started to skip because of her. He frowned at himself and faced the altar again. He felt the weight of Jess's eyes on the side of his face, but he refused to look at her.

He wasn't anywhere near ready to start another relationship, he knew that. He'd spoken to Martha every day since his release. Always in private. Always for only a few minutes, because she didn't seem able to do more than that.

Guilt gutted him as the pastor started speaking, and if Dallas were being honest, he never wanted to get married again. He simply wanted to find somewhere for him and his children to build a home and a life together.

Beside him, Jess texted, her fingers flying across her screen. Annoyance sang through Dallas, and he supposed he'd learned a few good things behind the fences and walls of the federal correctional facility where he'd lived. Number one was that he knew he didn't have to respond immediately to every message or text. Inside River Bay, such a thing was impossible, and Dallas found he really liked being unplugged from his phone, his laptop, his tablet, and the Internet.

He'd found himself slipping back into the same obsessive need to answer a text the moment he got it—the way Jess was.

He adjusted Remmy on his lap and glanced at his son, who sat on his left side. Thomas looked utterly bored, but he hadn't pulled out anything to entertain him. Dallas needed to tell him more about Nate, because the man was so exceptional on so many levels.

Looking back up to the altar, he listened as Ginger recited her vows to Nate, her auburn hair almost braided in the same way as the horse she rode. Dallas could only see Nate's profile, and he wished he could see his whole face.

"I promise to love you forever," Ginger said. "I don't have much else to offer you, but the day you came to this ranch changed everything for me." She smiled at him, and Dallas thought he caught a glimpse of what heaven must be like. Shining, angelic faces, with joy streaming around a person. Not necessarily from them, but almost like her happiness and love for Nate was a bubble where only she could exist, and she was trying to make sure everyone knew how she felt about him.

"I can't wait to be your wife and build our life together." She looked back at the pastor, and he turned slightly to Nate.

"Nathaniel has also prepared his own vows for Ginger."

Nate's horse shifted slightly, but Nate barely moved. He started speaking in the slow, deep, rich voice Dallas had heard him use in prison, though he did carry more of a cowboy lilt now than he had in the dormitory.

Dallas smiled, though the words sort of flowed in and around his ears. He could feel the love Nate had for Ginger, and Dallas wondered if he'd ever be able to feel like that about a woman again.

When he pictured the love of his life, she had dark blonde hair, dark blue eyes, and the name Martha.

At the same time, his eyes flitted back over to Jess—a brunette with only dark features and smattering of freckles across both cheeks. She was still texting.

"Can you stop that?" he hissed out of the corner of his mouth. "It's really distracting." And his best friend was saying his vows, for crying out loud.

Jess looked up at him, shock in her eyes. They glinted dangerously in the next moment, but she turned her phone over and laid it in her lap. They looked back up to the altar simultaneously, just in time for the pastor to say, "I now pronounce you man and wife."

Nate leaned over so far, Dallas thought he'd surely slip

from the saddle. He didn't, though, and as they kissed, Ted led the charge by yelling, "Aye, yai, yai!"

Dallas joined his voice to the cheering, and Remmy clapped her hands over her ears and said, "Daddy." Dallas let her down off his lap as he stood with many others. Nate and Ginger swung around on their horses, and the pastor had looped a braided rope around their wrists, which they raised up together.

Pure happiness radiated from their faces, and Dallas basked in the warm glow of it. He also really wanted it for himself, and again, he thought of Martha. He needed to call her as soon as he could find a spare moment to be alone.

Once Nate and Ginger had ridden away on their horses, the energy started to fade. Dallas suddenly felt the weight of the world descend on him again, and it was far too heavy for him to shoulder alone. But there was no one else to take even a piece of it for even a minute.

"Come on, guys," he said to his kids, and they stuck close to him as the crowd started to move in a herd toward the flaps in the tent that had been tied back.

Behind him, Ted said. "Missy, let's get the pool filled up, yeah? I feel like my skin is melting off." It was such a Ted-thing to say, and Dallas swung around and smiled at him.

"Who gets married in September in Texas?"

"Crazy people," Ted said, taking off his cowboy hat

and wiping his forehead. "Em and I chose the beginning of March."

"Smart," Dallas said, noting that Jess veered toward another door. He watched her go, a bit of guilt straining in his stomach. He probably shouldn't have snapped at her about the texting.

"Do you guys want to come swimming?" Ted asked, looking at Thomas and Remmy as they finally gained the doors and the crowd started to spread out.

"Can we, Daddy?" Remmy asked.

"Sure," Dallas said. "I think Aunt Amy bought you guys bathing suits." He refrained from tacking on the word, "Right?" as if he didn't know. He was ninety percent sure Amy had gotten swimming suits for his kids, because she'd had them for the bulk of the summer.

Remmy started skipping ahead of them, saying, "She did, Daddy. Mine's purple with pink stars."

Even Thomas looked excited about the prospect of a swimming pool, and as they approached the homestead, he went with Ted toward the cabins in the corner. A stand-up pool sat in the shade of a huge oak tree, and Ted said, "I'll get it going now. You guys go change." He paused and looked at Dallas. "I can take the kids for an hour or two," he said in a much quieter voice.

Dallas wondered if he wore his exhaustion on his face. He'd learned how to smother his emotions and cover everything up with a blank mask, almost from the first day he'd entered River Bay. But he'd obviously forgotten a lot already, in only a few days.

"You sure?"

"Sure," Ted said. "Go settle in. Shower. Whatever." He flashed Dallas a smile and started toward the hose.

Dallas went with his kids, and he helped Remmy dig through her suitcase until they found her swimming suit. He went out into the kitchen and asked a brown-haired woman if there was any sunscreen he could use on this kids.

"Sure," she said. "We have a cupboard we call the apothecary." She led him over to a cupboard next to the fridge and opened it. Bottles of every height and color stood there, with sheets of pills that could be pushed out of the foil on the back, and taller canisters of bug spray and sunscreen.

"Thank you," he said. "I forgot your name."

"Hannah," she said with a smile. He felt nothing for her, the way he had with Jess, and he wasn't sure what that meant. Probably that she wasn't texting during a wedding or yelling at him for cleaning up chocolate from the floor.

"Hannah, right." He took the sunscreen from the shelf and sprayed his kids. Then he went out the door that led into the garage and stepped toward the back yard. He paused at the corner and watched Thomas and Remmy run toward the other kids in the pool. Apparently, Ted had been nominated as the babysitter, and when he came out to the pool, wearing a bright lime green pair of swimming trunks, it was obvious why.

A couple of other women loitered on the back steps, clearly engaged in a conversation with one another. They looked a little bit like Ginger, and Dallas assumed they were her sisters. Part of him wanted to join the party in the pool, but the thought of changing his clothes and spraying himself with sunscreen made him want to sink to his knees and weep.

Ted's bellowing laugh filled the air, and Dallas grinned. His kids would be fine.

He went back to the room he'd been given to change in, wondering where he'd really be staying that night. This was the West Wing, and men didn't live on this side of the house. Instead of finding someone to ask, he simply closed and locked the door. He collapsed on the bed and pulled his phone from his pocket.

A sigh escaped from his mouth, and he thought about doing his best to fall asleep. In the end, though, he dialed Martha, his heartbeat bobbing into the back of his throat.

"Hey," Martha said, her voice far too chipper.

Instant annoyance flashed through Dallas. It seemed entirely unfair that she was off enjoying her life in Florida or Georgia or wherever she was, and he was here, exhausted and hot and trying to figure out how to be a dad all over again by himself.

At the same time, Dallas wanted her back in his life. Nothing made sense. He had no idea how his life had come to this bedroom, on this ranch, on this phone call. He'd felt like this before, because his first night in prison had provided him with the same out-of-body experience as he was having right now.

"Are you there?" she asked.

Dallas let his eyes drift closed as he said, "Yeah, I'm here."

"What's going on?"

"Just talk to me," he said. He'd asked her to do this many times for him in the past. When he'd lost a heart patient—the second child in a family with congenital heart failure—and he'd come home devastated, he'd collapsed on a bed very much like this one. He'd cried and cried, and Martha had simply sat with him and stroked his hair off his forehead until he quieted.

Then she'd asked, "Are you done crying?" in a kind, quiet, patient voice.

He hadn't answered, and he'd just asked her to talk to him. She'd told him that he had to go back to work, even though he'd said he didn't want to ever return to a hospital surgical wing again. He had to go back, because he had to help the others coming up behind him. He had knowledge others didn't have, and they'd have to learn it all over again.

He'd picked himself up, showered and slept, and gone back to work.

"I don't have anything to say," Martha said.

"Where are you?" Dallas asked.

"Dallas." She sighed. "I don't want to talk about this."

"I need you," he whispered, wishing he didn't. But he did. "I miss you. I—"

"Dallas," she said again. "Please, don't do this."

"Are you seeing someone else?" he asked.

"I'm not doing this," Martha said. "How are the kids?"

Anger drove out the soft feelings in his heart. He suddenly didn't miss her at all, and in fact, if he knew where she was, he wouldn't be able to stop himself from driving over there and throttling her.

"I have to go," he said. He hung up before she could protest, not that she would. And that would only hurt worse than telling her that the two children she abandoned were currently swimming in a pool and wondering where their mother was.

Dallas needed to figure out where he was going to go tomorrow. He needed to find a place to live, because the little money he did have would run out incredibly fast if they had to stay in hotels for long.

His back screamed at him as he stood up, and throbbed as he bent to get his laptop out of his backpack. Brent had given it to him, and gratitude streamed through Dallas. It wasn't enough to erase the pain his back, and he went out to the kitchen to get some painkillers from that cupboard full of pill bottles.

He'd just swallowed a few pills when someone came in the back door. Dallas really wasn't in the mood to talk to anyone, even someone he knew.

Jess came around the corner, and a physical groan actually came out of Dallas's mouth. He wasn't ready to apologize yet, and he turned away as she said, "Just the man I was looking for."

That got him to turn around, because he couldn't really determine her mood from the tone of her voice. She wore a smile that seemed a little predatory, and Dallas braced himself for something that would surely only add fuel to the fire already simmering in his stomach.

CHAPTER FOUR

J ess didn't like the stance Dallas assumed. One hip slightly cocked, arms folded, that glower in his eyes. Maybe she did like it. She wasn't sure. He definitely made something flutter somewhere inside her. She couldn't decide if it was her stomach or her chest.

It had taken a lot of nerve for her to come here and talk to him, but she reminded herself that she'd been asking Ginger for a man like him for months. Humiliation still ran through her, and she could still hear him telling her to stop texting during the wedding.

She had, and she supposed she could see things from his point of view. He simply didn't know that she'd been texting Emma about a salary for a mechanic. Then, after the ceremony, when she'd met Nate and Ginger in the stable, she'd gotten the go-ahead to hire him.

She'd swallowed her pride, and boy, that had been a big ball to force down her throat.

"Did you need something?" he asked.

"Yes," she said, realizing that she'd fallen into staring at him. He was pretty easy to look at, that was for sure. "I've been authorized to offer you a position here at the ranch."

He opened his mouth and then closed it again.

"As our mechanic," she said. "We're always a couple of steps behind with our equipment, and your skill with that air conditioner told me that you could get us caught up and keep us that way."

Dallas looked like she'd thrown her phone and hit him in the nose. He blinked a couple of times and leaned against the counter behind him.

"Do you have another job?" Jess asked. "The salary is pretty good, and it comes with a place for you and your kids to live."

His eyes widened even further, and Jess wondered why he hadn't changed out of his suit yet. She couldn't wait to get out of her dress, and her bedroom was only steps down the hall. Freedom. Relief.

She was so much more comfortable in jeans, a tank top, and boots, a cowgirl hat on her head and a pair of leather gloves in her back pocket. She could talk to the horses, and tell them about the wedding, and how beautiful Ginger was.

She could whisper about her own dreams and fantasies to ride one of them down an aisle to her waiting groom—or better yet, she could ride on the front of the saddle with her husband-to-be behind her.

"How good is the salary?" Dallas asked, pulling Jess back to reality.

"Sixty thousand," she said. "The cabin is out quite a ways, unfortunately, but it's a quick drive in. Five, maybe ten, minutes."

He looked like he was really considering it, and Jess wished it wasn't such a debate for him. "The cabin is here on the ranch?"

"Yes."

"How much of a cabin are we talking? There's running water and stuff?"

"Yes," she said. "It's one of the guest cabins we rent out, actually. We don't do as much of that in the winter, and Ginger is going to build more cabins here at the epicenter of the ranch. I'm sure you'll move into one of those once they're done." The ranch needed the money from the rentals, Jess knew that.

Hope Eternal was a great ranch, but it did take all the moving pieces and streams of revenue to keep everyone employed and the operation running smoothly. Ginger did an amazing job managing it all, though Jess knew each woman in the West Wing contributed mightily to the overall success of the ranch, herself included.

"Okay," Dallas finally said. "I can do that. Are we talking full-time work?"

"In the beginning, yes," she said. "Like, I said, we're behind on all of our mechanical work right now."

"Okay," Dallas said.

"Do you have a minute for me to take you out to the cabin? Emma will have your paperwork in the morning."

"Sure." Dallas started toward her, and Jess scanned him from head to toe.

"You don't want to change?"

He paused, his step slowing to a stop. "Yeah, I guess I better." A hint of a flush crawled up his neck as he pivoted and went down the hall toward the bedrooms.

Jess felt the oxygen drain from the room as he left, and she sagged against the kitchen island in partial relief and partial annoyance. She wasn't sure if she was irritated with herself or with Dallas, or with the day in general.

Dallas must've learned how to change in under thirty seconds, because he returned to the kitchen before Jess knew it. That, or she'd lost track of time while she stood in the kitchen, thinking about him.

"Ready," he announced, and Jess straightened and led him out to the garage. "I have to tell Ted where I'll be. Be right back." He veered left while she went right, where she'd parked in the driveway. A sense of self-consciousness slipped through her as she got behind the wheel. Dallas would be in this truck with her, and the cab was suddenly very, very small.

She even looked over to the passenger side of the bench, and she didn't think he'd fit on the seat. She'd once again lost time, and before she knew it, Dallas was opening the door and climbing in. He adjusted himself on the seat, and sure enough, those broad shoulders filled the whole space. "Ready," he said again.

Jess nodded, her voice suddenly on vacation. She got onto the dirt road that went west, toward the stables, barns, and equipment shed. As soon as she passed the shed that held the ATVs, she said, "That's where we keep our four-wheelers. We have a large building with our tractors and whatnot, and there's a small office there. One of the cowboys has been keeping the records there, so hopefully it won't be too much of a mess for you."

Dallas simply hummed, and Jess needed to fill the silence. She kept talking, detailing the beehives where they did their honey tours, the monarch butterfly programs they ran for the elementary school children, and the horseback riding lessons that Jess oversaw five afternoons a week.

Summertime was their busiest season for horseback riding, but they were busy year-round, as kids of all ages came after school for lessons.

Jess's truck chugged along, and she went too fast for the dirt road. She could feel the tires sliding on the loose gravel, and before she knew it, she'd taken a corner too fast and the truck slid sideways.

"Whoa," she said at the same time Dallas grunted and reached up to press his palm against the top of the door. "Sorry." She wasn't a great driver, and that was the last thing she wanted Dallas to know about her. She cast him a quick look, her face heating in less time than it took to breathe.

She came to a stop and gripped the steering wheel. One deep breath later, she lifted her foot from the brake pedal. The truck should've moved, but it didn't, and Jess's heart dropped to the soles of her feet.

"Oh, no," she said.

"What?" he asked.

"Sheila does this sometimes," she said, glancing his way again without truly meeting his eye. "I can get it going again." She leapt from the truck and leaned back inside to pop the hood. A wisp of smoke lifted from the seam along the front of the truck, and Jess paused.

She couldn't touch that, because it would be boiling hot. She'd put antifreeze in Sheila just a few days ago, and she couldn't be out already. A sweet, searing smell met her nose.

"Sheila?" Dallas asked, meeting her eyes across the hood.

"My truck." Jess indicated the vehicle. "We go way back."

"Well, she's on her last leg," Dallas said, eyeing the smoke.

Jess didn't want to believe that. She couldn't, because if she lost her truck, she felt like she'd lose the last piece of herself that she actually knew.

"I can take a look at her," Dallas said.

"It's way too hot," she said, darting around the corner of the hood to stop him. "I'll call Hannah, and she'll come get us."

"I can handle the heat," he said, nudging her out of the way. Sure enough, he fitted his fingers under the hood, released the catch, and lifted it up. He worked easily, as if working with machines was second-nature to him.

More smoke billowed out of the engine now that he'd released it, and he stepped back, waving his hand in front of his face.

"How did you do that?" she asked. "Open it when it was that hot?" She could feel the heat coming from the engine, and the hood should've scorched him.

"I've worked with a lot of hot things," he said, stepping up to the bumper.

Jess didn't want him examining Sheila. She had the distinct feeling she was about to be lectured for her care—or her lack thereof—of the vehicle, and she didn't want to hear it. "Really," she said. "I'll call Hannah to come get us, and I can get Spence to tow me back in with a tractor."

Dallas kept looking at the engine, but he kept his hands out. "All right." He turned and looked at her, and their eyes met. Though it was far too hot to stand here, smoke wafting around them, staring at him, she couldn't look away.

He finally stepped back, breaking the moment. Jess dropped her head and cleared her throat. "Right. I'm going to call Hannah." She turned her back on him, barely remembering how to use a cell phone as her brain misfired with the nearness of Dallas Dreyer.

"THANKS A LOT, SPENCE," JESS SAID LATER THAT night. She'd ridden out with him in the tractor, every moment almost like torture. They'd broken up weeks ago, and they'd said it wouldn't be awkward between them. She saw him around the ranch often, and when they were both working and busy, it wasn't awkward.

When she had to ask him for a favor, it was. When she had to ride with him for twenty minutes at the speed of a snail, it most definitely was awkward. She couldn't think of a single thing to say, and Spencer certainly wasn't helping to ease the tension in the tractor.

As he approached Sheila, he said, "You need to get a new truck," and glanced at her.

"Yeah," she said with a sigh. "You're probably right."

"My cousin has a dealership," he said. "We could go in one night after work, get some dinner...."

Shock moved through Jess. "Oh, uh, Spence, I don't think...."

"Yeah," he said. "I know." He came to a stop and looked at her fully. "I miss you."

"No," Jess said. "You miss having a girlfriend."

"No, I miss talking to you like we used to," he said. "We were friends, Jess, and now I've lost that."

She studied his face. He was a handsome man, and he shouldn't have any problem getting a date. In fact, in the past, he hadn't. She'd known about all of them, because they had been friends. "Okay," she said. "You're right. We should be friends. You used to tell me all about the women you were dating."

"Yeah," he said. "And you'd tell me about those British mysteries you love, and how you were going to get a corgi mixed with a poodle." He smiled at her then, and everything relaxed between them.

"I *am* going to get a corgidoodle," she said, smiling. "That's happening."

"Oh yeah?" Spencer challenged. "When?"

Jess looked away. "I don't know."

"I'm sure you'll make it happen," he said. He opened the door and got busy hooking up the winch to the truck. Conversation filled the ride back to the ranch, and Jess talked about the wedding and a colt she saw on the livestock board earlier that week. If Spencer had a weakness, it was horses, as he loved them almost more than life itself.

"I saw that one," Spencer said. "Too much leg."

"They always have too much leg," she said, teasing him. "Until they're three years old. *You* told me that."

Spencer grinned and shrugged. "Yeah, well, I just had a feeling looking at him."

"A feeling." Jess shook her head and said, "Take it to the big shed. Our new mechanic is going to look at it for me."

"Heaven help that man," Spencer said, and they laughed together. Jess was glad they'd been able to move past their awkwardness, because she had missed Spencer too. They walked back to the ranch together, and she waved to him as he continued toward the Annex.

She entered the West Wing, glad this day was done, but knowing that another one that would be just as busy and just as hot was coming tomorrow. A sigh filled her body as she went inside and found Hannah and Jill sitting at the counter, bowls of ice cream in front of them.

"Peanut butter cone crunch," Hannah said. "The Swann's guy came."

Jess wasted no time getting out a bowl and a spoon for herself. "I bet he did."

"What does that mean?" Hannah asked.

Jess looked at Jill, the two of them exchanging a look that said a lot. "It means you love Steve the Swann's man, and you order from him just to see him."

A scoff came out of Hannah's mouth. "I do not."

"And he won't ask you out, so you just keep ordering ice cream."

"It's good ice cream," Hannah argued.

"You've got to be more obvious about what you want," Jill said, joining the conversation. "Like, he obviously has your number. Maybe next time he comes, you can say something like, Would you like to use that number to take me to dinner?"

"That doesn't even make sense," Hannah said, gaping at Jill. "How would a phone number take me to dinner?"

Jess started to giggle, and so did the other two women. Before long, they were all laughing. Jess didn't honestly care if Hannah liked Steve and that was why she ordered super expensive ice cream from his truck. It was delicious ice cream, and it helped soothe Jess after a long day.

Her phone buzzed, and she flipped it over to catch Dallas's name at the top. She swiped and read the full message.

Thanks for the job.

A glow filled her, and she wasn't paying attention to Hannah or Jill as she quickly sent back, *Glad to have you. Can't wait for you to get started.*

She'd taken him out to the cabin in a ranch truck, and they'd made a plan to get started the next morning. Bill was going to meet them in the equipment office and go over everything with Dallas, and Jess was simply tagging along to introduce the two of them.

"Who texted?" Hannah asked.

"No one," Jess said quickly, flipping her phone over.

"Oh, yeah, seems like no one," Hannah said. "Look at her, Jill. She's turning purple."

"Stop it," Jess said, though the heat had rushed into her face. She did turn a shade of purple because of her naturally darker coloring, and she hated that her embarrassment stained her face so easily.

"A new guy?" Jill asked.

"No," Jess said. "How would I meet a new guy?" She rolled her eyes. Sometimes she felt chained to the ranch, but at the same time, she didn't want to be or do anything else.

"Lots of men at the ranch for the wedding today," Jill said. "In fact, I got the number of one of Nate's friends from White Lake."

"You did not," Hannah said, shock coloring every word.

"I did," Jill said, giggling. "It's only twenty minutes from here. Eighteen if I take a back road."

Thankfully, the conversation moved on, and the heat drained from Jess's face. Her fingers itched to turn the phone over when it buzzed again, but instead, she ate her ice cream as fast as possible and made a hasty departure from the kitchen so she could text Dallas in private, all the while wondering why she had to be alone to read and respond to *his* messages.

CHAPTER FIVE

O nce, Dallas had been able to handle a lot of things thrown at him. In surgery, any number of things could go wrong, and while a team of professionals all talked and gave statuses, he could focus on the veins and arteries on a screen. Nothing bothered him.

Prison had been the complete opposite of a heart surgery, and Dallas hadn't hated the slower pace of life behind bars. The boredom could get to a man, though, and though River Bay offered classes for its inmates, and Dallas had taken some, he wasn't what he would call overwhelmed or even that intellectually stimulated.

He walked around the ranch with Jess and a man named Nick, though she'd originally said Bill was coming. Apparently the other cowboy had been called out to a field with a couple of other men to address a broken sprinkler pipe.

No matter who he was with, Dallas felt like he'd landed on a different planet. Not only that, but neither Jess nor Nick spoke the same language he did.

Yes, he understood the words "horses" and "cattle" and "agriculture," but he wasn't sure how all the pieces fit together here at Hope Eternal.

Thankfully, he didn't have to know that. Nick, who was Ginger's nephew, would be running the ranch while she and Nate were on their honeymoon, and he didn't seem perplexed or stressed at all. He couldn't be more than twenty-five years old, and Dallas found himself marveling at Nick's calm demeanor.

He had a pretty German shepherd named Ursula with him, and Dallas found her intense and intimidating and welcoming all at the same time.

He'd left his kids in the cabin he'd been given, because Jess had said the tour would only take "an hour or so," and the cabin was far enough away from everything and everyone that Dallas didn't think anything would happen to them. Not only that, but Remmy hadn't even been awake yet.

As soon as he finished this tour, Dallas needed to get the kids and take them to get registered for school. They'd need more clothes, and school supplies, and the dollar signs just kept flashing in his head.

"Did you get that?" Jess asked, and Dallas swung his attention toward her.

No, he had not gotten anything. He glanced around to

see where they were, and they'd entered a small shed that smelled like gasoline and wet cement. "Tell me again," he said.

"Our ATVs are on a rotation for scheduled maintenance," Nick said easily. Jess looked a bit perturbed, but Dallas ignored it. He'd texted with her last night for over an hour, and he wasn't even sure what they'd talked about for so long. He'd told himself several times to stop messaging her, but then he'd send another text. She responded too, and he actually found her much easier to talk to when he didn't' have to look at her.

What that meant, he didn't know.

He had no idea what the feelings inside him were saying, and to add even more confusion to his ragged soul, he knew he wasn't over Martha. He couldn't start a real relationship with Jess right now, and he should've said so last night.

Instead, he'd asked her about ice cream, he remembered that. They'd talked about the job a little bit, and he'd signed the paperwork that morning with Emma. He had his old bank account, but there wasn't a branch in Sweet Water Falls, so he needed to get a new one open here.

He'd promised he'd call Amy and Brent too, and he hadn't done that.

His to-do list grew and grew, and the weight of it started to press down on him.

"Okay?" Jess asked, and he realized he'd zoned out again.

"Okay," he said anyway. "Got it."

"And back here," Nick said, leading him toward a hallway Dallas didn't want to go down. At River Bay, he would've never stepped foot down this hall—it was too dark and too narrow. Anyone could've been waiting for him in the shadows, and Dallas's heartbeat thumped loudly in his ears.

"We have our secret passageway to the main shed," Nick said, his voice getting muted as he entered what seriously looked like a tunnel. They hadn't gone down any steps though, so Dallas didn't really believe the hallway was underground.

He ducked his head, though he didn't need to, as he followed Nick. Jess pressed into the narrow alley behind him, and that only sent Dallas's pulse into a faster sprint.

"We have everything you need in here," Jess said, her voice echoing a little bit.

Nick opened a door right when Dallas thought he might start gasping for breath, and a bright rectangle of light filled the hallway. Relief filled him, and he didn't even care that the equipment shed smelled halfway between a gym full of sweaty socks, last night's dinner, and hot metal.

The shed was made of metal, and a special kind of heat filled the whole thing. "Wow," he said, looking up to the blue arched ceiling of the metal building above him. "This place is huge."

"It's so hot," Jess complained, already fanning herself

with a folded piece of paper she'd tucked into her back pocket a while ago.

"Well, Dallas can fix air conditioners," Nick said, beaming at him. "And I'd literally sacrifice one of my favorite goats if you could get Red Mama to run for more than ten minutes at a time."

Again with the nonsensical words. "Red Mama?" Dallas asked.

"She's the swather," Jess said as she rolled her eyes. "Nick and Spence name everything around here."

"Ted said he had to name the dogs," Dallas said. "So that's not entirely true."

"All the tractors and stuff," Nick said. "Ginger names every horse. And yes, Ted named the blue heelers. They love him." He reached down and patted Ursula, who hadn't had a problem walking through the secret passageway to the equipment shed.

"Is that the only entrance?" Dallas asked, starting to wonder if he shouldn't have signed the paperwork until he'd gotten the full layout of the job.

"Of course not," Jess said, and she seemed so annoyed with him. He looked at her, not sure why she would be. In his eyes, they'd had a great conversation last night, and she'd even smiled and said hello to him earlier that morning.

So what had changed?

"There's a big door over there," she said. "We usually have it open, as the tractors and trucks use it."

"And a door on each end," Nick said pleasantly. "And two on each side too." He pointed to them. "Let's go into the office, and I'll show you what Bill has been doing."

"All right." Dallas cast one more look around, counting the vehicles he could see. Eight. Maybe ten. This really was a full-time job, especially if none of them ran for longer than ten minutes at a time.

Worry started to eat at him. When would he have time for his kids? How was he supposed to raise them by himself *and* work around the ranch? In fact, he wasn't even sure how to do either of them singly, and a new kind of panic started wailing in his gut.

Nick led the way into a corner room that had no right to be called an office. Dallas had enjoyed an office in the hospital, and it could easily hold six of these rooms. It had been bigger than the cabin he'd stayed in last night too, and that moment brought crystal clarity to how different his life was now.

"Okay," Nick said with a sigh, stopping just inside the room. Honestly, he couldn't go in much further, but Dallas crowded in behind him, and Jess came in too, bumping into Dallas as she squeezed by him. Even Ursula came into the office, her ears perked up and her nose working overtime.

Something definitely smelled in here, and Dallas looked around, his skin starting to crawl. This whole place needed a thorough cleaning, and he was suddenly thankful for how tiny the office was.

"Bill's left notes." Nick handed him a yellow legal pad with black writing on it. Dallas looked at it, once again thinking that he'd left Earth in favor of some foreign planet far across the solar system, because this was definitely not English.

"What in the world?" he asked.

"Yeah, Bill's handwriting can be hard to decipher," Nick said, edging closer to him. "Once you get the lay of the letters, it's not too bad."

"Not too bad?" Dallas looked up. "I can't read a single word."

Nick took the top of the pad and leaned it toward himself. "Yeah, that top line says Gremlin oil change, six quarts, still leaking."

Dallas marveled at him, his eyes wide. He looked back at the notepad, trying to find a G at all. "Gremlin?" came out of his mouth, because he'd never met anyone who named their ranch machinery. Of course, he'd never really interacted with all that many cowboys, and right now, everywhere he looked, that was all he saw.

"Gremlin is the big green mower," Nick said.

Dallas shook his head slowly, his mind moving at ten times the speed. "I'm going to need a cheat-sheet," he said. "For all the nicknames of your vehicles. And what type they are." He had no idea what kind of tractor the Gremlin was, and he'd bet every last cent to his name that they didn't have the manuals anymore. They would at least tell him how much oil such a machine held, and how often to change it. The manual would list part numbers for belts and spark plugs, tires and pistons.

"I'll get Bill to come work with you on it," Jess said. She stepped back into his personal space, and he couldn't help catching a whiff of her sweet perfume. It was so different from everything else in this building, and Dallas looked up from the notebook again.

His eyes caught on hers, and while she had sparks shooting at him, he didn't think they were entirely unfriendly. "We've got feeding starting," she said. "You good here?"

Dallas's stomach tightened. She wasn't going to just leave him, was she?

Turned out, yes, she was. She left the office without even waiting for him to say yes, he'd be fine there. Nick grinned at him and said, "I'm so glad we've got you. Thanks for taking the job, Dallas."

"Yeah," left Dallas's mouth, though he didn't really direct himself to speak. Just like that, he was alone in the office, wondering what he was supposed to do now.

He took in the desk and noted there was no computer. He'd definitely need one of those. Someone should be monitoring the stock too, as he couldn't be running to town every day for the parts he needed.

Setting down the yellow pad, he went around the desk, which took up most of the space, and opened the top filing cabinet drawer. It squealed like nothing he'd heard before, and he flinched. Every folder and file and paper inside looked old, worn out, and grease-stained. What was all this stuff?

Sighing, Dallas closed the drawer and took a chance with his life as he sat in the chair behind the desk. It too protested being used, but he didn't care. He looked down at the desk covered in papers and dust and grime. "What have I gotten myself into?" he wondered aloud. He tipped his head back and looked up to the ceiling. It was much lower here than out in the main part of the building.

"Dear Lord, what have I gotten myself into?"

"I don't know my address," he said later that day, a healthy dose of embarrassment moving through him. "What should I do about that?" He looked at the blonde secretary who'd handed him a packet of forms to fill out so he could register Remmy and Thomas for school.

Thankfully, they'd be at the same one, and it was only fifteen minutes from the ranch. Missy went there too, and Connor, Nate's son, had started first grade a week or so ago.

Thomas had been unusually quiet all morning as Dallas had taken them to get a couple of new outfits and real backpacks that didn't hold their clothes. He'd gone to the bank too, and he'd splurged and taken the kids to lunch before finally stopping by the elementary school to get them enrolled.

Now, he simply looked at Dallas like he was the biggest failure on the planet. Dallas felt it keenly too, but he kept his gaze on the secretary.

"Oh," she said, clearly surprised. "Are you home-less?" She looked at Thomas, as if the fifth grader would tell her or otherwise exhibit some sort of sign of home-lessness.

"No," Dallas said, grateful he could answer in such a way. "We just got into town yesterday, though, and we're living at Hope Eternal Ranch." She didn't need to know it was a cabin out by some swampy areas. People obviously stayed there when they did the birdwatching or honey something-or-other Dallas hadn't listened to that closely. All he knew was that it didn't have a number on it that the USPS would recognize.

"Let's look that up," she said with a perky smile, and Dallas supposed someone should be glad to be in that school office. "I've got it right here," she said a moment later. She read it off for him, and he wrote it on the form. He didn't add the number of the cabin, though a big one had been nailed to the door. He could get his mail from someone in the West Wing, and his mind automatically went to Jess.

She'd definitely been frustrated or annoyed with him that morning, though he had no idea why.

He finished the forms, half of his mind on them and the other half on Jess. He turned them all in, and the blonde secretary said she'd get everything put into the system, and the children would have teachers ready for them in the morning.

Dallas nodded at her, put one arm around each of his children, and left the school. "Okay," he said, breathing out a big sigh as they approached his car. "That's done. What else do we need to do?"

Neither of the kids said anything, and Dallas looked at Thomas. "What's wrong?"

Thomas shrugged and went around to the passenger door. Dallas opened the back door for Remmy and waited for her to climb in and begin buckling her seatbelt. He got behind the wheel and started the engine so the air conditioning would start.

"Come on, guys," he said. "What's wrong?"

"It's just that...." Thomas started. He turned toward the window. "It's nothing."

"Remmy?" Dallas asked, looking at her in the rearview mirror.

"Tommy thought we'd be going back to Aunt Amy's," she said. "I'm just scared I won't like my new teacher."

Surprise shot through Dallas. "Why would we go back to Aunt Amy's?"

"Because she has a house," Thomas said.

"We have a house too," Dallas said, his defenses flying into place. "I need to sell the one in Houston, and then maybe we can get a real house here in town."

"Why can't we go to Houston?" Thomas asked.

The answer to that was far too much for a ten-year-old

to handle, so Dallas just said, "We can't, that's all." He flexed his fingers on the steering wheel and backed out of the parking space. "And Remmy, I'm sure you'll love your new teacher."

"I hope so," she said, and Dallas wished for simpler days, when he'd been six years old. All he'd thought about was going fishing, something his father had taken him to do every weekend and whenever they needed to de-stress and get away from the busyness of the world.

His heart beat in a strange way as he thought about his dad. He'd been so angry when Dallas had been indicted, tried, and convicted. Mad at the legal system. Mad at Dallas. Mad at the world. He'd never once visited Dallas at River Bay, nor had he ever taken one of Dallas's phone calls.

His mother had, and Dallas vowed to figure out how long it would take to get from Sweet Water Falls to Temple, where his parents lived. Where he'd grown up, and where two of his siblings still lived. Greg had called Dallas at Amy's the first night he'd been free. His sisters had texted, and he'd called his mom.

They hadn't made plans to get together, and Dallas now viewed that as a mistake. He needed to speak to his parents, especially his father, and start to repair what had broken. Wasn't that what he did for a living now? Make run-down and broken things come alive again?

"I'm sorry we can't go to Houston," he said quietly. "I'm sorry we can't go back to Aunt Amy's. But it's just the three of us now, you guys. Okay? And I'm not going anywhere. I've got a job, and I'm going to get you to school and back, and it's all going to work out."

Thomas looked at him, such hope in his eyes, and Dallas's heart bled for him. He had no idea what it would be like to have his mother drop him off somewhere while she left, never to return. He didn't know what Thomas had gone through when Dallas had gone to prison. He hadn't been the one on the outside, and he knew nothing had been easy for Martha, Thomas, or Remmy.

"Okay, Daddy," Remmy chirped, and Thomas nodded.

"Okay, Dad," he said.

Dallas managed to put a smile on his face, though his inner organs felt one breath away from collapse. His determination doubled though, and he nodded too. "Okay."

Now, if getting things back on track with his father could be as easy.

Or Jess, he thought, and he determined he'd call her the moment he could. With that new determination and drive inside him, Dallas headed back to Hope Eternal Ranch, suddenly realizing the significance of the name.

CHAPTER SIX

J ess *tsk*ed her tongue at Diamond Valley, the black and white horse she was training that morning. The mare didn't want to get close to the rail, despite Jess's assurances that it wouldn't hurt her. She'd get the equine there too, because Jessica Morales hadn't met a horse she hadn't been able to train.

She bonded with the animals easily, some deeper than others. She too tried to be present at every birth, and while she didn't have the final say on the horse's name, she definitely had input. She and Ginger had been working together at Hope Eternal for twelve years now, after Jess had left the wild world of horses up in Calgary.

She'd worked with the rodeo horses at The Calgary Stampede Ranch for five years before making the move south to Texas. And she'd gone to Calgary after a particularly observant cowboy had watched her work with a horse at a riding facility in her hometown of Bozeman, Montana.

Jess loved horses with her whole soul. She'd started at the riding facility when she was just twelve, mucking out stalls and sitting with pregnant mares to make sure they didn't get cast in the middle of the night. She'd heard horses scream when they got stuck when they rolled over and got their hooves against the wall. When they couldn't get up like that, the panic from a horse could curdle her blood.

She'd been riding since the age of four, when her father put her on her first horse and tethered the reins to his. He'd been a born-and-bred cowboy, and she'd loved spending time with him outside, on the small family ranch he ran all by himself.

She helped as she got older; all three of the Morales girls did. Jess was the oldest, and while she could've had the ranch in Bozeman, she found she didn't really want it.

Her phone buzzed in her pocket, but she ignored it. She couldn't focus on a conversation and training Diamond Valley at the same time. While in the ring with a horse, especially an agitated one, she had to keep her concentration on what was most important. The horse. Herself.

She tsked at Diamond again, pressing her further toward the rails with the long pole in her hand. Around and around the horse went, and after another ten minutes, she settled against the rail in a nice, even trot.

"There you go, girl," Jess said, smiling at her. She made the mare go around three more times, and then she pulled the pole in and lifted it straight up until it was vertical at her side. Diamond Valley stopped almost immediately, giving Jess and that pole the side-eye.

Rich knocked on the fence behind her, and Jess walked over and handed him the pole. "She did great today," she said.

"Seventeen minutes," Rich said. He only worked the ranch in the morning for about three hours. He drove a school bus the rest of the time, but Jess did like his quick smile and happy-to-help attitude. He worked with her and three other horses every morning, and Jess liked the routine.

Horses did too. Their brains were only the size of a baseball, and they were creatures of habit. They liked to be fed and exercised at the same time every day, and Jess found she did too.

"How's the rest of the string?" Rich asked as she climbed over the fence and they started around it together.

"Good," Jess said. "Bumblebee gave me attitude this morning about the saddle, but I'm wearing him down. All the temps came back normal. Noah's Ark won't leave his leg wrappings alone." She looked at Rich and rolled her eyes. "So good. Normal."

"I'll paint more of that cayenne pepper on them."

"I think he actually likes it," Jess said with a smile. She and Rich chuckled together, and she gathered the lead line for Diamond Valley from a hook on the wall, climbed back into the ring with the horse, and got the rope around her head. "Come on, sweetheart. You did so great today. Before you know it, you're going to be showing a little boy or girl how amazing the ranch is."

"She's going back to her stall?" Rich asked, taking the line from Jess as she left the ring.

"Bath today," Jess said. "Bill should have the stalls in our string done by then with fresh wood chips. Then yes, back in the stall."

"We need to work on that pasture rotation," Rich said.

"Yeah." Jess sighed, because there was always more tasks to do than hours in the day. "I'll pull up the one we've been using and get it started."

He nodded and veered left to take Diamond Valley down to the wash bays while Jess went right to go check on her men. They each worked with a string of horses, most of them much bigger than the one she oversaw. With over seventy horses at Hope Eternal, Jess had a lot of conversations each day, and the paperwork involved in their care could make the gruffest man cry.

Her phone buzzed again, and this time, Jess removed it from her pocket. Dallas's name sat on the screen, which caused a frown to pull at her eyebrows. She wasn't even sure why. She'd enjoyed texting with him last night. But this morning, when he'd shown up at the barn early, then barked at her and Nick that he really only had an hour for the tour, her annoyance with him had blossomed.

The call ended before she could decide to answer it or not, and she checked the other missed calls. She had three, and they were all from Dallas. Her heartbeat shot into a faster pitter, and she looked up as if someone would be able to hear it.

There was always activity in the stables, and today was no different. Men and women walked horses around. They fed them. They checked on them. They wrote on clipboards and left those by doorways. The riding lessons would begin in two hours, and most of the horses should be back in their stalls for a bit of rest before then.

Almost everyone in the stables only worked on the ranch part-time, and on weekends, Jess ran a skeleton crew to feed and water the horses, monitor their health, and rotate them out to pastures. Everyone took a break from training on Sundays, and Jess sometimes found an hour to go sit in church and listen to a pastor.

"Bootstrap is showing some signs of a cough," Giselle said as she went by Jess with a different horse in tow. "Tony said he's looking for you."

"Okay," Jess said absently. She didn't go find Tony though. She looked around again, as if she were trying to make an escape from the stable without anyone seeing her. She ducked down a small hallway between two stalls and pulled out her phone.

With a slightly shaking finger, she tapped to return Dallas's call.

"There you are," he said instead of hello.

Jess couldn't decide if he sounded frustrated or not. "Yeah," she said. "Sorry. I can't really answer the phone when I'm in the ring with a horse."

"Oh, sorry," he said. "I didn't know."

Jess leaned against the wall and pressed her eyes closed. "What's up?" She infused as much false brightness into her tone as she possibly could.

"Something's a bit off with you," he said, his voice lowering in volume and pitch. "I just wondered if I'd said or did something to upset you."

"No," Jess said, hating how two letters could be a lie.

"You sure?"

She shifted her feet, not sure what kind of game this was. How had he known she was slightly annoyed with him? And had he actually called to clear the air between them? Who did that?

"I mean, you were just a little...rude this morning."

"I was?"

"Yeah, you sort of snapped at me and Nick when we got to the barn, like we were holding you up or something. You work here now, Dallas. We did you the favor." She hated the words as they came out of her mouth. "That's not what I meant. I—"

"You did *me* a favor?" he asked. "Wow, I didn't know that. Thanks." His sarcasm wasn't lost on her. "I suppose I'll send you a bill for fixing the air conditioner in the stable then."

"Dallas." She sighed, because this conversation wasn't

going the way she'd thought it would. She honestly hadn't known why he'd called three times, and for him to simply find out how she was feeling didn't make sense to her.

"What?" he asked. "You offered me the job last night. I signed the paperwork this morning. I didn't know I was on the clock today. I have things I have to get done for my kids, and you said we'd start with a quick tour—which Jess, two hours is not quick in any definition I've found of the word—and I'd really start tomorrow."

"I know," she said, her voice barely above a whisper.

"So I get to be annoyed when you and Nick show up ten minutes late and then proceed to show me the most unorganized mechanical shed I've ever seen."

Jess toed the ground, her eyes trained on the dirt there though she could barely see it in the dim lighting down this hallway. Utility closets lined both sides of it, and they kept medical supplies, blankets, and other odds and ends in the cupboards.

Silence draped the two of them, and Jess felt like they were worlds apart. For some reason she couldn't name, she wanted to build a bridge to where he was and make things right.

"I'm sorry," Dallas said, plenty of resignation in his voice. "I guess we just need to communicate better."

"I'm sorry too," Jess said. "I didn't realize we'd—I'd— kept you from more important things." She wasn't a mother and never had been. She couldn't fathom what it took to keep children fed and well and happy, though she did help out with Connor from time to time. Now that the boy was in school, Nate didn't need as much help during the day, and there were plenty of people around the ranch in the evenings.

"It's okay," Dallas said. "I didn't mean to snap at anyone. I suppose I need to call Nick and apologize?"

"Oh, I doubt he noticed," Jess said, finally looking up as the conversation improved. "He's like a duck. Stuff just rolls off his back."

"Hmm," Dallas said. "What are you doing tonight?"

"Tonight?"

"Yeah, tonight. Say after dinner?"

"I don't usually do much after dinner unless there's an emergency in the stables."

"Maybe we could meet in that tiny room you guys called an office. I have some things I'd like to go over with you about the job."

Her heartbeat crashed against her ribcage. "You're not quitting, are you?"

Dallas laughed, and the sound of it lifted Jess's spirits even more. He had a deep, beautiful laugh, and she wondered if he'd had occasion to use it very often behind bars. She knew he'd just gotten out of prison, but she'd also worked with enough other men to know the ones from River Bay usually weren't too big of a threat.

Ginger wouldn't let them come to Hope Eternal if they were.

"No," he said between his chuckles. "But I need to do

some things in the morning, and I was thinking maybe we could meet tonight, and then I could take care of that stuff."

Jess noticed the vague nature of his statement, and while her curiosity skyrocketed about what "things" and what "stuff" he needed to take care of, she managed to keep her questions dormant. "Okay," she said. "What time tonight?"

"Seven?"

"Sure, see you then." The call ended, but Jess stayed in the narrow hallway, thinking. She sometimes got too wrapped up in her thoughts, and she finally forced herself to stop imagining what that night would hold. She'd find out when she showed up in the office in the equipment building at seven o'clock.

SHE MADE SURE SHE WAS EARLY THAT EVENING, BUT she still didn't beat Dallas to the office. He stood with his back to the doorway as she approached, turning before she could say anything. A smile crossed his face, but it didn't light up his eyes.

"Hey," he said, moving one paper behind another in a stack he held in his hand. "Why is none of this on a computer?"

"I have no idea," Jess said. "I'm not over mechanical or equipment."

"Who is?"

"Ginger."

"And she's not here," Dallas muttered, frowning at the file folder in his hand. He exhaled heavily as he set it on the desk. "Okay, so this is a huge mess. My guess is she hasn't had anyone over mechanical or equipment in a long time." He raised his chin. "Tell me I'm wrong."

Jess couldn't tell him that, so she lifted her own chin, her defenses kicking into gear. Ginger wasn't perfect, but she ran a good ranch the best she could. "You're not wrong."

He nodded and folded his arms, and wow, Jess could appreciate muscles like that. At the same time, his good looks and tall, muscular body was a huge distraction. She barely heard him as he said, "I'm going to need a computer. And all the manuals for every vehicle and machine on this ranch. Anything you've got." He indicated the filing cabinet behind him. "That's full of useless files we don't even need anymore. I need an inventory of parts, and contacts for ranch supply stores."

The list went on and on, and Jess finally started typing notes into her phone. She hadn't shown up with a notebook or anything, because Dallas hadn't given her any idea what to expect from this evening meeting.

Twenty minutes later, she had a comprehensive list of the things he needed, and she had no idea how to get him any of them. "Hannah's over the accounting," she said.

"She might know some of this, because she'll have to have paid for the parts."

"Great," Dallas said. "I can talk to her tomorrow."

"She works with the calves in the mornings," Jess said. "Then out of an office in the barn in the afternoons. Emma runs all the operations on the ranch. Hiring, which is why she has your paperwork. She oversees the overall budget on the ranch, and big-ticket items have to go through her. She might have records on the ATVs, tractors, trucks, and all the other vehicles we have here."

"Perfect." He had a notebook and scrawled something on it. When he looked up again, Jess forgot what they'd been talking about.

"Where are you from?" she asked.

Dallas blinked, his surprise evident on his face. Foolishness raced through Jess, but the words had been spoken.

"The Houston area," he said, his voice somewhat strained. "That's what I need to do in the morning. Call my realtor and put my house up for sale."

"Oh." Surprise wound through Jess now.

"Do I have to live on the ranch?" he asked.

"No," she said.

He nodded and made another note. "Once I sell my house, I'll probably find something better for me and the kids."

"Where's your wife?" she asked.

Dallas flinched, his eyes shooting back to hers again.

"You ask blunt questions, don't you?"

"I mean, I'm assuming you have a wife," Jess said. "Or had one." She shrugged though she wanted to tape her mouth shut. She did have a bit of a blunt streak, and she obviously needed help with censoring the things that came out of her mouth.

"I did." He cleared his throat. "I'm assuming you're going to have to clear all of the things I asked for with Ginger?"

"Yes," Jess said. "And Emma and Hannah. Computers aren't free, you know."

"Yeah, well, writing down the minimal maintenance you've done on three hundred thousand dollar vehicles— in handwriting no one can read—is ridiculous." His eyes flashed with something fiery, and wow, Jess wanted to get burned by it.

"If you want me to do this job," he said. "I need a computer. It's non-negotiable."

"I'll get it for you," Jess said. She leaned forward as he nodded and went back to his notebook, where he'd clearly put a list of questions.

"Okay—"

"Dallas?" she asked, interrupting him.

He lifted his eyes back to hers, and she sure did like the light gray depths of his. "Yeah?"

"Sorry," she said, her pulse hammering into her ribs, her throat, and her back. "One more question: Would you take me to dinner one night?"

CHAPTER SEVEN

"**D**inner?" came out of Dallas's mouth before he could even think.

"Yeah." Jess looked at him with those big, brown eyes, and he couldn't see straight. His thoughts jumbled, and he had no idea what was happening.

Several seconds passed, and finally, he seized onto something he hoped would get him out of this situation. "I have Thomas and Remmy," he said.

Jess nodded, ducked her head, and said, "Okay."

Instantly, Dallas wanted to explain everything about Martha. She'd asked about his wife—who was really an ex—but Dallas hadn't wanted to talk about her. He barely knew Jess, and in fact, they barely got along all that well. She had been circling in his mind all day, and he'd be lying if he said he didn't find her attractive.

Perhaps he'd even staged this meeting tonight, because

he knew there'd be less people around. He pushed that thought away, because it would take hours to determine if it was true, and Dallas didn't have that kind of time.

"Listen," he said, resigning himself to saying some things he might not otherwise. "I just got out of prison. You know that, right?"

"Yes," she said, still refusing to look at him.

"I did thirty months for insurance fraud and medical malpractice." His throat closed, but he swallowed and breathed and forced himself to continue, even when Jess looked up and met his eye. "Thankfully, the wrongful death suit was dropped." He looked away, but this office had no window to pretend to look out of.

"My wife's name is Martha. She came like clockwork to the facility, though it was a long drive for her. She brought the kids. Then...one day...." He shrugged, aware his voice had taken on a haunted quality. "She was gone. I got a message from her sister that said Martha had dropped the kids off at her place, and that she wasn't coming back."

A beat of silence filled the office before Jess said, "You're kidding."

"That was three months ago," he said. "The divorce is final, because I didn't contest it, and she didn't want custody. Very clean." He hated that with every fiber of his being. But how could he contest a divorce from behind bars? Martha had known he'd have no choice but to give her what she wanted, or he could lose the kids.

He drew in a deep breath and looked at her again. He'd learned to face his issues and problems head-on while in prison. He'd had a counselor work with him to do just that. "I hate to say it, but I'm not sure I'm over her yet. I don't think it would be fair to you to you know, go to dinner together."

"Okay," she said, those lovely eyes crinkling as she smiled. She reached across the desk and covered his hand with hers. "Thanks for telling me."

Sparks fanned through his fingers and up his arm. He hadn't been touched in a loving, kind way by a woman in far too long. That was all this chemistry between him and Jess was. His deprivation of affection. Nothing more.

He told himself that again and then again as he nodded. As the sparks caught into flames, he shifted his hand, and she moved hers back. Relief spread through Dallas, as did a heavy weight of disappointment. He wasn't sure what to make of either emotion, and he looked back at his notepad of questions. They suddenly didn't seem so important.

"If you can just get me a computer, I can get this all organized and up and running," he said. "It'll take a while, though. I want you—and everyone—to know that. I'm basically starting at zero here." He looked at the mess in the office. "Less than zero."

"I know," Jess said.

"You should've told me that," he said, looking back at her. "I feel a little tricked."

She nodded, her dark hair swinging with the motion. "I can understand that." She stood up and gave him a sober look. "That wasn't my intention, Dallas, honestly."

"I know," he said, because he believed she was being genuine. He still felt like he'd been presented with this amazing job that wasn't so amazing.

A smile appeared on her face, and it screamed of flirtatiousness. "When you're feeling up to it, you'll have to let *me* take *you* to dinner to make up for it." With that, she walked out of the office, leaving Dallas to wonder why he couldn't go to dinner with her right then.

Ted had the kids, and he'd told Dallas to take his time at the equipment shed. A quick text, and Dallas could drive into town with Jess and eat something besides a peanut butter sandwich or something that came out of a box.

He looked at his phone, his eye catching on the folder he'd pulled at random from the filing cabinet. By the time he stood up and moved to the doorway, Jess was long gone.

"Another time," he muttered to himself. He turned back to the office and surveyed it. He could sweep his eyes across the room in less time than it took to inhale, and he didn't see anything he couldn't leave until tomorrow.

He left the office too and walked through the insufferably hot equipment shed to the door. Outside, it was actually a little cooler, because a breeze played with itself as it raced around the ranch. He walked the distance back to Ted's cabin, where he'd left his car and his kids.

Ted had them all on the front lawn—Thomas, Remmy, Connor, and Missy—and he was currently putting on a show with the four blue heelers that liked to follow him around the ranch. Dallas had heard all about Paula, Simon, Randy, and Ryan in letters Ted had written him, and instantly his mood improved.

Ted had always been a fun-loving man with a big laugh, and Dallas had wondered how he could maintain that while in prison. Of course, Ted hadn't been beaten on his first day in River Bay, and he hadn't had to suffer with those injuries to this day.

Dallas groaned as he sat down on the front steps to watch Ted demonstrate how Ryan could sit, shake, and spin. He clapped along with the kids, and Ted grinned around at everyone.

"Done already?" he asked, taking up the other half of the steps as he sat beside Dallas.

"Yep," he said.

"Teddy," Connor said. "Can I get out one of those lemon pops?"

"Sure thing, bud," Ted said, standing up. "Take everyone with you and eat them on the back porch, okay?"

"Okay." Connor led the way inside the cabin, and Ted sat back down.

Dallas glanced at him, his feelings of inferiority rearing up and choking him. He wanted to ask Ted how he knew what to say and how he could deliver it with such happiness. Dallas had nearly snapped at Thomas that morning, and he'd had to apologize later.

"Now what?" Ted asked.

Dallas didn't look at him. "What do you mean?"

"I mean, what are you going to do now?"

"I got a job here," Dallas said. "Was that not obvious?"

"No, I know that," he said, his dark eyes finally hooking into Dallas. "Is that what you want?"

"Sure," Dallas said. "It's a mechanic job, which is exactly what I wanted." He didn't mention that he'd been considering opening his own shop. "I need to sell my house in Houston and get out of that cabin, though."

"Yeah, those birdwatching cabins aren't the nicest."

That was the understatement of the year, but Dallas didn't say more. The silence stretched between him and Ted, but it wasn't awkward. His back ached, though, and Dallas had to get up and get his kids to school in the morning.

He groaned as he stood up. "Thanks, Ted, but I better get going. Lots to do tomorrow."

"Yeah, sure." Ted stood too, his keen eyes missing nothing. "Do you have painkillers in that cabin?"

"No."

"Take some with you."

Dallas didn't argue; he simply followed Ted inside and accepted the pills. Ted smiled as he handed them over. "Must be bad."

"Why's that?"

"You didn't even argue."

Dallas swallowed the pills and met Ted's eye again. "I can do this, right, Ted?" He let so much vulnerability seep into his voice, and he knew he wore it on his face too.

"Of course you can," Ted said. "Listen, you lived in a dorm with fifteen other men. That was no picnic. You had to watch your back more than others, and it was already practically broken." He didn't smile or make light of what Dallas had been through. "This is fixing some tractors and driving your kids to school. You can do this."

There was so much more going on than just the surface things of fixing vehicles and taking care of his kids. He wasn't sure he knew how to do either of those things either, but they were certainly easier than trying to untangle the complex emotions surrounding Martha, his feelings of failure when it came to Thomas and Remmy, and this whole new attraction to Jess.

"Okay," Dallas said, because what else was there to say? He went out to the back porch, gathered his kids, and they made the ten-minute drive back to the cabin they could call home for now.

DALLAS SAT AT HIS DESK, THE LAPTOP ALREADY OPEN and waiting for him. He'd been working in the equipment shed at Hope Eternal Ranch for two weeks now, and Nate and Ginger were set to return that evening. He couldn't wait to show them both what he'd been doing.

Every vehicle the ranch owned had been put into a master spreadsheet. He'd found manuals and help pages online, and each one had a link for such things. He'd taken two of Jess's horse trainers to help him do the inventory on the parts, and he had a sheet for that too. He knew what he needed to order, and what they had on the shelves, for every machine on the ranch. All the vehicles. All the air conditioners. All the lawn mowers. Literally everything.

He'd taken his kids to school every weekday, worked as hard as he could during school hours, and drove back to town to get the kids. Sometimes Ted picked them up and that saved Dallas a forty-minute round-trip.

He really liked how all the cowboys and cowgirls at Hope Eternal Ranch helped each other, and his kids had fallen right into the group. He'd eaten at the West Wing a couple of times, and Remmy sat by Hannah and talked her ear off while the woman smiled, asked questions, and laughed.

Dallas had listed his house in Houston for sale, and the realtor updated him each day. Lots of showings. No offers. He wasn't getting nervous yet, because the housing market was in a slump right now, and Dallas's house was in a gated community and not something everyone could afford. It would take the right kind of buyer, and Dallas was committed to waiting it out.

He entered the paperwork from yesterday, finishing

the last one just as his phone rang. To his surprise, Alicia's name sat on the screen, and he quickly tapped the green phone icon to connect the call.

"Hey, Alicia," he said. "Tell me the good news." He felt more and more like his old self with every day that passed, though nothing had really been settled with Martha, and he still had a crazy attraction to Jess every time he saw her at the West Wing.

Their jobs didn't put them in the same places on the ranch very often, and if he saw her, it was always there, with lots of other people around.

"You assume it's good news," his realtor said with a laugh.

"Well, you updated me two days ago," he said, leaning back in his chair. His back reminded him that it didn't like that position much, and he sat up straight again. "So I'm assuming good news, although it could be bad." His heart skipped a beat. "Is it bad news?'

"No," she said. "You're right. Good news. I just got off the phone with another real estate agent. They took a couple through your house, and they loved it."

"That is good news," Dallas said, his pulse accelerating for a new reason.

"They're putting in an offer," she said. "I should have it by five p.m. tonight."

"That's *amazing* news." Dallas rose to his feet. He wanted to celebrate, and in times like this, he severely missed his wife. Fifteen years they'd had together. Fifteen years of always having someone he could talk to, share his fears and worries with, and enjoy a good meal together when things went their way.

Chris poked his head into the office, saw Dallas on the phone, and held up his hand as he backed out. Alicia spoke about how if the offer was good, they'd have twenty-four hours to accept it, and everything could be signed digitally, so he didn't need to come to Houston.

He hadn't gone to list the house either, as he hadn't wanted to make the trip. The furniture could stay, and Alicia had gone to make sure everything was clean and in order before her photographer had come to get the pictures for the listing.

Martha had left the house in good shape, and while Dallas knew he'd have to go to Houston to pack and move everything he owned, he'd bought himself a little time by turning the power over to his agent.

"I'll keep in touch," she said, and the call ended.

Dallas couldn't help the smile as it formed on his face. He had to celebrate with someone, and he looked back at the phone in his hand. He knew who he wanted to take for an expensive dinner so he could tell her the good news.

Jess.

"Can't do expensive," he told himself as he started typing out a text to her. *Hey,* he said. *Great news! My house is likely going to have an offer on it by tonight. Want to go to dinner with me to celebrate?*

He didn't think twice; he just sent the text.

He tapped the arrow back and sent a message to Nate and Ted, then one to just Ted, asking him if he could take the kids that night so Dallas could "go celebrate."

What are you going to do? Ted asked. *Congrats, by the way. That's big news. I know you hate that cabin.*

Dallas did hate the cabin. He had a nightly ritual of spraying for bugs, and he and the kids slept with mosquito nets over their beds. If they didn't, they had bites and bugs on them in the morning. He *needed* to get his children out of that situation.

That's great, Nate said on the group text. Ted chimed in there too, and Dallas was glad he had friends on the outside. No one else had called him, and he initiated all conversations with his family. For now, that would have to be enough, because Dallas didn't have any more to give.

He didn't have much in his energy reserves for a woman either, and he realized he should've just taken his kids to get hamburgers and French fries after school as a way to celebrate.

Jess hadn't answered yet. He'd just text and say that he couldn't because of the kids. He hated to use them as an excuse, but he would if he had to.

He navigated back to her text string and saw she had answered. He just hadn't seen it. *I'd love to. Seven? You'll come pick me up?*

His heartbeat slowed and thudded in his chest. He'd felt like this before, and he knew his attraction to Jess was more than the fact that he was a little starved for female attention.

Seven, he confirmed. *I'll come pick you up at the West Wing*.

Perfect, she said, sending a thumbs-up emoji too.

Dallas sank back into his seat, realizing that dinner with her *could* be perfect. His mind started to play all kinds of fantasies, and Dallas just let them roll through his mind's eye.

His phone rang, breaking him out of the trance he'd fallen into where he kissed Jess goodnight and floated back to his bug-infested cabin the happiest man on Earth.

"Hey, Ted," he said, forgetting what he'd asked the man to do for him that night.

"What are you doing to celebrate?" Ted asked, and he was clearly working somewhere on the ranch. The air blew across his receiver, and Dallas thanked the Lord above that he had an inside job on sweltering days like today.

"Uh." Dallas really wished he had a window he could pace back and forth to. He didn't see a way to keep it a secret. "I asked Jess to go to dinner with me."

A beat of silence came through the line, and then Ted burst out laughing. Dallas chuckled half-heartedly with him, not sure if Ted thought the idea of a relationship with Jess was ludicrous or not.

"Good for you," Ted said. "Really, Dallas. That's

great." He sounded genuine, and Dallas let his smile spread across his face again.

"You think so?"

"Sure," Ted said. "She's a pretty woman, and you're a great guy. Why not?"

"I don't know. Are there rules about dating here at the ranch?" He turned around to find Chris and Leon in his office now, and Dallas wondered how much they'd heard. His heart dropped to his steel-toed boots, and the three of them stared at one another.

"Not that I'm aware of," Ted said. "Bring the kids by whenever. Emma is making her braided breadsticks, and we're having spaghetti on the side." He chuckled again, and Dallas joined in with him.

He set his phone on this desk and faced his guys again. "Hey," he said. "What did you two need?"

"Who are you going out with?" Chris asked. He stood six feet tall, with linebacker shoulders, as he'd played football all the way through college. He hadn't been recruited into the NFL, and he'd traded his helmet for a cowboy hat. He'd been working at Hope Eternal for three years, Dallas had discovered, and he'd recently come over to the mechanical side of things after he'd had a run-in with Jess.

Dallas swallowed. "Uh, no one."

Leon looked at Chris, and Chris looked at Leon. "I swear I heard him ask if there were rules about dating here at the ranch." Leon's grin could only be classified as one Dallas would see on a Cheshire Cat. "Gotta be someone."

Leon had dark hair and eyes, and Dallas had learned that he'd been out with every woman on the ranch at least once—except Jess.

Dallas didn't know how he could tell them and not get daggered looks. They obviously didn't like her, and that suddenly struck him. *Why* didn't they like her?

Why do you? he asked himself, but he had no answer to either question.

He sat down at his desk. "It's nothing, guys. Do you have your schedules for today?"

"You're no fun," Chris said. "I came by to say I'm headed to San Antonio with Greg to get that load of hay. We're going to pick up the swather parts we need."

"Oh, perfect," Dallas said, pretending to look at something ultra-important on his laptop.

"And I came to talk to you about a couple of days off," Leon said. "My mother is having her gallbladder removed, and she needs someone to sit with her after she gets out of surgery. You know, the drugs make a person loopy."

"You have the paperwork?" Dallas asked, and Leon stepped forward and took a folded square of paper out of his pocket.

"Right here."

Dallas took it and unfolded it to find the dates. Not for another month. He tapped and clicked to get the calendar for the shop, and no one else had requested those days off. "You should be good," he said. "I'll put it in right now."

"Thanks, Dallas," Leon said. "I'll bet we can figure out

who it is," he said as he and Chris turned to leave the office.

"Yeah," Chris said, and Dallas expected their voices to get quieter the further from him the walked. But they didn't. In fact, it sounded like Chris was still in his office when he said, "I'm sure we can figure it out, Leon. Looks like a woman is coming this way right now."

CHAPTER EIGHT

J ess saw the two grease monkeys ogling her as she walked toward Dallas's office. She knew Leon and Chris, of course. She knew everyone who worked on the ranch. "Good morning," she said politely.

"Morning, ma'am," Chris said, twittering a moment later.

She paused and peered at him, something igniting in her blood. "What's going on?"

"Nothin'," Leon drawled. "What are you doing here?"

"I need to talk to Dallas," she said, ready for them to move on. Chris had moved over to mechanical after she'd had enough of his complaining in the stables. Ginger had reported that it was a much better fit for him, and he'd been doing well in the past year since he'd left her crew.

Of course he was, Jess thought. He didn't have a supervisor over here to answer to. At least not until she'd hired

Dallas. She tried to see past them to the office, and thankfully, Dallas filled the doorway.

"Go on, guys," he said. "You've got work to do."

Chris and Leon moved on, and Jess turned to watch them go, wondering what she'd done to them. Again. She'd simply asked for Chris to be transferred, and he had been. He still had a job, and he was better at it than he'd been with the horses.

Leon had worked his way through all the women here at the ranch, and Jess had been dating someone else when it was her turn. At least, that was what he'd told her. She'd been more disgusted with him for that than anything else, and perhaps she had told him she wouldn't go out with him even if he asked.

He never had, and she couldn't help feeling like she'd been slighted in some way.

"What was that about?"

"Nothing," Dallas said, touching her elbow. His skin seared hers, and she turned toward him. "What are you doing here?"

"I just came to see you," she said, smiling at him as she pressed in close to him to enter the office. "You got an offer on your house?"

"Not yet," he said. "But I should by tonight." He smiled too, and in Jess's opinion, he didn't do that nearly often enough. She didn't see him often enough to really know, though, and she decided on the spot to change that.

How, she wasn't sure, but if they started dating, surely she'd get to see him more.

She'd spent the last two weeks fighting with herself over whether or not she should even *want* to see him more. In the end, she'd always come back to yes, she wanted to get to know him better.

The problem was, Dallas was like a walled city. He didn't say much, and he was so busy that anything she did to pop into his life would be extremely noticeable. She'd settled for texting a little bit here and there and seeing him occasionally at the West Wing. He didn't seem ready for much more than that, and Jess had once tried to convince a man he was ready to date when he wasn't, and she didn't need to repeat that disaster.

He sat down in front of his computer, and Jess saw the quick flash of pain as it crossed his face. "You okay?" she asked.

"Yeah." He painted over the discomfort with a smile that could surely charm anyone with even one good eye.

Jess cocked her head, trying to see deeper inside him to what he wouldn't say. "We haven't talked as much lately," she said. "I was a little surprised to get your text."

"Were you?" The smile slipped away, and the more vulnerable version of Dallas Dreyer took over. "I've just been really busy with getting the new system set up," he said. "And the kids back in school, and...stuff."

"You say 'stuff' a lot," she teased, but it did annoy her somewhat that he couldn't be more specific.

"Do I?" His light gray eyes sparkled now, and Jess sure did like seeing that. She'd seen him with this glint in his eye when he laughed with Ted Burrows or when he smiled at something his daughter said during dinner.

"Yes," she said with a light laugh, beyond glad it wasn't a giggle. "You might want to work on being a little more specific tonight." She stood and lifted her hand in a wave. "I have to get back to my horses. I'll see you tonight."

"Okay." He stood too and took the couple of steps to the door. "See you tonight." He smiled her out the door, and Jess couldn't help the extra bounce in her step as she went back to Rich and a horse named Valley of Ferns, because of her feathery light, almost velvet, coat.

***

"Hannah," Jess said later that night, entering the other woman's bedroom. "Can I borrow that tank top with the blue ruffles?"

Hannah looked up from her tablet, surprise in her expression. Jess already wore a pair of tight, black jeans, and she needed something feminine and flirty for this date. Though Dallas had touched her elbow that morning, and he'd asked her to dinner to celebrate the offer on his house, he'd still been somewhat distant. It was almost like he didn't even see her standing in front of him, and she really wanted to open his eyes that night.

Hannah's gaze slid down to Jess's feet and back to her

curled hair. "Who are you going out with? You said you didn't meet anyone at the wedding." She got up off her bed and stepped over to her closet.

"I didn't," Jess said. "Well, I suppose you could say I did."

Hannah handed her the shirt, and Jess slipped out of her T-shirt and into the blue tank. It clung to her bust-line all the way down to her ribcage and then fell in ruffled layers to cover the top of her jeans. "I love that on you," Hannah said. "It's so good with your coloring." She smiled at Jess. "Who are you all dolled up for?"

"Dallas Dreyer," Jess said, trying not to feel so giddy. She'd texted him earlier that afternoon, and he'd responded with, *Driving to get the kids. Will see you in a few hours.*

She'd deflated a little, and she'd determined not to text him again. He could send texts too, and she didn't want to come on too strong. She'd been told she could be intimidating, and Jess usually wasn't afraid to let a man know how she felt about him.

"Dallas Dreyer?" Hannah's eyes opened a little wider. "Wow, Jess. He is a good-looking man."

"Why are you so surprised then?" Jess turned to look at the back of the shirt in the mirror on Hannah's closet door. It hung right, and she was glad she'd thought of this tank top. Hopefully, Dallas would like it.

"I'm not surprised," Hannah said. "That he asked you out. I'm surprised you said yes."

"Why?" Jess looked at Hannah fully now. They'd been working together on the ranch for years now, and they'd lived in the West Wing next door to each other for all of that time. Eight or nine years, since Hannah had come to Hope Eternal.

"He doesn't seem like your type," Hannah said, shrugging. "That's all."

"What's my type?" Jess asked, truly curious. "He's smart and handsome. He's hardworking. He's turned that equipment shed around singlehandedly in just two weeks." She was very impressed with Dallas, and surely Hannah was too.

"That's all true," Hannah said. "It's just...he has two kids, Jess. And he's an ex-con." She shrugged again. "I mean, I get that we don't judge men like him here, but you were never very interested in the guys we've had from the re-entry program before."

"He's not in the re-entry program," Jess said. "And I like kids." Dallas's were nice enough, and she didn't find them annoying like some of the eleven-year-olds that came for their first riding lessons.

"Okay," Hannah said. "Forget I said anything."

"Thanks for letting me wear this." She smiled at Hannah and down at the tank top. "You're sure it looks okay?"

"It looks amazing," Hannah said, looking at her again before she picked up her tablet.

Jess lingered for a moment, sensing something in

Hannah. "Hey," she said, sitting on the edge of the bed and looking at the brunette. Really looking. "What's wrong?"

Hannah shook her head, sighed, and then let her shoulders sag. Without saying anything, she turned her tablet toward Jess, so she could see what was on the screen. Warm Hearts sat there, their highly recognizable logo with a handprint placed over a heart right at the top of the page.

Jess sucked in a breath, her eyes round as she looked from the screen back to Hannah.

"Why are you signing up for this?" she asked.

"Because Jill met Mike at the wedding, and now you're going out with Dallas, and Ginger is married now, and Emma's engaged, and I just...." She blew out her breath and rolled one shoulder again. "I'm just lonely, and I want to meet someone too." She turned the tablet back to her. "So I'm signing up for this thing. If someone messages me, and I'm not interested, I don't have to answer."

Jess had never used a dating app, and she was truly surprised Hannah would. She could hear the loneliness in her friend's voice though, and Jess didn't know how to make her feel better. She wasn't great with feelings and explaining them to herself or someone else.

"I love you, Hannah," she said, and the other woman raised her eyes to Jess's again. She stood, bent down, and hugged her, glad when Hannah sniffled and said, "I love you too, Jess. Have fun tonight."

The doorbell rang just as Jess said she would, and pure terror tore through her. "It's him, and I don't even have shoes on yet." She darted out of Hannah's bedroom and into hers, her mind quickly moving through her available footwear. Almost anything would go with a pair of jeans and a tank top, but Jess wanted to stand out.

She felt like she had to with Dallas, and she quickly stepped into a pair of black sandals that added a couple of inches to her height. Nothing too drastic, and nothing she couldn't walk in for the whole night. In fact, she'd once gone dancing in these sandals, and her feet hadn't complained once.

She hurried out into the kitchen to find Dallas standing there, chatting with Jill. He wore a pair of jeans too. Nothing too fancy, and nothing too light. He'd put on cowboy boots, and for some reason, Jess found that adorable. He was definitely more mechanic than cowboy, but she sure did like the idea of a cowboy mechanic, so she clung to that.

He wore a dark purple shirt with only a couple of bright yellow stripes across the chest, and if Jess hadn't found him appealing before, the cowboy hat he wore tonight would've changed her mind. Big time.

He caught her staring at him, and he reached up and touched the brim of that dark, delicious, cowboy hat with two fingers. She got herself moving in the right direction, her smile genuine and real as she approached.

"Hey," he said. "Don't you look great?" He grinned at

her and reached for her hand. She willingly laced her fingers through his, snaps and crackles and pops moving through her whole body. Her teeth almost chattered from the electricity bouncing between them, and when she met Jill's eyes, it was obvious she could see something happening between the two of them too.

"Thanks," Jess said, grinning from Jill to Dallas. "You look amazing too."

Dallas ducked his head as if examining his own clothes, as if he hadn't dressed himself. "I cleaned my car and everything."

"Let's go then," Jess said. They turned toward the front door, and she had to let go of his hand. Thankfully, he took her other one as they walked away from Jill, and once they settled in his car he gave a nervous chuckle.

"You wouldn't have wanted to get in this thing a couple of hours ago. The kids eat in it every day, and wow, my children are slobs."

Jess laughed with him, glad things seemed to be easy with him.

She quieted and as they left the ranch, he said, "I haven't been on a date in a very long time, Jess," he said. "I hope you'll forgive me if I mess it up."

"Dating is like riding a bike," she said. "It'll come right back to you."

"Do you go out a lot?" he asked.

"I wouldn't say a lot," Jess said, glancing at him. She also didn't want to talk about her romantic history on the first date. No need to get into the specifics of her failures and shortcomings so soon. No, she wanted to hide those for as long as possible.

"More than me," he said. "I'd been married for fifteen years. Martha and I dated for a year before we finally got engaged."

Jess didn't like that word "finally" in there. She shook her hair over her shoulders, realizing that she'd forgotten to put on earrings. A flash of regret hit her, because she wanted to be and look her best tonight.

"How long...?" She let her question hang there, because she didn't want to continue it. "You didn't want to get married?"

He glanced at her, but Jess just played with the end of a piece of hair as if she didn't care. But honestly, she did. If he wasn't looking for a committed relationship, she might as well go back to the West Wing right now.

"Martha stalled for a while," he said. "She wanted her father's approval, and I hadn't applied for medical school yet."

Ah, so status was important to his ex-wife. "She didn't file for divorce until you were about to get out?"

"Yes," Dallas clipped out.

That made perfect sense to Jess, but she wasn't sure Dallas had gotten the memo yet.

"Who's the last guy you went out with?" he asked, his voice still on the outer edge of angry.

"Spencer," she said.

Dallas looked fully at her, not bothering to watch the road. "Spencer from the ranch, Spencer?"

"Yes," Jess said, her chest filling with a chill. "It didn't really work out. He's like a brother to me."

"Did you kiss him?"

"Yes," Jess said. "It was awkward and horrible."

Dallas started to chuckle, the sound morphing into full-blown laughter. As he quieted, he said, "If it's like that when I kiss you, just tell me, okay? I haven't kissed a woman in a while either."

Surprise moved through Jess. "Are you planning on kissing me tonight?"

"I don't know," Dallas said. "I guess that depends on how well the date goes."

"It's the first date," she said.

"Yeah," he said, clearly not getting it.

"Maybe I don't kiss on the first date," she teased.

Dallas's cheeks took on a pinkish hue, and he chuckled again. "Good, that'll take the pressure off me for a while."

Jess crossed her legs in the front seat of his small sedan, wondering if he could see her yet. "I mean, I've been known to kiss on the first date, if I really like the guy."

"Oh, boy," he muttered. "Now I've got two standards to live up to."

She laughed with him, and the moment he parked in the parking lot of Red Light Ravioli, she knew she'd kiss him that night if he even attempted it. He was easy to talk to, and real, and handsome, and no matter what Hannah said, Dallas was exactly Jess's type.

"Tell me a little about prison," she said as she took his hand and they went inside the restaurant to get a table.

Dallas just stared at her and said nothing. He waited until they had a table and had ordered drinks before he even looked her way again. "I don't really want to talk about my time in prison," he said.

"How long were you there?" Jess asked.

"Thirty months."

Jess nodded, thinking of all she could do and had done in two and a half years' time. She'd heard a couple of Nate's stories from the River Bay facility, and she decided that if Dallas wasn't comfortable sharing about it yet, she shouldn't push him.

He winced as he shifted to get his phone out of his back pocket. "I set my kids' notification to something special," he said. "I hope you understand that I need to have this out sometimes."

"Of course," she said, admiring him and his devotion to his kids.

"Okay." He took in a long breath and looked at her. "So, Jess, how's Buttermilk doing?"

He wanted to talk about horses? She supposed he had asked her where she'd grown up and about her siblings in texts over the past couple of weeks. Still, she didn't want to talk about her job—or anything ranch-related at all.

"Good," she said. "Did you get the offer?"

"Oh," he said, a bit of life and energy coming into his eyes. "Yes, it came through about four-thirty. It's a full price offer, and I already accepted it." He glanced up as the waitress arrived with their drinks. He lifted his to his lips and took a long drink of it.

"That's great," she said. "Houston, right?"

"Yep," he said, nodding. "I'm going to have to get up there and go through everything."

"That doesn't sound fun," Jess agreed, though she honestly had no idea what it would be like to live through a divorce and have to go back to the house she'd shared with her husband, box everything up, and clean everything out. Alone.

Moving was hard enough, and to add that emotional weight to it felt entirely unfair to her. She reached across the table and covered one of Dallas's hands with both of hers. "I'll go with you, if you want."

"Thanks." He cleared his throat. "I'm going to ask Nate and Ted to go. With the three of us, it'll go fast." He nodded, keeping his head down so the brim of his cowboy hat blocked his face from her view. "But I'll probably need help with the kids."

"Lots of people to help with that."

He lifted his eyes to hers. "Do you like kids, Jess?"

"Yes," she said, disliking how she had to defend herself again tonight. "I really like your kids, Dallas. They're great."

"Thank you," he said, smiling softly. "I'm still figuring

out a lot of stuff. Parenthood isn't something you learn once and you're good to go."

"I'm sure that's true," she said. "My mother sometimes says I was the easiest and the hardest to raise."

"Oh, I can see you being the hardest," he said, the mood at the table lightening considerably.

"What does that mean?" she demanded in mock outrage. She squeezed his hand and let go, pulling hers back across the table.

"It means you have fire inside you," he said. "That doesn't like to be tamed."

Jess considered him, because he'd just spoken straight to her soul. "Do you like women with untamable fire inside them?"

"Yes," he said simply.

The waitress returned for their orders, but Jess hadn't even picked up the menu yet. Dallas hurried to do so, and they quickly decided on what they wanted to eat. The conversation turned to his kids, and how school was going for them. He came alive when he spoke about the mechanic work he did in the equipment shed, and she even got him to say, "I taught classes in prison for the other inmates."

She learned a lot about him, including that he didn't speak too fast or too slow. He cleaned his plate, claiming that his pine nut and pesto ravioli was some of the best pasta he'd ever put in his mouth, and that he had quite the dislike for popcorn.

"It always gets stuck in my teeth," he'd said, and that had made him more human in Jess's eyes.

The waitress had just asked, "Dessert for you tonight?" when his phone rang. He reached for it while Jess considered ordering one of every dessert on the menu just to prolong the time she had with him at dinner.

"It's Martha," he said, already sliding out of the booth. "I have to take this. I'll be right back." He swiped on the call as he stepped away, but Jess could clearly hear him say, "Hey, sweetheart," in a tender voice he surely only used for those he loved.

Jess sat back in the booth, dumbfounded. She managed to wave away the waitress and say they just needed the check.

Sweetheart.

Martha.

She was his *ex*-wife, but Jess got the very real feeling that Dallas did not think of her as his ex-anything.

In fact, everything in his life would go back to normal if he could get Martha back. Perhaps that was what he'd been trying to do these past couple of weeks when he'd been too busy to text her back.

"He answered a call from her while on a date with you." Jess sighed, negativity crowding into her lungs. She wanted to flee this ravioli restaurant and never come back. That was a real shame too, because it was one of the better places to eat in Sweet Water Falls.

The check arrived and Jess quickly pulled out her

card. She had to get out of there. She didn't see where Dallas had gone but it hardly mattered.

While she waited for her card to process, she dialed the one person she knew would come get her no matter what. No matter where.

"Spence," she said when her best friend picked up. "I need you to come get me in town." She stood up and shouldered her purse, sticking the card in her back pocket when the waitress returned with it.

Sweetheart.

Martha.

"What a fool you are," she muttered to herself as she wove through tables and toward the exit. She definitely wasn't going to get her kiss, and she thought back through her relationships, trying to find one that had ended before the night had.

She couldn't think of one, and just when Jess had thought she'd experienced it all in the dating pool, she could now add the humiliation of having her date answer a phone call from his ex-wife with the words, "Hey, sweetheart," to her list of misfortunes.

Disasters.

Follies.

Unluckiness.

Or maybe, just maybe, she had really bad taste in men, and she should never trust her own feelings again.

CHAPTER NINE

"No, Martha," Dallas said as firmly as he could. She'd often told him that he spoke in a rough, rugged voice that made her feel like he was angry with her. She'd coached him for a decade to have a better bedside manner. So he knew he could definitely add some bite to his tone. He sincerely hoped she could hear it right now.

"Dallas," she slurred, and he severely regretted taking this phone call. He turned and looked down the street where he'd been slowly walking. The restaurant was only one storefront down, so he hadn't gone too far. "I just need a little to tide me over."

"You're drunk," he said, not for the first time. "We're not talking about money until you're sober." His pulse fired in his chest, because he knew exactly what Martha was like when she drank too much. It wasn't pretty, and he was beyond grateful his children didn't have to be with her right now.

Guilt stung him right behind his lungs. He should be home with his children, making sure they were okay and well cared for. Helplessness filled him, but it didn't change his mind. "Besides, Martha, I have no money. I've only been out of prison for a couple of weeks."

"But you sold the house in Houston," she said, and in that sentence, she sounded almost normal.

He cocked his head to the side. "How did you know that?" The house was in his name; she wasn't anywhere on the title or contract, so she hadn't had to sign anything.

"Josh told me," she said, adding a giggle to the words. "He takes good care of me, Dally. Like you should."

Ice ran through his veins, because he knew Martha was on something stronger than the wine she liked with dinner—and sometimes for a long time after eating. She only called him by that ridiculous nickname when she was completely wasted.

He had no idea who Josh was, but everything in Dallas's life started to collapse. For some insane reason, he'd actually thought he and Martha could fix things between them. Ridiculous, he knew. Crazy. He had no right to hope for such a thing, when she'd abandoned their children, and he'd signed the divorce papers.

Did he really think they'd get remarried?

The pinch that started in his chest said yes, he'd

thought that. It grew and grew until a deep, dark hole had taken the place of his stomach and lungs. His heart struggled to beat against the foolishness and pain pouring from that hole, and the only things keeping him from swearing at his ex-wife, hanging up, and leaving town was Jess inside the restaurant, and his children waiting for him back at the ranch.

"I have to go, Martha," he said with as little emotion as he could.

"You owe me some of that money," she said. "That was my house—"

Dallas pulled the phone from his ear and jabbed at the red phone button to hang up. He still heard her say, "—too, and I deserve—" before her voice muted.

"You deserve what, Martha?" he asked bitterly. "You don't *deserve* anything. You abandoned our children at your sister's house without a word to me. No conversation. Nothing. You're a coward who ran away. You care more about yourself than anything and anyone else."

His chest heaved, and a storm raged in his whole being, body and soul.

Another couple walked past him, but he felt completely alone. He clenched his fists around the phone, wishing something would break. The case or his bones, he didn't care which. Somewhere far away, in the back of his mind, he remembered a conversation between him and his counselor at River Bay.

There will be times where you're treated unfairly, Dallas. How do you think you'll feel?

Angry, Dallas said. *I hate things that are unjust.*

You'll be an ex-con. Some people won't want to hire you when they find out.

Dallas had nodded. In prison, he'd accepted that. In prison, it was easy to talk through a situation and come to a conclusion on how he'd act. In prison, he'd been safe from real-world situations, ex-wives, first dates, and science homework he thought was stupid.

He did employ the breathing techniques his counselor had taught him, and slowly, Dallas came back to a place inside himself that wasn't about to punch at a brick wall until it came down. He turned back to the restaurant where he and Jess had enjoyed a nice meal together and went back inside.

The booth where he and Jess had been sitting was empty. He came to a complete stop, watching as the busboy wiped the table and stepped away. He had no idea what to do now, and he turned in a full circle, expecting to see Jess waiting for him somewhere.

She wasn't, and he met the eye of the woman at the counter who'd seated them. He retraced his steps to her. "Did you see where she went? Did she pay?"

"She left about twenty minutes ago," the woman said. "I'm sure she paid, because we don't have any tables that left without paying."

Dallas just nodded, his voice suddenly gone. His throat had narrowed so much, he could barely swallow as he left the ravioli restaurant and looked up and down the street. He didn't see Jess anywhere, and he hadn't seen her pass him either. Of course, he also hadn't realized he'd been gone for as long as twenty minutes, so anything was possible.

Still, he reasoned. If she'd come outside, she'd have seen him standing on the sidewalk. He hadn't moved that far away from the restaurant.

He worked up enough saliva to swallow, and then enough courage to dial Jess's number. It rang and rang, and she did not pick up. He mentally beat himself up for answering Martha's call. What was Jess supposed to think about that?

Dallas shook his head, irritation with his ex growing inside him again, and his annoyance with Jess multiplied too when he called her a second time with the same results as the first.

He sent her a quick text. *Listen, I'm sorry. I shouldn't have taken that call. Where are you?*

She read it, and Dallas stared at the phone, willing her message to come in. Should he go back to the car? Call her again?

"What you should've known," he muttered to himself. "Is that life was going too good, Dallas. You should've seen this coming."

He disliked the negativity in the statements, and he could hear his counselor admonishing him for always expecting the worst life could give him. But Dr. Pelltri hadn't lived Dallas's life. He didn't understand that life *had* kicked Dallas around quite a bit.

It sure did seem like every time things started to look up in Dallas's life, there was something or someone to pull him back down. He'd started attending religious services while at River Bay, and he honestly wasn't sure how he felt about God.

"Why did she have to call right then?" he asked, tilting his head toward the sky. He wasn't sure if God could hear him, or if He even cared. "Why did I answer?"

No one gave him any reasons or answers for either of his questions, but his next one—*Where was Jess?*—appeared on his screen.

I'm back at the ranch already, Dallas.

He tapped to call her again, praying with everything inside him that she'd answer this time. To his great surprise, the call connected though Jess didn't say anything.

"Hey," he said, relief filling the three letters. "I'm sorry, Jess." He found he didn't have anything else to say. He wasn't going to tell her about Martha, and that meant there wasn't anything to tell. "I shouldn't have answered the phone. I'm sorry."

She still said nothing, and Dallas's heart wailed at him.

What the message was, though, Dallas didn't know. His brain blanked, and he simply stood in the middle of the sidewalk, the Texas heat baking him, and waited for Jess to say something.

"What did she want?" she finally asked. "No, you know what? That's not the question I want answered."

Dallas swallowed, because he'd heard Jess talk in this clipped, irate tone before—when he'd delayed her before the wedding. She hadn't been happy then, and she most definitely was not happy now.

"Are you over her, Dallas?"

"Yes," he said, believing himself for the first time. If Jess had asked him that only an hour ago, he wouldn't have known what to say. *Maybe? I hope to be one day? No, not at all, because I'm still hoping we'll make things work between us?*

Any of those would've been true.

But now he knew she had another man in her life already. One who was supplying her with drugs and alcohol, and one who'd probably put her up to calling Dallas and asking him for money.

That was all Dallas had ever been good for when it came to Martha. Money.

Bitterness coated his mouth and throat, and while he'd felt the emotion before, it had never been this strong and this tinged with dislike.

"Are you sure?"

"Yes," he said again.

"Why did you call her sweetheart when you answered then?" Jess asked. "While you were on a date with me. A date *you* asked me to go on, Dallas."

He thought for a moment. "Reaction," he said. "Habit."

"Really?" Her sarcasm wasn't that hard to hear.

"Really," he said, not wanting to fight about this. "Are you really back at the ranch already?"

"Yes."

"How'd you get there?"

"I called Spencer," she said.

Humiliation ran through Dallas, along with a healthy dose of frustration. "Spencer, huh?"

"Don't say it like that," she said.

"Like what?" Dallas challenged as he started toward his car. No reason to stand out in the heat if he didn't need to wait for his date.

"I'm *not* seeing Spencer."

"Yet he's the first one you call to come get you. Why not Hannah? Or Jill? Emma? Ginger?" Anyone who wasn't a male she'd been out with before. Someone she hadn't *kissed* before.

"Jealousy is not a good look for you," she said.

"You either," he fired back, instantly regretting the words. His head still felt too hot as he sank into the driver's seat, but he managed to say, "I'm sorry. Okay? I made a mistake and I'm sorry," in a kind, normal voice.

He started the car and reached to turn off the radio.

"Can I please come explain it to you in person?" He didn't know what he'd do if she said no. Get his kids and go home, he guessed. He didn't see Jess that much around the ranch. He could avoid her easily, especially once he moved out of that cabin.

"Jess?" he asked above the sound of the air conditioning blowing full-blast in the car.

"Okay," she said. "I'll be in the stables."

"Thank you," he said.

"Don't thank me yet," she said, and Dallas almost chuckled. Instead, he said goodbye and looked out the windshield at the ravioli restaurant where they'd eaten. They'd been about to order dessert when Martha's call had come in, and Dallas sprang back out of his car and hurried inside.

"I need one of every dessert you have," he said. "To go, please."

––––––––

THIRTY MINUTES LATER, DALLAS ENTERED THE stable, immediately wondering where Jess would be. He'd not spent much time here at all, something he needed to change. He did remember that she'd been working with a horse named Diamond Valley, because she'd gotten the horse to do what she was supposed to in a much quicker fashion than Jess had originally thought she would.

A cowboy walked toward him, and Dallas dang near tripped over his own feet when he recognized Spencer. The other man slowed and said, "You're looking for Jess," easily. "She's out in the paddock with Diamond and Bumblebee."

"The paddock?" Dallas asked, wondering what Jess had said to Spencer. The other man wasn't looking at Dallas funny, nor did he seem like he'd found Jess in a bad state.

"Yeah, just go straight and back outside." Spencer turned and pointed to the big double doors on the other side of the stable. "Then turn left and go all the way to the end of the building. You can't miss 'er."

"Thanks." Dallas got himself moving, hearing the other man's footsteps recede in the other direction. He turned and looked over his shoulder to catch Spencer leaving the stables and turning toward the homestead. He seemed like a nice guy, and Dallas knew both Ted and Nate liked Spencer a lot. Connor especially liked him, and he was good with kids.

Jess had said he was like her brother, so maybe Spencer hadn't asked any questions. But if he really was like her brother, shouldn't he be overprotective of her, not showing Dallas exactly where to go?

He shook his head, trying to get the thoughts to leave. He didn't care what was going on with Jess and Spencer. She'd said they weren't seeing each other, and he either believed her or he didn't. He wanted to believe her, so he didn't need to spend any more time thinking about it.

He found her right where Spencer said she'd be too, her right hand stroking the side of a beautiful horse's face. She had one foot up on the bottom rung of the fence as she leaned close to the horse as if she were whispering secrets in its ear.

"Hey," Dallas said as he approached, and Jess lowered her hand as she looked his way. She wore a somber look, and she was beautiful in a way that made Dallas's tongue too thick for his mouth.

He knew she loved horses, and she was very good at her job. Maybe she didn't get along with everyone, but he'd never seen her treat anyone unkindly, even his mechanics who clearly didn't like her much.

"I'm sorry," he said again, lifting the oversized paper bag he carried. "I got dessert."

She looked from him to the bag and back. "You thought you could bribe me with desserts?"

"Yes," he said simply, letting a smile touch the corners of his mouth. "Would that work?"

Jess stepped off the bottom rung and tucked her hands in her back pockets. "Depends."

"On what?"

"What kind of dessert?"

Dallas let the smile spread across his face then. "Well, Miss Jessica Morales. I think I'm in luck, because I got one of everything. There's bound to be something you like in here."

What he really wanted was something that would help her forgive him, and as he pulled out the seven-layer chocolate mousse cake, he watched her eyes light up.

Bingo.

CHAPTER TEN

"I want another bite of that cream cheese square," she said, waiting for Dallas to lift the plastic container and hand it to her.

He'd been talking for twenty minutes while they sampled all eight desserts he'd brought back to the ranch. She'd taken him into the office in the barn, where Hannah did a lot of her work. Jess would have to make sure she swept all the crumbs and powdered sugar from the desk, or Hannah would be dealing with ants, and then Jess would have to deal with Hannah's wrath.

"I'm sorry," Dallas said for probably the sixth or seventh time. "I thought it must be something I needed to know, because Martha never calls me." He ducked his head and took another bite of the white chocolate raspberry cookie. Jess hadn't liked that much, but Dallas sure seemed to.

"And to be completely transparent, Jess, I thought that, because I'm the one who's been calling Martha."

"You have?" Jess reached her fork toward the cream cheese square again. The crust was part blondie, part cookie, and part nutty, and utterly fantastic. A layer of vanilla cake sat on that, with a layer of cream cheese that wasn't quite cheesecake texture. It was sweet and savory and salty, and her favorite thing he'd brought.

Or maybe she'd liked the chocolate cake the best. It was hard to pick something with no chocolate over something practically oozing hot fudge, but Jess was seriously considering it a toss-up at the moment.

"Yes," Dallas said. "To keep her updated about the kids. That I got them in school. That Remmy had grown three inches in the past few months. That sort of thing." He looked away and dusted off his hands. "She obviously doesn't care, but I thought she did."

Jess nodded. "I'm sorry she doesn't care."

Dallas met her eye again, and that same electric pulse that had always existed between them zinged through her bones. She'd been hurt and angry an hour ago. Spencer had wondered why she needed a ride, and she'd simply said her ride wasn't reliable. Jess hadn't volunteered any further information, and Spencer hadn't asked. He'd already been in town, which had allowed her to get back to the ranch in record time.

She'd gone immediately to her horses, as the equines always made her feel better about herself, even when she made rash and irrational decisions. He'd told her a couple of weeks ago he wasn't over his wife, and now he was saying he was. She'd been whispering about it to Diamond when he'd arrived, and Jess really wanted to believe his feelings had changed in the past fourteen days.

"I think she's mixed up in something," Dallas said, his voice almost a whisper. "She wanted money, from the sale of the house."

Jess cocked her eyebrows. "How did she know about the house?"

"Someone named Josh." Dallas shook his head, clearly in pain. Jess had never been married, so she couldn't even pretend to understand all the emotions of a divorce. She knew she saw a good-hearted man in front of her, one who was just trying to do the right thing.

"Dallas," she said gently. "I'm sorry about Martha."

He looked up, his eyes wide, hopeful, and filled with vulnerability. "Thank you."

"I also need to apologize," Jess said, looking down at her cream cheese square again. "I shouldn't have assumed the worst and ran out. That wasn't very nice of me."

"You don't need to apologize."

"I think I just sort of...I don't know." Jess could see herself sitting in the booth alone after hearing Dallas answer the phone with the word "sweetheart." She floated above the situation, watching herself sit there and talk to herself, then call Spencer, pay the bill, and leave the restaurant.

She hadn't looked for Dallas at all, and she'd gone down the street to the corner, where Spencer had picked her up only a few minutes later. They'd gone back to the ranch, and he'd said nothing to her. She obviously wasn't very distressed on the outside, though Jess felt like she'd messed up once again. She'd somehow miscommunicated to Dallas that she wasn't interested. Or that she wasn't patient. Or forgiving.

She wanted to be all of those things, and though they'd just had a good talk, she still felt like she was operating from a completely different book than he was.

"It's okay," he said. "You really don't need to apologize to me. You didn't do anything wrong."

"I did, though," she insisted. "I judged you, and I shouldn't have. I left, when I should've stayed to have this exact conversation." She shook her head. "You said you weren't ready to go out with me a couple of weeks ago, and then you asked tonight, and I should've known that meant you were over your wife. I'm sorry too, Dallas. Will you forgive me?"

"Of course," he said. "Does that mean you forgive me?"

"Yes," she said, feeling them both take one giant step toward one another. For her, though, there was still a massive barrier keeping them on opposite ends of the spectrum.

"Dallas," she said slowly. She was full and starting to get a buzz from the high sugar consumption, so she didn't dare take another bite of any dessert. "I think I need to know about prison."

He nodded. "I've told you why I was there and what happened with Martha."

"I think I got three or four sentences," she said. "I need more."

"More of what?" he asked.

"You were a surgeon, right?"

"Yes."

"What kind?"

"Heart surgeon," he said.

"Someone died?"

His jaw clenched, and he nodded. "Some of my patients died, despite my best efforts. It's the worst feeling in the world to know you're not good enough when so many people are counting on you."

Jess didn't know what that kind of pressure felt like either. She'd always been accepted in her family, and she'd been good with horses for her whole life. Her father said it was a gift she'd been born with, and she'd never doubted him.

"But someone died, and someone thought it was your fault," she said.

"Yes," he said. "I got sued; the hospital where I worked did too. There was a malpractice issue, and then the sister of the woman who died filed with the insurance company too. I guess I signed the papers, because I was desperate to help the family. I wanted them to know I still cared, that I hadn't done anything wrong on the operating table." He shook his head. "Always read what you're signing, Jess. By me signing that paperwork, I was essentially saying that the insurance should pay for this woman's death, and that was fraud. I thought I was signing a form for her medical care, not her death benefit."

"That's not your fault."

"Doesn't matter," Dallas said, his voice low. "I signed the paperwork. It's amazing how quickly fires can start, by seemingly simple decisions."

Jess could only nod, though she didn't have the personal experience Dallas did.

"I didn't go to court," he said. "I couldn't put the family through it. So I signed the medical malpractice admittance, got fired to save the hospital, and agreed to sign for insurance fraud if the same charges were brought against the sister and they dropped the wrongful death suit. Otherwise, I said I would take them to court over the insurance issue."

Jess didn't know what to think. She didn't understand the ins and outs of the law. She didn't even know any lawyers besides the ones that Ginger had to deal with on occasion as she took men for the Residential Reentry Program.

"They must've agreed," she said.

"They did," he said. "I got thirty months for the two charges. The sister got fifteen for her role in the insurance fraud."

"Wow," Jess said, noting that he'd stopped eating too. "And what about your limp? Did that come from prison or before?" She watched the surprise roll across his face, followed quickly by a dark look that only stayed for half a breath.

"I limp?"

"Only a little," she said. "Only when you get up after sitting for a while." She shrugged to try to downplay it, as Dallas was obviously sensitive about it. "I've seen it once or twice."

A frown had gathered between his eyebrows, and he studied the desktop for several long seconds. "I got beaten my first night in prison," he said. "River Bay is a low security facility. Most of the guys there are like me—white collar criminals caught up in something illegal, but not violent. Not a lot of drug charges. Hardly any weapons. No sexual assaults. It's mostly businessmen, guys who used to own businesses, or someone who made a couple of bad decisions that were bad enough to put them in prison for a while."

"It's still prison," Jess said, mostly to prompt him when he didn't go on.

"That it is," Dallas said. "And there are still gangs in River Bay, and a man still needs to watch his back." His facial features had hardened, but he didn't back down from this conversation the way he had previously. "I didn't know all of that, and I got jumped my first night there. The leader of the gang at the time wasn't happy that I'd put his sister in jail. I was nearly unconscious by the time Nate got there."

"Nate? Ginger's Nate?"

Dallas nodded, everything on his face softening. "He came, and he got the others to leave me alone. I'm not even sure how, and every time I ask him, he just says it doesn't matter. He and Ted took me to the infirmary and patched me up the best they could. I saw the doctor the next day, and I had a broken finger and two fractured ribs. Everything else was muscle and skin pain. Lots of cuts and bruises. It took me a long time to heal, because of the ribs, mostly. My back has been messed up since, and I suppose it does cause me to limp a little bit when I get stiff."

Jess reached across the corner of the desk and put her hand over his. "I'm sorry, Dallas."

"Nate watched out for me after that. I watched out for him and Ted. There are a couple of other guys in our band of brothers—Slate and Luke—and I worry about them. Luke especially. He'll be alone in River Bay for three months after Slate gets out."

"Do you still talk to them?"

"Inmates only get fifteen minutes for a phone call," he said. "I've spoken to Slate once, and he said Luke hasn't said anything, but Slate's worried about him in there alone."

"Why are they in there?"

"Slate ran a bank in San Antonio. A huge branch, and

he processed fraudulent transactions over Christmas for an organized crime family."

"What?" Jess asked.

"Yeah, it sounds bad," Dallas said. "But it's not. He just didn't know what he was dealing with. He got a list of transactions to be completed from what he thought was a reputable company. He processed them. Later, he found out that he'd stolen over a million dollars from seventeen businesses in some mall in the city. He got four years. He'll be out in seven or eight months."

"Wow." There was so much Jess didn't know.

"Luke is a boxer," he said. "A good one too. He was working his way up through the ranks to becoming pro, when someone he knocked out sued him for excessive violence. I guess the guy had suffered permanent brain damage. He sued Luke and the referee who didn't call the match before this guy got pulverized. He's only been in a year or so. Has another year to go, I believe."

Jess couldn't even imagine being in jail for fifteen minutes, let alone fifteen months. Everything was easier for someone not living through it, and she wished she had more life experience so she could relate to Dallas a little easier.

She couldn't help feeling like she'd put more distance between them because of her behavior that night. The last thing he needed was someone running out on him, especially someone who should've stayed to get his perspective on the situation.

"I've got to get my kids," he said, starting to clean up. Jess helped, snapping lids closed and loading the leftover treats into the paper bag.

"Will they eat these?" she asked.

"Yeah, sure," he said. "Kids love sugar." He grinned at her, the moment starting out flirty and fun and quickly sobering. "Jess, would you like to maybe start spending some time with me and my kids?"

"Yes," she blurted, before her mind could truly latch on to what he was asking. "I'd like that."

He nodded, his smile plain on his face. "Okay. I'll ask them what they want to do, and if it's okay if you come along."

"Oh, so I'm going to be the tagalong. Is that it?" She picked up the bag. "If that's the case, I get to tell them about these treats."

He laughed and took the bag from her. "That's not the case at all." He slipped his hand into hers next, and they started the walk back to the homestead. The night had darkened while they'd been inside the barn eating too much sugar, and Jess sighed as she looked up into the sky. It was deep purple and blue and black, and she found it absolutely wonderful.

"The sky in Montana is twice as big as this one," she said.

"Is that so?" he asked, and he sounded so Texan. "I thought everything was bigger in Texas."

Jess giggled and kept her eyes on the skies, looking for

the first twinklings of the stars. "Everything but the sky, Mister."

"I suppose that's why they call it Big Sky country."

"That's right."

"Did you like living in Montana?"

"Sure," she said. "My dad has a small ranch there. We all worked it."

"You just have sisters, right?"

"Two sisters, yes," she said. "I'm the oldest."

"I think I could've guessed that," he teased, and Jess laughed again. "You didn't want his ranch?" he asked. "Or would he not pass it down?"

"He would," Jess said, suddenly thoughtful again. "But no, I don't want it. I left Montana to work in Calgary with the rodeo horses for a while. Then I came here. I love it here. I love training horses. My dad's ranch is more of a cattle operation, and my sister has taken it over for my parents."

"That's Abi, right?" Dallas asked.

"Yes, Abi," Jess said, thinking of her younger sister. "She's just a few years younger than me. Almost engaged to a guy name Huey."

"Ah, right," Dallas said. "I think you mentioned the almost-engagement in a text. Still not a thing?"

"Not yet," Jess said with a smile. "But Nia is convinced it'll be soon, and she said I'll be the first to know." She wouldn't really be the first to know. Abi would obviously know, and Nia, and their parents. It was only

Jess who wasn't in Bozeman anymore. For a moment, homesickness descended on her, and she let it flow through her while she and Dallas walked through the stunning night.

"At least you talk to your sisters," he said, breaking the enchanting moment.

"You don't?" she asked. He'd said little about his family, the same way he'd said little about his time in prison.

"I talk to my sisters," he said. "And my brother. And my mother. But not my dad."

"Where are you in the order?" she asked.

"Second. Olive is three years older than me at forty-three. Judy is thirty-five. Greg is thirty-two. They're all married, with kids."

She heard what he didn't say—*like me, once.*

The lights above the garage came on as they sensed Jess and Dallas's movement. "Have you tried talking to your dad?"

"Yes," Dallas said. "I've called him three times since I've been here. My mother finally said he's just not ready."

"I'm sorry," Jess said, thinking there was simply another thing she couldn't relate to. She spoke to her parents and always had.

"It's okay," he said. "He's stubborn, but I have to believe he'll come around. I might go up to Temple when I go to clean out my house in Houston."

"Oh, that's a good idea," Jess said. She paused in the light of the garage. "Well, I'm this way."

"Thanks for going out with me tonight," he said, releasing her hand and smiling at her. "I hope we can do something again soon. Maybe without the phone call from my ex and you getting a ride back here with yours."

She gaped at him for a moment, and then the pair of them both started laughing. "What a disaster," Jess said. "Right?"

"Oh, I don't think so." Dallas took her into his arms, and that got her to sober right up. He was so strong, and smelled so good, and Jess closed her eyes and just let herself be with him for a few moments.

He cleared his throat, fell back half a step, and swept his lips along her cheek. "I'll talk to you soon, okay?" He put more distance between them while her skin felt like something fizzy was bubbling through it.

"Okay," she finally said, and he turned and went up the back steps to the deck at the Annex. She watched him until he went inside, a loud burst of noise escaping the door when it was opened.

She went up the few steps and into the West Wing, no noise greeting her. It wasn't that late, but the kitchen sat in darkness, with only the light above the stove to show the path to the hallway that led to the bedrooms.

She'd just reached hers when Hannah opened her door. "Jess," she said. "How did it go tonight?"

"Good," Jess said, trying to keep her voice light.

"Listen, I just wanted to say that I'm an idiot." Hannah folded her arms and leaned against the wall. "I shouldn't have said Dallas wasn't your type."

"Oh, it's fine," Jess said. "You know I do what I want anyway." She grinned at Hannah, who smiled back. She was much more reserved than Jill, and she didn't quite have the confidence Jess did.

"That you do," Hannah said. "I'm still in awe of that, by the way."

"You could do it too," Jess said, nodding into her bedroom. She needed to get out of these jeans and into something with a more forgiving waistband, especially after all that cake she'd consumed. "Who do you want to go out with?"

"I don't know," Hannah said. "I met a guy at church a couple of months ago, but I haven't seen him since."

"What about someone here?" Jess asked, unbuttoning her jeans.

"Here?" Hannah sounded like she'd seen a ghost. "Really, Jess?"

"Sure," Jess said. "Spencer is great. He'd go out with you. Bill. Jack."

"Okay, Bill is way too old for me."

Jess laughed and pushed her jeans off her ankles. "He is not," she said. "Spence is older than him."

"You're kidding."

"Spence is almost forty," Jess said. "How old do you think Bill is?"

"I don't know." Hannah sat on Jess's bed while she pulled on a pair of stretchy pants. "Fifty?"

"Oh-ho-ho," Jess chortled. "Don't ever let him hear you say that. Bill is thirty-six, Hannah. He's actually younger than you."

"You have got to be kidding. He has a full head of gray hair."

"It's silver, baby, and a lot of women like that." Jess sat cross-legged on the bed. "So Bill or Spencer? Or what about Steve-the-Swann's-guy?"

"Steve has a girlfriend," Hannah said, casting her eyes down. "And I can't order any more ice cream from him, because I made a huge fool of myself to find that out."

"Hannah," Jess said, smiling widely. "Why haven't I heard this story?"

"Because it's embarrassing." Hannah looked up and shook her head. "I'm not telling it right now."

"All right," Jess said. She could get the story later. "So Spencer or Bill? We can make a plan and you can ask one of them tomorrow."

"Tomorrow?" Hannah squeaked.

"Yes," Jess said, deciding for her. "Tomorrow. Hannah, you want to go out with someone. You know you do. Time to be brave and *do* something."

"Be brave," Hannah said, reaching up to tuck her brown hair behind her ear. "Do something."

"Spencer or Bill?"

"You know what?" Hannah asked, a new spark entering her eyes. "Let's go with Bill."

Jess raised her eyebrows but kept her smile in place. "Wow, Bill. I was not expecting that."

"Really?"

"You just said you thought he was fifty years old," Jess said.

"Yeah, well, you said his hair was silver, not gray, and maybe I am one of those women who like that." She grinned then, and all Jess could do was laugh and shake her head.

"Okay, so we just need a good plan for you to talk to him alone...."

CHAPTER ELEVEN

Dallas grabbed as many bags as he could carry from the trunk, telling Thomas and Remmy to do the same. They'd been to the store three times that day already, and he was not going back for a fourth time. Whatever they didn't have, they could survive the night without.

He never wanted to unpack another box, but he knew he had a lot more boxing, taping, and moving in his future. He'd signed the agreement to sell his house in Houston three weeks ago, and he only had eight more days before the buyer would close.

Ted and Nate were going with him to go through the whole house in just two days, and they were planning to get it done in a weekend. Dallas hadn't exactly told them how big the house was, nor what condition it was in. The first item he knew; the second he did not. Martha could've packed everything they owned and taken it with her, but somehow Dallas doubted it.

She'd called him twice more since his date with Jess, and wisely Dallas hadn't answered the phone unless he was alone. She'd asked for money both times, and Dallas hadn't known what to tell her. He'd asked her where she was living; she wouldn't tell him. He'd asked her who Josh was; and she'd clammed right up. He'd asked her what she was doing for a job, and she'd actually scoffed, as if working was far beneath someone like her.

Dallas heaved a sigh as he lifted the grocery bags he carried onto the countertop in the new house he'd rented for him and his kids. "Oh, boy," he moaned. "That was a lot of cans."

Thomas put his sacks up on the counter too, and Remmy came in toting a gallon of milk and a bunch of bananas.

"Let me, Smalls," Dallas said, taking the gallon of milk from her before she dropped it. He'd seen what happened to the plastic containers milk came in when they hit a hard floor, and it wasn't pretty.

He looked around the house, starting to feel like it was coming together. They'd brought over the majority of their stuff last night, and he'd let Thomas pick which bedroom he wanted. All three of them sat down a hall that dead-ended into a linen closet, and forked left into the master bedroom and right into two other, smaller bedrooms. Thomas had taken the one at the back of the house, and

Remmy had come into Dallas's room in the middle of the night, claiming to be afraid of being the closest one to the front door.

He'd let his daughter sleep in his bed with him, because it was a new place, and he could. In the end, Thomas had been in the big bed in the morning too, and Dallas didn't know when he'd come in.

They'd spent today at school and work, and once Dallas had picked them up from school, they'd started shopping.

He started unpacking the groceries and telling Thomas what to put where in the pantry. He gave Remmy the things she could put in the fridge, his mind on Jess. They'd gone out twice more too, and his children had started horseback riding lessons with her as well. Dallas loved walking out to the corrals about five to watch them dismount.

Remmy especially loved the lessons, and she gave Jess a big hug around the middle every time she got off her horse—aptly named Princess. Remmy skipped everywhere on the ranch, and Dallas's heart had started to heal a little bit with his daughter's joy.

Hannah had offered for both of them to be in the after-school honeybee program, and Dallas had readily accepted. Any time he could keep the kids out on the ranch until he finished work was a win in his book. They seemed to enjoy the ranch even without an activity to do, and Dallas could often find them playing in the fields surrounding the homestead or in Ted's cabin with Missy and Connor.

"What do we want for dinner?" he asked as he started folding up their recyclable grocery bags.

"Pizza," Thomas said. "Can you order, Dad?"

"Not pizza," Remmy said, making a face. "We had that last night. There's still some in the fridge."

"Just the kind with nothing on it," Thomas said, shooting a dark look at his sister. Dallas didn't particularly want pizza again either, and he wouldn't eat the plain cheese leftover in the fridge. He also didn't want to cook, and he'd literally stage a riot if he had to leave the house again.

He looked from his son to his daughter and back, wanting them both to be happy. "What about—?" Before he could finish, the doorbell rang, and someone knocked a moment later.

"I'll get it," Dallas said, and he left his kids standing in the kitchen at the back of the house while he went past the dining room table and a couple of loveseats to the front door. He opened it, pure surprise mingling with happiness when he found Jess standing there. "Well, howdy, pretty lady." He reached up to tap his cowboy hat, a grin forming on his face instantly. "What are you doin' here?"

She lifted a baking dish, and he reached to take it from her, because she also had a bag of groceries hanging from her wrist. He caught the scent of garlic and chicken as she said, "I brought dinner. I figured you guys would be hungry and not have much in the house."

"We've been to the store three times today," Dallas said. "But somehow, I didn't buy anything that was ready to eat."

"Now you don't have to." She smiled at him as she squeezed past him and into the house. She looked around, taking in the floors, the furniture, the fine craftsmanship in the beams in the ceiling. "Dallas, this place is amazing."

"You found it," he said, following her. "So thanks, by the way. It is pretty amazing." It wasn't the seven-thousand-square-foot monstrosity he had in Houston, and Dallas had thanked the Lord for that every night since he'd seen this place.

He certainly didn't need all that space, and this three bedroom, two and a half bathroom house with half an acre of land was perfect for him and his kids. They had a yard to play in, and Remmy was already asking for kittens. Thomas was violently opposed to that, and he wanted a dog, of course.

Dallas sided with Thomas on that one, but he didn't think any of them were ready for a pet. He was still trying to make sure he sent his children to school on time looking like they had someone who cared about them.

"Jess brought dinner," he said, taking the baking dish into the kitchen.

"Bread," she said, finally abandoning her scrutiny of the house. "Salad. Brownies. That's chicken Alfredo."

Dallas took the tin foil off the dish to the sight of the creamiest, cheesiest pasta he'd ever seen. His mouth watered, and he knew his kids would like this. "Did you make this?" he asked.

"It's the one thing I know how to cook." Jess beamed at him and started fiddling with the buttons on his stove. "This bread needs five minutes to toast, and dinner is served."

"Tommy, get us some plates," Dallas said. "Remmy, you get the punch out." He busied himself with opening the bagged salad and drooling over the brownies. He got out silverware and set it next to the plates his son had retrieved. He took out a knife and cut the brownies, putting big pieces on each plate.

Jess turned from the stove and paused. "What is going on here?"

"We're having dessert first," Dallas said, picking up two of the plates. He nodded to the other two before he moved to the table. "Who wants this one?"

"Me!" Remmy danced over to him and climbed into the chair. He set her brownie in front of her and left the other one on the table. He returned to the kitchen to finish the salad and make the punch. He took everything to the table, as his momma had taught him how to have a family meal at a real table. Growing up, all Dreyer's were expected to be at the dinner table at six-thirty, barring an emergency.

Dates and jobs had been exceptions. Hanging out with

friends was not. His mother simply said to bring them along, and she'd often fed twice as many children as she'd actually given birth to. Dallas had loved having his friends over for dinner, because his momma was a good cook.

His heart squeezed at the thought of her, and he knew it was a sign that he needed to call her. He should probably get up there with the kids one of these weekends, and he decided he'd call her after dinner that night.

"Let's say grace," he said, glancing at Jess. She'd mentioned church before, but Dallas had never actually seen her attend. He swiped his hat from his head and looked at Thomas. "Your turn, Tommy."

"Dear Lord," Tommy started, bowing his head as he spoke. "Bless this food. Thank you for Jess for bringin' it. We're glad to have our own house without the bugs. Bless Mom. Bless Dad. Help me to get a good grade on my science test on Friday, and help Remmy to forget about gettin' a cat. Amen."

"Amen," Dallas said, glad Thomas had at least remembered the bit about Jess bringing the food.

"I'm not going to forget about a cat," Remmy said, reaching for one of the toasty pieces of garlic bread.

Dallas grinned at her and then Thomas, wondering what he thought about his mother. *Bless Mom.* What did that mean?

Dallas hadn't gotten any extra airtime in the prayer. *Bless Dad.*

He needed all the help he could get, and he looked at

Thomas and asked, "What's the science test about on Friday?"

A COUPLE OF HOURS LATER, HE EASED OUT OF Remmy's bedroom and closed the door behind him without making a sound. Exhaustion pulled through his whole body as he went back into the main area of the house and found Jess putting the rest of the pasta in his fridge.

His heart slipped between beats at the sight of her there, and he keenly remembered having a good woman in his home, helping with the kids, cleaning up dinner, and being his best friend.

He paused at the end of the hall and watched her turn toward him. "Thank you," he said, his mouth suddenly dry as his fantasies started down a path that ended with kissing her goodnight. He'd entertained such thoughts on all of their previous dates, but he hadn't quite pulled the trigger yet.

Their last date had been on a Sunday afternoon, and when they'd returned to the ranch, a picnic had been in full swing on the front lawn at the homestead. They hadn't had any privacy, and Dallas definitely needed to be alone to kiss Jess.

"Of course," she said.

They moved toward one another, and Dallas wrapped

her in a hug, everything inside him sighing.

"You're going to Houston on Friday, right?" she asked.

"Yes," he said. "We're leaving at noon to get a jump on the weekend."

"Take me to dinner tomorrow night then?" She leaned back and peered up at him, and Dallas couldn't look away from her deep, beautiful eyes.

"With the kids?" he asked. He was already leaving them with Amy and Brent that weekend, and sometimes the constant juggling of his parental responsibilities weighed on him like a noose around his neck.

He quickly dismissed those feelings, because his children were not a burden. He refused to think of them that way, even for a moment.

"Sure," Jess said. "I'd love to go with the kids. Do you... what have you told them about us?"

"Not much," he admitted, another sigh pulling through his body. He looked away, out the back window to the large back yard that already needed to be mowed. "I should probably say something, huh?"

"Probably," she said. "I mean, how would you phrase that?"

He looked back to her, the feel of her arms around him suddenly registering twice as strongly in his mind. "Hmm, that's a good question." He smiled at her. "I think I'd use the word girlfriend if you're not averse to that."

Jess's eyes sparkled, but she did not smile. "I don't think so, cowboy," she said.

"No?" Dallas asked, liking this game and the way she teased him.

"You haven't kissed me yet," she said. "It's not the first date, and I think kissing comes before that specific label."

Dallas didn't waste another moment. He adjusted his hands along her waist, leaned down, and touched his mouth to hers, letting his eyes drift closed. Pure heat stole through his body, pumping out in waves with every beat of his heart.

He deepened the kiss, because he hadn't had the soft, caring touch of a woman in a long, long time. Jess matched his movement, absolutely no complaining coming from her. Thankfully, Dallas had managed to land the kiss without making a fool of himself.

Her fingernails traced up the sides of his neck and over his ears, causing a shiver to move through Dallas's shoulders and down his spine. He wasn't sure if this relationship was wise or not, or if he was moving too fast after his divorce or not. All he knew was he wanted to keep kissing Jess.

So he did—at least until Thomas said, "Dad? Can you come help me with my window?"

Dallas sucked in a breath and jumped away from Jess in the same motion, his heartbeat booming in his throat, his ears, and his skull. "Sure," he said, his voice far too high to be normal. Had his son seen them kissing? They'd been standing right there in plain sight.

"What's wrong with it?" he asked as he strode away

from Jess still standing in the kitchen.

"I can't get it closed," Thomas said. "I thought I wanted it open, but it's still too hot."

Dallas followed his son into the bedroom and got the window closed. He tucked his son into bed and kissed his forehead. "See you in the morning, bud."

When he returned to the living room, Jess stood near the door, her purse over her shoulder. "You're going?" he asked.

"I think so," Jess said, tucking her hair behind her ear.

Dallas wanted to do that, but he approached with caution. "Tomorrow night is still good? We can just go straight from the ranch if that works for you. Whenever we're all ready."

"Sure." She looked up at him, something vulnerable and beautiful in her expression. "And you can use that label." A smile touched that pretty mouth, and all Dallas could think about was kissing her again.

Instead, he employed his Texas gentleman genes and reached to open the door behind her. "Great," he said. "I'll talk to the kids on the way to school in the morning." How he would do that, and what he would say, he had no idea. He'd never had to do anything like this before, and he felt like he'd just boarded a boat with no bottom.

"Great, see you tomorrow." Jess stretched up and pressed her lips to his again, and Dallas growled deep in his throat, one hand sweeping around her and keeping her right where he wanted her.

CHAPTER TWELVE

J ess could kiss a man like Dallas all day and all night. He knew how to make a woman feel sexy and strong all at the same time. His body was warm against hers, and he tasted like the brownies he'd eaten as an appetizer and as a dessert.

"You should definitely go," he said, his voice ragged and hoarse.

"Mm." Jess drifted out the front door and down the steps. When she got to her car, her good sense returned, and she turned back to wave to Dallas. He stood in the doorway and watched her, lifting his own hand to say goodnight.

Jess had known him for a week and a month, and while she wouldn't classify their relationship as being that old, she felt like she knew him really well. He worked hard on the ranch, and everyone in the equipment shed respected him. He didn't say anything that didn't need to be said, and she'd never seen anyone as dedicated to their kids as he was.

He really had a way with them, whether he knew it or not, and Jess loved working with them on their riding lessons and eating with them when they stayed for dinner in the West Wing.

Remmy had warmed to her instantly and easily, but Thomas still hung back. She wasn't sure what she expected from the ten-year-old, and she told herself that they didn't have to be best friends instantly. He was a quiet, reserved boy who liked horses and dogs, being outside, and math and science. She'd listened to him talk about the genetics unit they were doing in school with excitement. So much excitement that she'd found herself smiling and wanting to be involved with the unit on cross-pollinating plants.

She got up the next day and worked with her horses. She checked in with the kids after their horseback riding lessons, and Remmy didn't come skipping over to her like usual. She did do that to her father, and Dallas scooped his daughter up into his arms, smiling as he said something to her.

Remmy giggled and responded, then they both looked at Jess. Dallas kept his daughter on his hip as he came closer. "See? She's not going to bite."

Remmy looked at Jess, and Jess just looked back.

"Daddy says you're his girlfriend now," the little girl drawled.

"Is that what he says?" Jess asked, grinning at her. "What do you think of that?"

Remmy shrugged, and Dallas did the same. He set the girl down, and she ran toward Nate, who'd just arrived back with another group, including Thomas.

"I told them this morning," he said. "Remmy didn't know what to think. She asked if she couldn't hug you anymore or if you only liked me and not her now."

Jess didn't know what to say. How could she explain what dating meant to a six-year-old? "And Thomas?"

"He said, I knew you were kissing her last night, Dad." Dallas chuckled. "I asked him what he thought about that, and he said kissing is gross."

"Oh, well, I disagree with him about that," Jess said, watching the boy dismount. He took his horse's reins and walked him back to the group, handing them to Spencer.

"Me too," Dallas murmured. "But I did tell him I wouldn't kiss you in front of him again."

"Good plan."

Thomas approached, and Jess asked, "How was it, Thomas? You're on week four, right? Did you get to go up the hill?"

The boy's face lit up and he nodded. "Yeah, and I got Ginger to do it before any of the other riders."

"You did?" Jess looked over to the tawny horse named

Gingerbread Castle. "That's amazing. Ginger is kind of a softie, so I'm surprised she went first."

Thomas looked at where Dallas held Jess's hand. Instinctively, she tightened her fingers in his, and he squeezed back. "What time are we going to dinner?" he asked.

"Six-thirty," Dallas said. "I have to get back to work for a minute, and I'll come find you."

"I'm going to go ask Missy about her oral report," Thomas said, walking away. "Okay?"

"Okay," Dallas called after his son, and they stood there and watched for a few more seconds.

"I think that could've gone better," Jess said.

"He just doesn't know what to think," Dallas said. "And he's not happy he has to stay with his aunt and uncle this weekend instead of coming out here."

"We'd take them," Jess said. "Me and Emma and Hannah."

"I know," Dallas said, and that was all. His ex-wife's sister was coming, though, with her husband, and Dallas's stance on that hadn't been swayed no matter how many people offered to help him with his kids this weekend.

"I do have to get back to work," he said. "I'll see you in a bit, okay?" He swept his lips across her forehead, and Jess nodded as he walked away from the corrals and toward the equipment shed. When she turned back to the mass of horses and all the kids who'd arrived for the next riding session, she caught Spencer staring at her.

He looked like a combination of Thomas and Remmy —partially indifferent and partially like he was afraid to come talk to Jess. Her heart sent out a couple of extra beats, and she turned away from his curious stare. She didn't have to explain anything to anyone, least of all him.

He'd asked why she'd needed a ride home the first time she and Dallas had gone out, and she'd given him an excuse about not having a reliable ride. Was it her fault if he assumed her truck had broken down again?

Guilt dug at her though, all the way back to the West Wing. She showered quickly, because she didn't want the scent of horseflesh to go on her date with her that night. Dallas would likely carry the hint of grease with him, as he didn't have the luxury of showering before dinner. She didn't mind; she simply wanted to look and smell her best.

She put on a pair of long, white pants that flowed around her legs as they were wide. She imagined herself a beachcomber, and she'd paired the pants with a pale pink blouse that left her shoulders bare and accented the darkness in her hair and eyelashes.

She'd put her semi-permanent lip stain on last night after she'd gotten home from Dallas's new rental, and that meant her lips were the perfect shade of pink for tonight. She evened out her skin tone with a few brushes of foundation, added some color back to her face with some blush, and looked at her hair.

"What do I do with this?" she asked. She had half a mind to cut it all off, because then she could style it with a blow dryer and call it good the way Jill did. As it was, she spent the next twenty minutes taming her thick hair with a round brush and a hair dryer.

Hannah came down the hall just as Jess finished. "Going out with Dallas?" she asked, taking in Jess and her fancy, non-ranch clothes, her shiny hair, and the makeup.

"Yes," Jess said. "With his kids."

"Oh, wow," Hannah said, her eyebrows going up. "That's a big step."

"Yes," Jess said. "It is."

"Wear my silver flats," Hannah said. "They'll look amazing with those pants." She went to get them, and Jess slipped them on. They were perfect, and she thanked Hannah.

"What about you and Bill?" she asked. Their plan of attack had worked, and he'd asked her out last week.

"First date is Saturday night," Hannah said. "You'll be doing my hair, so don't forget."

They laughed together, and Jess promised she had not forgotten about doing Hannah's hair for her first date with Bill.

At precisely six-thirty, she went outside to find Dallas and his kids. They came walking down the road from Ted's, and Jess watched them talk to each other. Remmy looked up and caught sight of Jess. In the next moment, she started skipping toward her, a huge smile on her face.

"You're so pretty," Remmy said, and she came right

over to Jess and hugged her, the way she had after riding lessons.

"Thank you," Jess said. "You're beautiful too." She peered down at the little girl, seeing only pieces of Dallas in the child.

"Good evening," Dallas said, his voice deep and welcome in Jess's ears. He looked at Thomas, who rolled his eyes.

"You look nice, Jess," Thomas said in a deadpan.

"Thank you," Jess said, finding something so funny about this exchange. She tried to smother her laughter, but it came bubbling out anyway. Dallas joined in, but Thomas obviously didn't get the joke. Remmy just looked back and forth between her father and Jess.

Dallas embraced her and whispered, "You don't look *nice*, Jess. You look like a million bucks."

She giggled and ducked her head, feeling warm from head to toe with his compliment. In that moment, she knew dinner with his children would go just fine and that she would have more than this one opportunity to get to know his children and allow them to get to know her.

THE WEEKEND PASSED IN AN UNBEARABLY SLOW WAY without Dallas around. Jess spent Friday night with the women in the West Wing, and it almost felt like old times. Ginger made her famous cowboy caviar dip, and Emma pulled out all the stops with a smoked beef brisket. Her daughter made cookies, and as they played card games and talked, Jess told about her date with Dallas and his kids.

Everyone listened and supported her, and while Jess sometimes felt on the outside of the women at the ranch because she'd rather spend time with horses, that night, she didn't. She felt loved and accepted.

Saturday passed in a blazing haze of horseback riding lessons that seemed to go on and on, and then flat ironing Hannah's hair until she wanted to scream. Sunday morning dawned early for Jess. She had a buyer coming to look at two of her horses, and she wanted to get them cleaned up, fresh on all the commands, and ready for the ten o'clock appointment.

"All right," she said to Prancer and Buttercup. "He's coming to see you today. You have to show him how good you are." She put them both in the ring and walked them around and around. She startled them with plastic bags and a slamming door, and they both barely looked up.

They were two of her best riding horses, and the man coming to see them that day wanted them for tourist riding. They had to be calm and gentle. They had to be patient. They had to be perfect.

She put them in the wash bay and gave them each a bath, combing the water from their hair and then drying them completely in the air walkway. She put a bow in Buttercup's hair and told Prancer how handsome he was.

She'd just put them in the pasture and run back to the

homestead to greet Bruce Washburn when she saw a truck pull into the gravel lot in front of the house. Trepidation moved through her, because she hated being late.

Jess increased her pace, though she still had a least a couple hundred yards before she'd reach the far lawn surrounding the house.

A man got out of the car, but it wasn't Bruce. She'd sold horses to him before, and Hope Eternal had bought some from him too. He ran a horseback riding tour of the Texas Hill Country, and though it was a few hours away, most people in the horse business knew one another.

Jess frowned as she realized she should've known the truck didn't belong to Bruce. There was no horse trailer attached, and he always came prepared to purchase.

This man had a head full of dark hair, and he wandered to the fence that separated the gravel lot from the grass and put one foot on the bottom rung. He watched the house for a moment, then pulled his phone out and looked at it. He tapped and swiped and tapped some more, finally sending something. He lifted the phone and took a picture of it.

Jess's feet finally touched the lawn. Over the summer, Emma had had some trouble with one of her ex-boyfriends, and Jess's face grew hotter with every step she took. "Can I help you?" she asked.

The man finally looked her way, and he clearly didn't mind being seen. "This is Hope Eternal Ranch, right?"

"Yes," she said. "We don't have any programs running on Sundays right now."

"I'm looking for someone," he said. "I heard he works here."

"We have a lot of men who work here." Jess stopped several paces away and folded her arms. "Who is it?"

"Dallas Dreyer," the man said, and Jess's heart somersaulted in her chest.

"He's not here today," Jess said, because she couldn't deny that Dallas worked there. She hadn't lied; Dallas wasn't at the ranch today. He wouldn't be tomorrow either. He'd told her about the phone calls with his ex-wife, and Jess narrowed her eyes at the man.

"If I can get your name and number, I'll pass it along to him."

"I don't need you to do that," he said. "When will he be back? Tomorrow?"

"He's out of town for a day or two," Jess said, evading the question. He was. He had been. He, Ted, and Nate were driving back to Sweet Water Falls tomorrow, and then Dallas had taken Tuesday off as well so he could manage whatever he might bring back from Houston.

The man nodded. "Well, then, I suppose you can tell him that Josh came to see him."

"Will he know who you are?" she asked. "Were you in River Bay with him?"

The man's eyebrows went up, and he cocked his head

at Jess. An icy sensation flowed over her, and she suddenly had a bad feeling about this guy.

"No," he said. "I'm a mutual friend of his wife's."

"Ex-wife," Jess said automatically. "Dallas is divorced." She realized how she sounded, so she quickly shrugged one shoulder. "At least that's what he says."

"She is his ex," Josh said. "We just need to meet to settle a debt."

Jess didn't know what to say to that. Nate had had debts he'd had to take care of once he'd been released from prison too. Maybe Dallas had a similar situation. "I'll tell him," she said. "He has your number?"

"No, but I'll get in touch with him." Josh nodded and turned back to his truck. Jess watched as he got behind the wheel and backed away. He seemed perfectly at-ease, but something about him made Jess's skin crawl. Maybe the way he was so in control of the situation, like nothing could ruffle him though he was the outsider here.

Dallas claimed to not know where his wife was, and yet Josh had showed up here, looking for him? Something wasn't right here.

Jess had vowed not to text or call Dallas incessantly while he was out of town, dealing with something huge that he didn't want to deal with. But she pulled out her phone and dialed him, thinking he needed to know about Josh as soon as possible.

CHAPTER THIRTEEN

Dallas had no idea how he and Martha had accumulated so much stuff. Why did they need three living rooms full of furniture? Couches, loveseats, armchairs, ottomans, rugs, lamps, entertainment centers, and decorations. Holy cow, the decorations.

Dallas hadn't even realized how many Martha put out. She had little pillows for the Fourth of July, and rabbit figurines for Easter. The Christmas decorations took up an entire closet under the staircase, and with every door Dallas opened, he found more stuff he didn't want.

He and the kids had been getting by for just over a month now, without any of this stuff. He didn't need it. He didn't want it.

Unfortunately, the house had to be cleaned out. Dallas was making quite a bit with the sale of the house, but his credit cards groaned at him every time he even took out his wallet. He needed to pay all of those down. He needed to get a new car. He needed to have some savings so he wasn't living hand-to-mouth every two weeks.

Part of him wanted to throw everything away. Call a truck and have someone come pick it all up. But Dallas saw dollar signs everywhere in the house, and he knew the job he'd brought Ted and Nate to do was suddenly much different than boxing up everything he owned and trucking it south to Sweet Water Falls.

He'd make more money selling it here in the city, and Dallas needed the money. When they'd arrived on Friday afternoon, he, Ted, and Nate had decided quickly to host a weekend sale that was really an open house. People could come see the furniture, the decorations, the dishes, any of it. If they wanted it, all they had to do was name a price.

Dallas had taken a ton of pictures and he'd posted them everywhere online that he could think of. The online classifieds. The yard sale pages on social media. The estate sale sites for the City of Houston.

Nate had a realtor friend in the area, and he'd called to let him know about the big sale. Hans had used his network to get the word out, so come Sunday morning, when Dallas opened the front door, he found a line of people.

"Oh," he said, and he called over his shoulder. "Ted, Nate, it's game time."

The woman at the front of the line looked beyond hopeful, and she held up a picture of the four-poster bed in the master bedroom. "I want this, and I'm willing to pay two thousand dollars for it."

"Sold," Dallas said, and he realized he might need a way to itemize what he'd sold already so he could avoid hurt feelings and possible fights if two people wanted the same thing. He decided to stay by the door and greet each person, then ask what they were looking for.

The second person in line had also printed a picture, and it was of the dining room table and chairs. "Is this solid wood?" he asked.

"Yes," Dallas said. "It was custom-made at the Boulevard." Martha had paid five figures for the dining set, and they'd entertained surgeons, hospital administrators, and other VIPs at the table.

"It's a Doug Rutheford piece, isn't it?"

"I believe it is," Dallas said, something jogging in his memory.

"I'll take it for eight thousand," the man said, his eyebrows up.

"Sold," Dallas said again, marveling at how well his idea had worked. One by one, more people stepped up to the front door. Some said they were just browsing. Some had specific items and prices in mind. Those items he sold immediately if the price was even close to fair. Those who wanted to wander and browse had to check with him, Ted, or Nate first, as Dallas had started a sheet with the things he'd sold as people walked through the door.

Mid-morning, his phone rang, and Jess's name sat on

the screen. He didn't answer, because a group of three women had just arrived, and they wanted to see the wardrobe in the master closet. Dallas gave them to Ted, who started to lead them through the house.

His phone rang again, and again, he saw Jess's name. "Nate," he said, and his friend came over to man the front table they'd set up after realizing how this sale should be handled.

Dallas swiped on the call and said, "Hey, Jess, I'm in the middle of something really big."

"Sorry," she said. "I'll talk fast." She started a story about a dark-haired man named Josh, and that was when Dallas started blinking to keep his vision working properly. Martha had mentioned Josh a couple of times.

"He didn't say what he wanted?" Dallas asked when he sensed the story was almost over.

"He said you two needed to settle a debt."

Fear ran through Dallas in cold waves, and he was glad he'd wandered away from Nate and any shoppers. "I don't owe anyone any money," he said.

"He said he'd get in touch with you," Jess said. "He was kind of creepy, Dallas. That's why I called. I thought you should know."

"Thanks, Jess," he said at the same time he heard someone shout. "I have to go. I'll call you tonight." He hung up and turned toward the commotion. A woman faced a man, and they both had one hand on a piece of art Dallas had bought during a hospital auction, years ago.

"I've been standing here for ten minutes with this painting," the woman said. "You can't just waltz up and claim it."

"Yes, I can," the man said. "I checked with Nate at the front door, and he said it hadn't been claimed."

"*I* claimed it," the woman said. "I just haven't seen one of them to make it official."

"Can I help you?" Dallas asked. They both looked at him with relief in their eyes. They both started talking over one another, and Dallas found he had very little patience for either of them.

"You checked with Nate?" he asked the man. "You got the tag?"

"That's right." He held up the pink post-it note that had Nate's handwriting on it. It said, *Painting in hall beside kitchen.*

"Ma'am," he said. "I'm sorry, but talking to the front table and getting a tag is the procedure we've been using."

"I was waiting here to talk to one of you," she protested.

"Have you seen the library?" Dallas asked. "There are at least half a dozen paintings in there, most better than this one."

"The library?" she asked, and Dallas led her to the sprawling room filled with books no one had ever opened. Several items had tags on them, claiming them for people. But none of the paintings had been taken.

"Oh, my," the woman said, and she started examining

the pieces. "This is an Andy Warhol." She turned to Dallas with wide eyes.

"Yes, my ex-wife loved his work," Dallas said. In the time it took to blink, he could see the anniversary where he'd presented that painting to Martha. She'd been over the moon, and Dallas had too—because he'd loved her so much and all he'd ever wanted was for her to be happy.

"I want this," she said, already moving to the next painting.

"Ma'am," he said as kindly as he could. "You have to get the tag from the front table. Someone could be getting it now."

"Not again," she said, and she practically sprinted from the library. Dallas just watched her go, trying to remember if he'd ever been that excited about the art hanging in the library. No, he had not.

He returned to the front table to help Nate, and the woman after the paintings had five tags with her as she hurried away from him once more.

"This is incredible," Nate said. "What a great idea. We don't have to move the stuff, and you're making a lot of money."

"I need it," Dallas said, looking down at the sheet. His mind seized onto numbers, and they just made so much sense to him. In only a few seconds, he calculated that he'd made over seventy-five thousand dollars in just over two hours.

And he had many more ahead of him before he could

truly relax, especially if the mysterious Josh knew where he worked.

Josh didn't call Dallas, nor did he show up at the ranch again. He wasn't loitering outside Dallas's house on the outskirts of town, and as one week became two became three, Dallas started to put the man out of his mind.

He hadn't spoken to his ex-wife since the closing on the house either, and he wondered if she'd found someone else to fund her habits. Dallas wasn't going to do it, he knew that. If Martha wanted to be on the fast-track to self-destruction, there was little he could do about it except withhold the cash she needed for the pills and alcohol she favored.

He couldn't believe she'd abandoned their children, their marriage, and their house for her vices. She'd made such great progress over the years, and they never kept wine in the house. If she drank, it was only socially, and only at restaurants.

He kept in touch with her sister, but Amy hadn't heard from Martha in longer than Dallas had. As October became November, he started to put her out of his mind completely, which was a good thing as he prepared to go visit his parents and siblings in Temple.

The day finally arrived, and Dallas loaded up the pies

he'd bought from Emma and told the kids to put their suitcases in the back of the SUV. He put his in too, glad he'd bought a new car that could hold luggage without making it a workout to get it in and out.

"Seat belts," he said as he got behind the wheel. It was almost four hours to Temple, and his mother was serving Thanksgiving dinner promptly at one o'clock. If she hadn't changed while Dallas had been in prison—and he didn't think she had—they'd probably start eating at twelve-thirty.

He and the kids were on the road by eight, and he didn't let his lead foot take over. He was in no hurry to get to his parents' house and then wait around. That was the worst part about Thanksgiving meals—the visiting before and after. He just wanted to eat and run.

He wouldn't be doing that this year, though. He and the kids were staying for the whole weekend, and Dallas had been hoping and praying to rebuild bridges and make amends while he was in Temple.

His skin itched with every mile that took him closer to seeing his father for the first time in years. He still hadn't spoken to him, and Dallas suddenly wanted to protect himself and his children from a potentially volatile situation.

"Guys," he said. "I haven't seen Grandpa in a long time." He looked in the rear-view mirror to see if Remmy had heard him. She'd looked up from her coloring book, so

Dallas assumed she had. "Did Mom take you to see my parents ever?"

"No," Thomas said. "Just Gramma Fran in Florida."

"Mm," Dallas said, his mind spinning. Martha hadn't gotten along particularly well with Dallas's father, so it wasn't terribly unsurprising that she'd chosen to take the kids to see her mother. At the same time, Thomas and Remmy were his parents' grandchildren too, and he thought Martha would at least make an effort. Everything about Martha required effort, but only to make it look like everything was so effortless.

"Does he still have Scottie?" Thomas asked, his face brightening.

"I haven't heard that he died," Dallas said, though that didn't mean much. He'd been talking to his siblings via text since his release, and they seemed interested in having him in their lives again. He called his mother, and she'd been the most forgiving and the most accepting. "So I'm sure he still does."

His mother would've told him if Dad's dog had died. The canine went everywhere with Dallas's father, even down to the barbershop to get a haircut.

Because he didn't want to get there too terribly badly, the miles and hours passed quickly. Before he knew it, he was pulling into the long driveway and parking his new SUV beside a couple of others.

He hadn't even gotten out of the car yet when he heard someone call his name. He looked up to find Olive running down the steps to greet him. His whole heart beat like a drum, the skin around it oh-so-tight and someone banging on it with a lot of force.

He got out, and Olive was upon him in the next moment. "Dallas," she said. "You're here." She hugged him tight, and then tighter. "You look so good." She stepped back and looked him up and down, tears in her eyes. "I thought you might be permanently injured or something."

Dallas smiled at her and kept his chronic back pain to himself. "Come on, guys," he said to the kids. "You know Aunt Olive."

Remmy, always the more adventurous child, got out of the SUV first. She hugged her aunt, and by then Greg, Dallas's brother, and Judy, his other sister, had come outside too. Dallas knew he was the last to arrive, and while that had used to bother him, now it didn't. He'd made excellent time on the drive, and it was before noon.

He looked up to the porch while his siblings' kids started talking to Remmy and Thomas, and he found his mother standing there. She held one hand pressed over her heart as she cried.

"Momma," Dallas said, suddenly needing nothing more nor less than a good, long hug from his mother. He took the steps two at a time, noticing how white her hair had become before he swept her into his arms.

He buried his face in her neck and breathed, getting the floral scent of her favorite perfume, a hint of something green as she tended to an herb garden the size of a small farm, and the soft, powdery scent that belonged to all women over the age of seventy. "Momma," he said again, pulling back to look at her.

She placed one hand on the side of his face and gazed at him, tears still running down her face. "Dallas Alexander," she said, her Texas drawl really lengthening the syllables in his name. "It's so good to have you home again."

"It's so good to be home," Dallas said. The scent of butter and roasted turkey wafted out onto the porch through the open front door, and Dallas's mouth watered. He'd skipped breakfast in his haste to get on the road and because of his nerves. "Where's Daddy?"

"He's tinkering this morning," Momma said. "You know where to find him."

Yes, Dallas did know. He turned back to his children, who wore smiles and spoke with the cousins they hadn't seen in so long. "Do I have time?" he asked.

"Yes," Momma said. "Go now, Dallas, and get it done."

"Yes, ma'am." He touched the brim of his cowboy hat, noticing how his mother's gaze lingered there for an extra moment. No, he'd never worn a cowboy hat for longer than it took to go trick-or-treating, but they were dead useful around the ranch, and he found he really liked wearing the hat.

He retraced his steps down to the sidewalk and went around the side of the house opposite the driveway. In the back corner of the back yard sat a shed, and his father went there when he wanted some peace and quiet, or when his brain had started to work on a new idea for a new fishing fly, and when he wanted to make those flies.

His father loved to tinker with things too, and he'd once taken the toaster apart to see if he could put it back together. His workshop smelled like feathers and fishing line, and Dallas had always loved going out there with his dad.

Now, he stopped outside the closed door and raised his fist to knock. His father didn't answer, and Dallas figured he knew who stood out here while he waited in there. The stubbornness of people sometimes fascinated Dallas, and his heartbeat stormed in his chest. His father clearly didn't want to see him. Why should Dallas force a reconciliation upon him?

"It's not about him," Dallas muttered to himself. He had to feel like he'd done everything he could to make things right between him and his dad. And that required going into the shop without being invited.

He pushed open the door, surprised at the blast of heat that came out. It was almost December, but certainly not cold enough to pump the heater the way his dad was. "Daddy?" he asked, and his father turned from the tall workbench where he attached feathers, threads, chenille, hooks, and other items to make the flies he used to fish with.

Their eyes met, and so many things were said. Dallas

could hear the last thing his father had said to him, and it crushed his chest as strongly now as it had then.

You've ruined my name.

His father had taught all of his children growing up that they might not have much money, but they had something far greater. They carried the blood of great men and women in their veins, and it meant something to be a Dreyer.

Remember whose name you carry, his father had said so many times. *It's my name. It's Grandpa's name. Your great-grandmother's. We're all counting on you to be a good citizen. Honest. Upstanding. Helpful. That's what Dreyers do. It's who we are.*

No one in the Dreyer family had ever gone to prison before, and his father could convey how disgusted, disappointed, and downright angry he was by simply saying Dallas had ruined his name.

Dallas had tried to apologize then, but his father hadn't wanted to hear it.

"Hey, Daddy," he said, taking a step and letting the door close behind him. "What are you working on?"

His dad looked back at his workbench as if he'd forgotten where he was. Perhaps he had; his father seemed to have aged a decade in the thirty months Dallas had been in prison. He's always been mostly bald, but now his hair existed in a dull shade of gray. His skin, which had seen too much sun in its life, seemed to sag everywhere. He wore a blue T-shirt and a pair of jeans, and Dallas wondered how he could survive with the heat as high as it was in the shed.

"Wooly buggers," he said. "And some mayflies."

"You like the mayflies."

"The fish like the mayflies," Daddy said.

Dallas dared to go over to the workbench, and he stood beside where his father sat on a high stool. He had little bits of everything on the bench, and how he knew where to put what, Dallas didn't comprehend. He supposed making flies for fishing for his father was a lot like being a mechanic for Dallas.

The knowledge of it just existed inside his head.

"I'm really sorry, Daddy," he said. "I know you might not be able to forgive me for a while, but I really hope you'll try. I've been doing good things in Sweet Water Falls. The kids and I have our own place. They're never late for school. I run the entire mechanical repair shop at a decent-sized ranch."

His father said nothing as he reached for a pair of pinchers and picked up a tiny piece of feather for the mayfly he was working on.

"I'm trying to restore the family name," Dallas said. "Honestly, Daddy, I am."

His dad looped a wire around the feather and the hook, the fly already starting to come together. "I know you are, son," he said, his voice gruff and low.

Son.

Dallas's whole world shifted with that one, three-letter-word.

"I love you, Daddy," he said, his voice a whisper.

"I love you too, Dallas." He stood, and their eyes met again. So many things paraded across his father's face. Dallas felt the stomping boots in his own soul, taking out the parts that were dark or rotten.

They embraced, and his dad clapped him loudly on the back. "It's taken me a long time to realize that you're a good man," he said. "Who just got caught up in some bad things."

Dallas thought that summed up what had happened fairly well, and he just held tightly to his father, this hug almost better than the one he'd gotten from his mother.

Almost.

"I heard you have a girlfriend," Daddy said as he stepped back. He cleared his throat and made a big show of rubbing his eyes, as if that would somehow convince Dallas that he hadn't wept a little bit.

Dallas simply wiped his eyes, because his tears of gratitude had managed to leak out too. "Yeah," he said. "Her name's Jess."

"Why didn't you bring her?"

"Uh...I don't know." The truth was, Dallas wasn't even sure his father would talk to him. He wasn't sure what kind of reception he'd get at all, and he wanted Jess to meet his family when things were as good as they could be.

"We're going really slow," he added, because that was true too. He and Jess had agreed that they didn't need to rush into anything. They could enjoy getting to know one another, and she could take her time getting to know the kids. They'd gone to dinner, to movies, even to a theme park together, and the four of them got along great.

Remmy liked Jess the most, but even Thomas would answer her questions, especially if they were about science. Jess was no idiot, and she'd realized quickly how to get the boy to open up.

Dallas had loved her in that moment, but he knew he wasn't *in love* with her. He liked her a lot, sure. The kids did too. But they all needed more time to get to a place of love.

"Going slow is probably a good idea," his dad said. "I suppose your mother will need help with carving the turkey." He looked at Dallas. "Take your time with Jess if you need it, son," he said. "If she's the one, it'll work out."

"Thanks." Dallas wasn't sure what he was thanking his father for. Perhaps just letting him into the shed and then forgiving him so easily. Dallas knew it hadn't been easy for his dad to get to that point, and he knew he still had a long way to go to show that he was a Dreyer, and that that meant something.

He couldn't wait to call Jess and tell her how things had gone with his father, and he supposed it meant something that she was the one person he wanted to share his good news with.

CHAPTER FOURTEEN

Jess refused to allow herself to look toward the clock hanging in the stables. Dallas would call her when he got back to town. They'd spoken that morning, and he'd said he was going to eat breakfast with his family and then hit the road. From Temple, Sweet Water Falls was just under four hours, and he had children who might need to stop.

She missed him, that was all.

Jess knew it was a little bit more than that, as she'd had a serious discussion with Dallas when he'd brought up the idea of going to see his family for Thanksgiving. She'd thought he was inviting her along and wanted to know her opinion on what they should do.

Turned out that no, he just wanted her opinion on what *he* should do. He'd told her that he didn't get along great with his father, and perhaps him making the drive and showing up for the family feast would put too much tension and awkwardness on everyone else, himself included.

Once she'd learned that, she'd been flustered. He said he wasn't ready to introduce her to anyone in his family yet, and Jess supposed she could respect that. She'd spent a lot of time thinking about her family, and if she was ready to take Dallas home to meet them.

She honestly didn't know. She hadn't quite made it to this stage of a relationship before. Once Christmas arrived, Jess would be in purely uncharted waters, as by then, he would be the longest romantic relationship she'd ever had.

Her stomach squeezed, and she moved down the row of stalls to the next one. "Hey, Momma," she said to the horse there. Her real name was Weeping Willow, but she was due with a foal in a few months. Jess stroked Willow's neck and up to her ears. "You doing okay today?"

The mare blew her breath through her lips, and Jess smiled at her. "Yeah, I can imagine." She wasn't exactly sure what the horse had said, but she didn't think Willow was very comfortable these days. She'd started getting bigger and bigger, her belly obviously swollen with new life.

Jess thought about Thomas and Remmy and the candy turkeys she'd bought for them. She hadn't been able to give them to the children before they'd left to visit their grandparents, and she mentally reminded herself to take them with her to Dallas's that night.

"Maybe you won't go," she told herself.

During their serious talk, they'd agreed to go slow. Jess had been fine with it at the time, but lately, she felt like she initiated every conversation. She was the one stopping by his office during the day to see him. She was the one bringing him and the kids dinner and staying to watch a movie or play a board game. She was the one texting him questions about heart surgery, or prison, or tractors, or his kids, or dogs.

He responded, and he sometimes asked her about Montana or her time in Calgary with the rodeo horses there, but not much. Jess felt like her life was very boring—that she herself was very boring—and soon enough, Dallas would realize it and break up with her.

At the same time, Jess wanted time to get to know Dallas and his children. She wasn't just taking on a boyfriend or a husband. She'd be a mother to two kids instantly, and she had a lot to think about when it came to this relationship.

Thomas and Remmy deserved a mother figure who loved them deeply, as they'd already had a lot of trauma surrounding their family life. Jess didn't want to add to that; quite the opposite, in fact. She wanted to allow them the opportunity to heal from that, and she knew that would take time.

Dallas had called a few days ago to say his father had received him better than Dallas could've hoped for, and Jess couldn't stop smiling about that. He'd also said he'd seen some things in his son he hadn't realized, and that he wanted to look into getting someone for the boy to talk to once they returned to Sweet Water Falls.

Jess didn't know much about therapy or therapists, but Nate did, and she was sure Dallas would get the help he needed.

She hadn't seen anyone fishy hanging around the ranch. No one had come looking for Dallas in weeks now, and she'd stopped asking about his ex-wife. Still, a certain sense of curiosity ate through her from time to time, and Jess couldn't stop herself from looking at the clock.

Only noon.

She sighed and moved down the row to the next horse. She didn't mean to lunge for her phone when it chimed, but lunge she did. Dallas's name sat on the screen, and she smiled widely as she swiped and tapped to open the message.

Dinner tonight? he'd asked. *Just me and you. I'm feeling disconnected from you.*

She couldn't type out the word *yes* fast enough, and he sent back a smiley face and nothing more.

"At least he can feel it too," she muttered to herself. That meant something, right? She asked horse after horse as she visited them to make sure they were all doing well, and then she went back to the West Wing, where Ginger and Nate were hosting the final stage of the cook-off they'd started on Thanksgiving night.

They'd taken all the leftovers and separated them into

individual portions with turkey, mashed potatoes, yams, cranberry sauce, stuffing, and gravy. They'd challenged three people to come up with the best use of Thanksgiving leftovers in a "battle to the death," that had really ended in laugher and some of the most delicious mashed potato cakes Jess had ever tasted.

Emma had entered, of course, as she was a whiz in the kitchen. Spencer had thrown his hat into the ring, and Jess had actually been impressed when his dish had won the first round. Not just scraped by but won.

The last two contestants were Hannah and Bill, and Jess had watched them perform a delicate dance in the kitchen as they sliced, diced, baked, and broiled their way toward ranch fame.

Emma had come in second to Spencer's Thanksgiving pot pie, complete with flaky sweet potato crust and "stuffing bombs" that were really just mashed potatoes and stuffing bound together with flour and egg and fried. He'd done something magical with the spices, though, and they were the perfect thing to dip into the creamy sauce of the pot pie and pop the whole thing in her mouth.

Those two had advanced to the next round, along with Bill. He'd slung his arm around Hannah when the announcement was made, and they'd laughed together while he pressed a kiss to her temple.

She'd seemed so happy, and Jess was happy for her.

Round two had been yesterday, and Bill had been

eliminated when he forgot about his mashed potato "toast points" and not gotten all of the ingredients on the plate.

"All right, all right," Nate said, holding up his arms. Folding chairs had been set up and furniture rearranged so people could sit and view the cooking. "We've got Spencer Rust on this side of the kitchen." He indicated Spence with a huge smile on his face. The assembled crowd went wild, and Jess moved out of the way as Ted and Missy squeezed into the kitchen behind her.

Three more cowboys followed, and Jess figured she better get a seat now or she'd be standing to watch the cook-off.

"And Emma on this half of the kitchen," Nate said. More cheers filled the room, and Jess added her voice to those siding with Emma. In moments like these, Jess didn't miss her family. She had a new group of people she belonged to here at Hope Eternal Ranch, and she sometimes marveled at how well Ginger integrated everyone into the ranch, no matter how small their role was or how short their visit lasted.

Jess wanted to build something like that for her own family, but she didn't know how. She lived too far away from Montana, but her thoughts lingered on Dallas, Thomas, and Remmy. Perhaps if they became a family, they could start to build a place where all were welcome, no matter what time of day, what condition they were in, or how far they still needed to go to make things right.

Ginger had started taking men from the Bureau of

Prisons as a way to make ends meet on the ranch, but Jess had seen her heart grow and expand beyond belief as everyone who'd been on the ranch for any length of time could see that it was about more than money now.

Jess's own heart and mind had been opened in ways she'd never thought possible, as she hadn't given dating Dallas a second thought, at least not because he was an ex-convict.

People made mistakes.

She knew she did, and she wanted to believe that with some effort and some honest sincerity, those wrongs could be righted.

She faded into the background by taking a folding chair on the side of the room as Nate and Ginger tag-teamed explaining the rules. She'd been present for both of the other rounds though—as had everyone else—so going over the rules wasn't necessary. They did it though, and then Nate circled the long kitchen island and said, "Ready, set, cook!"

Emma and Spencer flew into action, and Jess clapped along with everyone else. They had an hour to present their best Thanksgiving Day leftover meal, and the excitement would wear off in about two minutes.

Only when Ginger would pretend to be a television host and go into the kitchen to ask questions would the crowd be stimulated again, and Jess looked down the row to where Jill sat with Michelle and Nick. She scooted down to the next empty chair and smiled at Jill.

Nick leaned over her and said, "We've got a friendly competition going on Spence."

"What about him?" Jess asked, watching him pull a mixing bowl toward him and dump all of his mashed potatoes into it.

"If he wins, Ginger said she'll host a Christmas giveaway." He grinned like Santa Claus had come early.

"And if he loses?" Jess asked, wondering if she could cheer against Emma.

"Nothing." Nick shrugged and looked back into the kitchen. "I want that giveaway," he said. "Her dad used to do them, and he gave out envelopes of money."

Jess smiled, but deep down, she didn't think Ginger would do that. Hope Eternal was thriving now, but not to the point where she could just give away everything.

Her attention wandered until the last five minutes, when both Nate and Ginger went into narration mode. Finally, the last second ticked away, and both Emma and Spence had put their plates on the front of the island. They hugged, both of them laughing, and went to stand beside their plate of food.

"Judges," Ginger announced, putting the big bowl of folded papers between the plates. Jess had not been called to judge yet, but anyone could taste the food once the winner was declared. That was how she'd gotten half of that perfectly fried mashed potato cake. Her stomach rumbled for lunch, and she hoped she'd get called to judge now.

Ginger pulled out the first name. "Nick."

He whooped and bolted to his feet. Jess already knew who he was going to vote for, and he hadn't even tasted the food yet. She shook her head and dutifully clapped as Nick made his way to the front of the room as if he'd already won a huge prize.

"Missy," Ginger called, and Jess saw the votes get tied up.

Spence started to protest, but Ginger silenced him with a look. She pulled the last name out of the bowl, and read, "Jess."

Surprise and dread moved through her, and she stood up. Everyone watched her walk to the front and pick up a fork.

"What do you have?" Nate asked Emma.

"This is a turkey cordon bleu," she said. "With a slightly sweet cranberry gravy sauce, twice-fried potato cubes, and a sweet potato glaze."

Jess looked at the beautiful plate of food. The turkey had been rolled in dried stuffing crumbs, which was pretty ingenious in Jess's opinion. She wasn't sure about the cranberry gravy, but the moment she put a bite of the meat, cheese, ham, and sauce in her mouth, she was sold.

The potato cubes practically melted in her mouth, and they had a burst of cheese inside them too. The glaze on the outside of them was almost crispy, producing a soft and hard texture that Jess really liked.

Nick liked it too, she could tell.

"Spence?" Ginger asked.

"I've got a turkey pie," he said. That was it. It was actually in a pie plate, with whipped mashed potatoes that looked like buttercream frosting. When he cut into it, Jess found he'd used the stuffing for the crust, and layered turkey over that. The whole thing was covered in gravy, cranberries, and then the potatoes.

It certainly wasn't as inventive or as sophisticated as Emma's. It did taste good, though.

Jess conferred with Missy and Nick, and they voted the way she expected them to. They both looked at her while Ginger said, "Judges?"

She stepped back in front of the crowd. Nick said, "Spencer," and the crowd went wild.

"Emma," Missy said, and more cheering met Jess's ears.

Silence draped the kitchen then, and Jess rather liked the power she held in her hand. She looked at Emma, then Spencer, then Nick.

She couldn't help herself, and she had to vote with her conscience. She opened her mouth and said, "Emma."

The room erupted, both with happy cowboys and cowgirls, and unhappy ones. Jess shrugged at Nick and went to tell Spence his food was really good. He was good-natured about it, and others came up to sample the food too.

Jess slipped away after that, as she had a date she needed to get ready for. Dallas hadn't said what time he'd

come to get her, and her texts to ask him went unan-
swered. They'd gone to dinner right after work in the past.
Sometimes later at six-thirty or seven.

Jess didn't panic at five. Or six. By seven, when she'd
been ready for over two hours and had a dozen unread
texts out to Dallas, her annoyance with the man had
grown wings and taken flight.

"Don't text him again," she told herself in the quiet
stillness of her own room. "Don't call him. He has eyes."

At the same time, she worried that something bad had
happened to him or the children. Perhaps they'd gotten in
a car accident. Perhaps they'd been delayed due to traffic
or a freeway closure.

Her mind went round and round, and she got up to
match her body movement to the way her brain couldn't
settle. She paced from one end of her room to the other,
desperate for someone to just tell her what to do.

No one did, and Jess had to make her own decision.
She dialed Dallas, her heart beating in her throat. Once,
twice, three times, and finally he said, "Jess, I have ten
seconds. I'm fixing a truck to pay off Martha's debt. Can
we reschedule?"

CHAPTER FIFTEEN

Dallas hung up the moment Jess said yes. The last thing he needed was for Josh to catch him on the phone. He shoved the device in his back pocket, wiped his hands on the rag he'd been using, and turned back to the driveway.

He and the kids had been home for less than an hour when someone had knocked on their door. Josh himself had stood there, and Dallas had only known panic as severe two other times in his life. First, when he'd been arrested and charged with a wrongful death suit. Second, the first day he'd entered River Bay and been beaten to within breaths of his life.

A man like Josh Hurley had done that, and Dallas could see the malice in the other man's eyes the moment he'd opened the door. He'd closed it just as fast and moved his children into the master bedroom. "Don't come out," he told them. "No matter what. Promise me right now."

They'd both promised, and Dallas had locked the door behind him. By the time he made it back to the living room, Josh was yelling and kicking at the door. Dallas had opened it again, because while he had enough money now, he didn't need to be replacing the door on this rental house.

"What do you want?" he asked.

"I need you to fix my friend's truck." Josh indicated the white one-ton truck in the driveway, a muscled, tattooed man leaning against the driver's door.

That had been four hours ago. Josh had given a steady stream of rules as Dallas went down the front sidewalk to the truck, and one of those was no phone calls and no texts. Dallas's phone had already been on silent, so no one knew about all of Jess's texts.

His heart pounded again, because he didn't know how this situation ended. He'd been forced to use the bathroom on the side of the house, with Josh watching him from the corner. The truck had multiple problems, and Dallas had fixed three of them already, after a trip to the automotive store.

"What's left?" Josh asked as he came up beside Dallas. His shoulder ached, and a steady pain radiated up and down his spine.

"The radiator." Dallas didn't look at the other man. He

hadn't explained much more than Martha owed him some money, and she couldn't pay it. So Josh was going to get what she owed from Dallas. When Dallas had asked how much she owed, Josh wouldn't say.

He'd said he'd ask how much fixing the truck would be worth, and then he'd know if Martha was out of the woods.

Worry kicked through Dallas again, because he hadn't heard from Martha in a while. One look at Josh, and it was very easy to imagine her being in very real trouble. He stood a couple of inches taller than Dallas, and while Dallas had worked out in prison, this guy worked out before breakfast, afterward, at lunchtime, and well into the evening. He also had a mean, squinted look about his eyes, and Dallas had known guys like him in River Bay.

He did not care who he hurt, as long as he got what he wanted.

Right now, he wanted Dallas to fix Mario's truck. The other man had gone in Dallas's house, found something to eat, and put on the TV. A vein of anger pulsed just beneath Dallas's skin, and he kept it there.

Nate had taught him how to do that. How to hide how he really felt until he could release it. How to deal with people he'd rather not deal with and make them think he didn't want to be anywhere else, even if he didn't like them.

"It's a complicated process," Dallas added. "Because of where it is in this model. Labor-intensive."

"How much longer?"

"At least an hour," Dallas said, and he worried about his kids. They hadn't had dinner yet, and their lunch had been snacks and beef jerky from a gas station halfway between Sweet Water Falls and Temple. Thomas knew to be quiet, but Remmy was six years old, and Dallas almost started crying thinking about her in his bedroom, scared, hungry, and worried.

"I need to go see my kids," he finally said.

"No," Josh said. "Get this done, and we'll leave you alone."

Dallas did what he said, but he knew Josh and his friends wouldn't leave him alone. They knew where he worked. They knew where he lived. If they knew those things, they knew where the kids went to school, and they knew where his parents were.

Fear accompanied his every move, and just over an hour later, the radiator was done.

"How much?" Josh asked. "Would you charge for everything you did?" Mario stood next to him, his arms folded and his biceps huge.

Dallas looked back to the truck and considered all he'd done. "If I owned my own commercial shop or you took it to someone like that, that job would've easily been four grand."

Josh looked at Mario, who nodded just once.

"We'll take it off Martha's debt," Josh said, starting for the passenger side of the truck.

"How much does she owe you?" Dallas asked. "You know we're not married anymore, right?" In so many ways, his life with Martha had been broken. At the same time, he knew they'd be inseparably twined for the rest of his life.

"She owes a lot," Josh said. "Your wife likes the speeders, and they ain't cheap."

"She's not my wife," Dallas called after him. "I don't owe you anything." Plus, Josh could continue to show up, day after day, and say Martha owed him something and Dallas wouldn't know. He'd been given no ledger or sheet. Just Josh's word.

Josh paused at the front bumper and looked back at Dallas. "She said you'd take care of her," he said. "Are you saying you won't?" He took one menacing step back toward Dallas. "Because that changes how she's treated, you know."

Dallas swallowed. "Where is she? What have you done to her?" He didn't want to care, but the truth was, he did. He'd care about anyone who'd gotten themselves into the situation that Martha obviously had.

Addicted to something hard core. No way out. No money to pay for the habit.

His compassion warred with his fury, and that caused his fingers to curl into fists.

"She's safe," Josh said coolly. "For now."

"I want to talk to her," Dallas said.

"We don't control who she talks to," Josh said. "If she's

not answering your calls, man, that's her decision." He knocked on the hood of the truck, and Mario started it. Josh got in, and Dallas listened to the engine purr as he backed out of the driveway.

He wanted to race down the street after them, shouting threats and telling them never to come to his house again. Men like Josh did what they wanted though. They took what they wanted, because they thought it belonged to them.

Dallas spun back to his house and dashed inside. He went to the master bedroom and knocked on the door, saying, "It's Daddy, Thomas. Open the door, bud."

Several moments later, the door swung open, and his son's tear-stained face appeared. He looked resolved and stoic, but Dallas saw all the turmoil beneath the mask. "I'm sorry." He swept his son into his arms and held him tight. "Remmy, come on." The sobbing little girl came over too, and Dallas held them each with one arm, as tightly as he could, right against his chest.

"It's okay now," he whispered. "It's okay now. I'm here, and it's okay now."

⸻

A couple of hours later, Dallas stood in the doorway of his bedroom and watched his children sleep in his bed. Martha had not answered his calls that night, and he was currently listening to Ted talk about his options.

"We need to find her," Ted said. "Get her out of there. Find out what she owes, and pay it off. Then they'll leave you alone."

"Okay," Dallas said. "Nate?"

"I hate this plan," Nate said, his voice echoing because Ted had the two of them on speakerphone. "But Teddy's right. The only way this goes away permanently is if the debt is paid and done."

The three of them knew more about debts being paid than most, that was for sure.

Dallas wanted to ask about Jess, but he kept the question beneath his tongue. He'd call her next. He kept his voice low as he asked, "How do we find her?"

"We know people," Nate said. "Right, boys? We all know someone a little shady from our time in prison. Maybe now's when we work the system we lived inside for a while."

Dallas frowned, but he didn't confirm or deny what Nate had said. Everyone in River Bay had a past, that was for sure. Some had done bad things, but most of the men there had made bad choices, which lead to bad things happening, which lead to their incarceration. They weren't inherently bad men.

"I can call Jesus," Dallas finally said. "But he's probably not even in the country anymore."

"Can't hurt to try," Nate said. "If this is the only way you're going to get out from under this...." He let his words hang there, and Dallas hated this feeling of being trapped between two impossible solutions.

His lungs hardened, and all he could see was the horrible, red-rimmed eyes of his children as they melted into his arms. He would *not* put them through that again, which meant he could not allow Josh to "drop by" his house again. Or his workplace, his parents' house, or anywhere else he and his kids might be.

"I'm going to call him right now," Dallas said.

"I've got a friend in law enforcement that could help," Ted said. "And about two dozen of the best lawyers in Texas who know how to find people online. I'll put some feelers out."

"I'll call the Warden," Nate said.

Dallas turned away from his sleeping kids. "The Warden?"

"Yeah," Nate said. "We've stayed in touch, and he's dead useful with stuff like this. He has ears in places no one else does."

"I bet he does," Dallas said. He hadn't been close to the Warden, and he hadn't known anyone had. The Warden held himself apart from everyone, and Dallas had dealt with him several times because of the beating he'd taken.

"Let's talk tomorrow," Nate said.

"You sure you're okay there tonight?" Ted asked.

"There's room at the ranch," Nate said. "We can make sure no one comes near you or even onto the property."

"I'm okay," Dallas said, though his gratitude for his friends couldn't be quantified. "But thank you."

"I'm going to come stay with you," Ted said. "He has two kids. He shouldn't be alone."

Dallas let him and Nate talk to each other, though they were talking about him, without saying anything. This was just another one of those times where he had to let someone else take care of him.

Nate had done it in River Bay. They'd all looked out for each other after that. He thought of Slate and Luke still behind bars, and then Ted said, "I'll be there in twenty minutes, Dallas. What do you need?"

"Could you stop and get some Frosted Flakes?" he asked. "My kids love those, and we're out."

"Sure," Ted said. "Anything else?"

"No, I think that's all." He drew in a deep breath. "And guys, we've got to go check on Slate and Luke."

"Yes," Nate said instantly. "Let me call the Warden and find out about the next family day."

"Okay," Dallas said. The call with his friends ended, and he took a deep breath. If he didn't make his next call right now, he wouldn't do it. He thought of Jess, but he scrolled through his list to find Jesus's number. They'd been in the infirmary together for a few days in the first six months of Dallas's stay at River Bay, and they'd bonded a little bit.

His line rang and rang, and no one answered. He didn't get a disconnect notice, but his heart still fell toward his shoes. His feet hurt. His back hurt. He hadn't been anticipating driving for four hours and then working on a broken down vehicle for five more.

He'd missed his date with Jess, and his children had been abandoned once more. Fierce anger burned through him, and he started to dial Jesus again. He wasn't going to let this drop, even if the conversation would be hard to have.

Before he could connect the call again, his line rang, and Jesus's name sat there. Hope shone brightly in Dallas's soul, and he quickly connected the call. "Jesus," he said.

"Amigo," Jesus said, holding onto the O for a long time. "What's up, bro?"

"Jesus," Dallas said with a chuckle. He cast a quick look behind him at his sleeping kids—his angels—and softly stepped out of the room. "I'm looking for my ex-wife," he said as he went down the hall. "And you're sort of the expert at finding someone who doesn't want to be found."

"Not sort of the expert, *muchacho*. I *am* the expert."

Dallas laughed with Jesus, and said, "All right then. Can you help me?"

THE NEXT MORNING, TED SAT AT THE KITCHEN TABLE with Thomas and Remmy, all three of them eating through an entire box of Frosted Flakes. Dallas lingered in the kitchen, a hot cup of coffee in his hands, watching them.

Ted was such a big teddy bear, and everyone he met loved him. Even stoic, masked Thomas had smiled the moment he saw Ted in the kitchen. They'd been laughing about something one of Ted's dogs had done a couple of days ago for ten minutes. Dallas watched the clock, but he honestly didn't care if the kids went to school today.

By the time he'd gotten off the phone with Jesus, it had been too late to call Jess. Nate had texted to say he'd spoken with Ginger, and they wanted Dallas to take a couple of days if he needed them to make sure his family was safe.

He wasn't going to the ranch today. He was going to rekey the house and tell the landlord that he'd done it afterward. He was going to install cameras in the eaves just to make sure he knew who was coming and going around his house. He didn't care if he had to donate the new locks and camera equipment to the landlord; he needed to keep his kids safe.

"Daddy, will you do my hair?" Remmy asked, climbing up on a barstool. "We have a magician coming today."

He wasn't sure how the two things were related, but he pushed away from the counter and approached his daughter. He bent to get the hair kit out of the cupboard under the sink and opened it. "What am I doing?"

"Can you do the half-braid?" She peered at him over her shoulder, and she was the cutest thing on the planet. He loved her dark eyes and light skin, that smattering of freckles across her face, and that adorable Texas accent.

"Yeah," he said, pulling out the comb and the water bottle. He could braid so much better now than he'd been able to two months ago, but it required wet hair to get just right. "When is the magician?"

"After lunch," she said.

"Good," Dallas said. "Because we're already late for school."

"We are?" Remmy peered at the clock while Thomas got up and put his cereal bowl in the sink.

"I'll go get my stuff," he said. "Sorry, Dad."

"I don't even care if you go today," Dallas said. "In fact, I'd love to just keep you with me all day, so I know you're safe."

Thomas hesitated, clearly the idea of skipping school appealing.

"I can't miss, Daddy," Remmy said. "We do a spelling test on Monday, and the magician."

"Do you want to miss the magician?" Dallas asked his son as he started to spray his daughter's hair. "I'm assuming it'll be a whole-school assembly."

"I mean, I don't really care," Thomas said.

"You don't have to go," Dallas said, meeting his son's eyes. "We can take Remmy, and then come back here."

"Okay," Thomas said, detouring back to the table and Ted.

"I want to go, Daddy," Remmy said, looking at him with wide eyes.

"I just said you could," he said. "Now face the front so I can part your hair." He worked with the comb deftly now, pulling it from her ear and up to the crown of her head. He brushed down the rest, noting how thin and wispy her hair was. He gathered the top into a ponytail and split it into three pieces and began to braid them together.

He finished the job in a few minutes, feeling the weight of Ted's eyes on him. "There you go, bug. Go get your bag and put on some clean clothes too."

Remmy skipped off to get the job done, and Dallas looked at Ted, who grinned. "You just did your daughter's hair in a braid."

"Yeah," Dallas said.

"How'd you learn how to do that?"

"I watched a lot of videos online," he said with a smile. "And she sat still for me for a lot of practice sessions."

Ted stood up and took his bowl to the sink too. "That's amazing, Dallas. I barely recognize you."

"I wasn't a father in prison," he said simply. He took Ted's seat and looked at his son. "What do you want to do after we drop off Remmy?"

"I don't know."

"We could go to the trampoline park," he said. "Or get a real breakfast that isn't made of only sugar." Dallas still hadn't eaten, and he could go for pancakes and bacon. "Or just come back here and watch *The Last Airbender*."

Thomas looked up at Dallas, and he definitely had the same light eyes Dallas saw whenever he looked in the mirror. He had most of Dallas's facial features, but his hair was dark like Martha's.

"Can we get breakfast and bring it back?" Thomas asked.

"The pancakes will be soggy," Ted said. "And the eggs cold."

"We could call for delivery," Dallas said. "They have apps for that these days."

"Sold," Ted said, groaning as he sat at the table.

"You literally just ate half a box of cereal," Dallas said, grinning at Ted.

"Yes, and in another hour, I'll need a stack of pancakes with blueberry syrup." He grinned back at Dallas, who shook his head.

Ted's phone rang, and he checked it. "Oh, this is my old boss." He jumped up and walked away, saying, "Counselor," in a booming voice.

Remmy came skipping down the hall. "Ready, Daddy."

"All right." Dallas also groaned as he stood up, his back still twitchy from yesterday. "Let's go guys." He nodded to

Ted, who was on the phone in the living room. The three of them were quiet on the way to school, and Dallas got out and opened the back door for Remmy, giving her a tight hug with the words, "I love you, Rems. Have a good day. I can't wait to hear about the magician."

"Okay, Daddy."

He marveled at the resiliency of six-year-olds, and he cast a long look to Thomas, still sitting in the front seat of the SUV. He sighed, wishing his son could shrug off last night as easily as his sister had.

"All right," Dallas said on the way back. "*The Last Airbender* and pancakes?"

"Yes," Thomas said, finally cracking a smile.

Dallas returned it and swallowed. "Are you okay, Tommy?" he asked. "I was thinking maybe you'd like to go see someone. Talk about Mom, and Aunt Amy, and what happened yesterday. You know? Just someone who won't judge you, or give you any suggestions, or anything. They could help you and help you make sense of your life now."

Thomas nodded, but he didn't say anything.

"Think about it," Dallas said. "It might be good for you." Dallas thought it might be good for *him* to talk to someone too. He could get some help for his current problems. He reminded himself that he had Nate and Ted, and they had a solution they were working toward.

His conversation with Jesus had been great, and the man said he'd been living in Miami. He had a lot of contacts down there, and he said he'd be back in touch with Dallas once he had more information.

They returned to the rental, and Dallas sat on the couch with Ted while Thomas got the movie set up. He ordered the breakfast foods they all wanted, and with the movie going and Thomas all curled up in the recliner, he looked at Ted.

"What did your friend have to say?"

"He's got a PI in Florida who says he's seen Martha down there."

"Really?" Dallas asked, shocked by that news. He supposed her mother lived in Florida, and it felt like someone had flipped a switch and flooded his mind with light. She was probably living with her mother. *Using* her mother.

Instant anger flowed through Dallas again, and he set his jaw. "Once we find her, then what?" he asked.

"Then we get her out," Ted said. "Pay off the debt. Be free."

"Free," Dallas echoed, wanting that so badly. He remembered every single day of the thirty months he'd spent in prison, and he'd yearned to be free then too. This wasn't nearly as confining as River Bay, but he still felt trapped.

"Once we find her, we'll go," Ted said. "Okay, Dallas? Don't think about it too hard. We'll all go, and we'll get her out."

"I don't think she wants to get out," Dallas said. "That's the problem."

"Yeah," Ted said. "But you need her to get out, so we'll do what we can."

"Okay." He focused on the movie, hoping Ted would get the message that he didn't want to talk about this anymore.

Several minutes later, the doorbell rang, and Ted got up with the words, "That should be the food." He stepped over to the door and just stood there.

Dallas stood too, watching as Ted moved out of the way to reveal a gorgeous brunette standing on his front porch. "Jess," he said, casting a glance to Thomas. "I've got to talk to Jess for a minute, okay, bud? Ted's going to sit here with you."

"Okay, Dad."

He met his friend's eye and went past him to join Jess on the porch. "Hey." He gathered her into his arms as Ted closed the door behind them, giving them a measure of privacy.

Jess said nothing, but she clung to him in a way that made Dallas feel special and important.

"I'm sorry about last night," he said.

"What happened?" She stepped back and looked at him, a questioning look on her face.

Dallas sighed and ran his hands through his hair. "Uh, I'd rather not involve you."

"Involve me?" Her dark eyes flashed, and Dallas saw lightning and thunder in her expression.

"Jess," he said. "I just...I'm looking for Martha."

Horror crossed her face, but she wiped it away quickly. "Okay. I get it. I see." She started down the steps, obviously headed back to her car.

"Jess?"

"She was your wife, and you want her back. I get it." She tossed the words over her shoulder like they meant nothing to her, and it took Dallas a few moments to make sense of them in his head.

By that time, Jess had made it back to her car. She sat behind the wheel already. Dallas went down the steps in a jog and hurried toward her. "Wait, wait," he said. "That's not true at all."

All of her windows were up, and she glared at him through the glass. He put both palms against the glass, and said, "Jess, wait. You're wrong."

She cracked the window and he continued, almost desperate for her not to drive away believing he was looking for Martha because he wanted her back. "I don't want Martha back. I need to find her so her thugs will stop bothering me."

Jess simply stared at him. "Her thugs?"

"I couldn't take you to dinner last night, because when I got home yesterday, there were two guys here, and they made me work on their truck for five hours. I locked the kids in the bedroom to protect them, and they were terrified and crying by the time I finished after eight p.m."

Jess killed the engine and got out of the car. She stared at Dallas, her eyes wide. "Are you serious?"

"Yes." She couldn't leave, not over this.

"You're not trying to find Martha?"

"I am," he said. "But not to get her back." He tentatively reached out and brushed her fingers with his. "I just...need to find her and get her out of whatever situation she's in. Otherwise, that Josh character that showed up at the ranch could continue to make my life difficult."

Sudden worry hit Dallas again. "And yours," he added. Perhaps it was better if she left in a rage and never spoke to him again. His heart wailed, because it had just found another rock and another hard place to exist between.

"You didn't come to work," Jess said, her voice feeble.

"Thomas wanted to stay home from school," Dallas said. "We're just hanging out. Ted's here."

"Yeah, I saw Ted." Jess blew out her breath and looked away. "Okay, well, as long as we're okay."

"I think we're okay," Dallas said. "What do you think?"

She wouldn't meet his eye again, and Dallas finally reached up and gently guided her face back to his. "Jess?"

"I feel like you said yesterday," she whispered. "Disconnected."

"Do you have a few minutes?" he asked. "Come in and

sit with me." He watched the indecision rage across her face.

She finally nodded, and Dallas tucked her into his side and led her back to the house. Fierce determination filled him. He was not going to let Josh or Mario take what he'd been building. Not his relationship with his children, and not this beautiful woman at his side.

Find Martha, he thought. *Get her out. Pay the debt.*

Be free.

CHAPTER SIXTEEN

J ess told herself not to worry about not being in the spotlight of Dallas's life. He had a lot going on right now, and she didn't need to be front and center. She kept her head down, and she went to work everyday.

Dallas texted her every morning to let her know if he was going to be at work that day or not, and if he was, what they should do for lunch. She sometimes took lunch to his office, and he sometimes joined her in the West Wing.

Those thirty minutes every day became the basis of their relationship, and as the days and weeks passed, she started to wonder if that was all she'd ever get with him.

They hadn't spoken about the holidays, though Jess's mom had called and asked her to come to Montana for the Morales family celebration. With only a week to go until Christmas, Jess had to make a decision.

She worked at the desk in the kitchen, working on the

schedule for her trainers, as well as the horseback riding lessons. A new batch of kids started once the New Year did, and while Emma usually helped with this schedule, she'd been busy planning her wedding and Jess had volunteered to do it all this time.

"Jess!"

She turned and dropped her pencil at the sound of Remmy's voice. A smile filled her face as well as her soul. "Hey, sweetie."

The little girl flew into her arms, already talking about something that had happened at school that day. "And this boy—his name is Mickey, you know like the Mouse?—and brought in a real, live rat for show-and-tell. It squeaked and everything, and it had this long, long tail. He actually held it by the tail, and we all got to touch it."

"That's amazing," Jess said, beaming at her. "Was he slimy?"

"No," Remmy said with a giggle. "His tail didn't have any hair though."

"So it must've been slimy," Jess said, still teasing Remmy.

Remmy laughed and shook her head. "No, Jess, it was just kind of weird."

"I bet."

"You'll come to my birthday party, right?" Remmy looked at her with all the hope and innocence of a six-year-old, and Jess's whole heart expanded for the girl. While she hadn't seen Dallas a ton, she had spent some more time with his kids.

She'd taken Thomas shoe shopping when Dallas had to work a fifteen-hour day to get caught up on all the things he'd fallen behind on after taking time off.

He hadn't updated her about Martha for at least a week now, and she looked up to find Dallas standing there, watching her and Remmy and grinning.

"Of course I will," Jess said, focusing on Remmy again. "When is it?"

"January seventh," Remmy said. "The party is that night."

"At your house?"

"Yes," Dallas said, stepping forward. "Our place. Remmy's favorite food is—"

"Tacos!" the little girl shouted, and Jess flinched away from the sound. "Daddy's ordering a *lot* of tacos."

Jess grinned too, wishing a lot of tacos would bring her the same happiness it brought Remmy. "That's amazing," she said. "I love tacos too."

"Ask her," Dallas said, and Remmy turned to look at her father. Jess did too, noting the half-serious look on Dallas's handsome face. Something sharp stung her, and she realized how much she missed him. Maybe she'd taken too big of a step back. Maybe she'd overestimated how overwhelmed he was.

When Remmy turned back to Jess, she wore some of the seriousness in her gaze too. "Will you make the cake?"

Surprise shot through Jess and lifted her eyebrows. "Your birthday cake?" She switched her gaze to Dallas as if to ask, *Really?*

"Yes," Remmy said. "Daddy says you're good at baking."

Was she? Had she ever told Dallas that? She couldn't remember. She was no whiz in the kitchen, she knew that —and Dallas did too.

"Sure," she said anyway. If she couldn't do it, Emma would help her, and Emma *was* a genius with baked goods. In fact, Jess should just ask Emma to make the cake up front.

"Is there a theme we're working with?" she asked.

"Disney princess," Dallas said. "All the little girls will be dressed up in princess dresses for the party."

"No boys coming?" Jess asked, smiling at Remmy.

Remmy shook her head. "Nope. Girls only."

Jess tried to see the tall, broad-shouldered mechanic who wore a cowboy hat everywhere he went amidst a bunch of six-and-seven-year-old princesses, and somehow he fit right in.

She wouldn't, but she didn't want to dwell on that right now. "Disney princesses," she repeated. "Which one are you going to be?"

"Belle," Remmy said instantly. She played with the ends of Jess's hair. "Her dress is yellow."

Jess grinned at her and pressed her forehead to Remmy's. "Is your daddy the beast? Or Thomas?" She giggled with the girl, and Remmy felt like she fit right in Jess's life.

She looked up at Dallas, wondering if he did too. She couldn't have Remmy without him, and she felt like an idiot for getting attached to the girl when her relationship status with her father was so tumultuous.

"Okay," Dallas said. "Rems, you have homework for tomorrow, and Jess has work to do."

The little girl slipped from Jess's lap, and she stood as Remmy skipped past her dad and down the hall. She watched him watch her until the back door closed, and then he met her eye.

"Do you have a minute?" he asked, extending his hand toward her to hold.

Jess nodded, easily putting her hand in his. She let him lead her through the house to the rarely-used front porch. Ginger kept a bench there, and Dallas let out a long sigh as he sat down. His hand in hers never wavered, but he took several seconds to breathe before he spoke.

"Jess, the boys and I have to go to Miami."

"Okay," she said, her chest vibrating. "Why?"

"We found Martha." He looked at her. "She's in a bad way, Jess, and she won't leave on her own."

Everything inside Jess laced tight. "What makes you think she'll go when you get there?"

"She won't," he said. "It's not going to be easy."

Worry accompanied the tension radiating through

Jess. "And then what? You're going to bring her back here?"

"Yes," Dallas said. "She needs to be in a drug and alcohol treatment facility, and I'm going to check her into one of those."

Jess nodded, because she didn't know what else to say or do. It felt like Dallas was bringing home his mistress and expecting the three of them to live under the same roof.

That made no sense, because it wasn't like she and Dallas lived together. They weren't even close to talking about something serious.

The closest they'd come was him asking her if she'd like to get to know his kids better, and that was months ago.

She looked at him, the storm in his soul so easy to see. "Dallas," she said carefully. "We're still okay, right?"

"Of course," he said. "Once I get through this, things will go back to normal."

Normal. He'd been using that word since Thanksgiving, but Jess honestly didn't know what it meant anymore.

"I don't think that's true," Jess said slowly. "There will be a new normal, Dallas." One with Martha in it, and part of Dallas's attention forever on his ex-wife.

Selfishness strung through Jess. She reminded herself that she'd made the choice to start dating Dallas and get to know his kids. She thought of Remmy and the birthday cake she'd just committed to making. She did love the little girl, and she enjoyed Thomas too. With time, she knew the boy would finally open up to her completely.

"That's okay," he said. "I've had a lot of new normals, Jess. I'd love to have the chance to build one with you."

"Is that true?" she asked.

"Of course it is." He searched her face, trying to find something Jess hadn't been able to discover herself. "What are you worried about?"

She couldn't say Martha, and it wasn't really his ex-wife anyway. Jess felt like she'd just stepped onto a turning point, and what she said next would determine the path of their new normal.

"I'm worried that you aren't ready for a new normal," she said. "Because you still have so much from your old normal to tie up. I'm not blaming you." She spoke softly. "Our relationship is my longest, Dallas. I'm falling for you, and I'm scared that even if you could fall in love with me, that you're simply not in a place to do it."

Dallas's jaw jumped as he pressed his teeth together. "I don't know what to say."

"You asked me what I was worried about. That's what I'm worried about." Her chest seized as she realized that her fears and concerns about their relationship were one hundred percent true. He hadn't refuted what she'd said.

"I think we should wait until I do tie up everything," he said. "And then you can decide if the new normal is what you want."

She nodded, once again not sure what else to do. She

didn't want to break up with Dallas. He was easily the one single man she'd connected most with in her whole life. Didn't that mean she could give him more time? More chances?

"I hate to ask this now, but I was hoping you would come stay at my place and take care of the kids while I'm gone."

Jess jerked her attention back to him. "You want *me* to take care of your kids?"

"Yes." He smiled. "Remmy loves you, and you'll be able to see if you really want to spend more time with them in the new normal."

"I already know the answer to that, Dallas," she said.

"Nate said he'd talk to Ginger, and Ted with Emma, to help you."

"When are you guys going?"

Dallas didn't answer; instead, he leaned down and kissed Jess. She was aware of the scent of him, the warmth from his body and mouth, and the instant way her heart melted into the kiss.

"I'm going to miss you, Jess," he whispered, lightly touching his lips to her cheek, jaw, and earlobe.

Heat flared through her whole body, and she actually giggled as he pulled away.

He lifted his arm around her shoulders, and she sighed as she settled into his chest. She wanted more moments, minutes, and months with Dallas Dreyer. Moments like this, where there were no white trucks to fix, no locks on doors to keep crying children safe, and no worries that every time he went home, he'd find some angry man demanding something from him.

Jess hadn't even realized how stressed she'd been until that weight had been removed from her shoulders. "I told you about the horse show, right?" she asked.

"Yes," he said, his voice low and his mouth right against her temple. "January twentieth, in San Antonio."

"You and the kids could come," Jess said, though she knew he wouldn't commit to it. He didn't know what tomorrow would bring, or Christmas, and he couldn't make a judgment about January twentieth.

"I'll look at their calendar," he said. "Thomas has a band concert in January sometime."

"Okay," she said. "You never said when you were going to Miami."

"Tomorrow, Jess," he said. "We're leaving in the morning."

She stayed very still for a few seconds. "You don't give a woman much time to prepare, do you?"

"All you need is clothes," he said. "I'll change the sheets for you in the morning, and you can sleep in my bed." He kneaded her back into his chest when she started to rise. "Fair warning, though. Both kids usually end up in the bed with me."

"Oh, wow," Jess said, because she hadn't shared a bed with anyone in decades. "Do you think they'll do that with me?"

"I guess you'll see," he said, chuckling. "You can take them back to the ranch if you want. They know where their suitcases are and how to pack. School is out at noon tomorrow, and then it's the holiday break."

"Right," she said, suddenly needing to start writing down some details. "Allergies or food things I need to know?"

"I made you a sheet," he said. "Thomas has therapy on Monday."

"You won't be back by Monday?" That was four days. What did they need to do for four days in Miami? Another dose of fear reminded Jess that she had no idea what they were getting into.

When Dallas said, "We don't know, Jess. I've told Nate and Ted that I absolutely have to be home by Christmas, so I know it won't be longer than that."

"My mother asked me to come for Christmas," Jess said. "I was going to talk to you about it."

"Yeah?"

"Yeah," she said. "I know you can't go, but I think I will. If you're back."

"I can't imagine we'll even be gone until Monday, but I did make you a quick cheat sheet of Thomas's and Remmy's favorite places to order. I'll leave you money for that. And there's just the one appointment on Monday."

"The kids would like to go horseback riding, I bet," Jess said.

"Absolutely," Dallas said. "And Thomas has been

talking about a friend named Henry that you'd probably score some points with if you let him come over."

"Henry," Jess said. "Got it." They fell silent again, and Jess closed her eyes and enjoyed being with Dallas. She thought she'd like to bottle moments like these and unstop them when the hard times came, because she knew there was a dark, brewing, bubbling cloud on the horizon. She just wasn't sure when it would burst and send down the winds and rains.

CHAPTER SEVENTEEN

Dallas followed Ted off the plane, his backpack already hitched over his shoulders. The flight from San Antonio to Miami hadn't taken nearly long enough, because Dallas wasn't nearly settled enough.

They had some idea of what they were getting into, because the Warden had been the one to identify the drug gang that Martha had gotten involved with, and he'd described them as "nasty."

Jesus had also provided a lot of information about Josh, who wasn't the leader of the gang, but he was the one who did the dirty work. Dallas had thought it sure was a long drive to bring a broken down truck from the tip of Florida to the Texas Coastal Bend.

He surely had gotten that truck somewhere else, because it had had a lot of problems.

Josh was unmarried, not addicted to the stuff his goons

sold across the city, and the enforcer within the group. He'd been in prison before, and he wasn't afraid to go back. That was the main difference between him, Nate, and Ted, none of whom wanted to ever see the inside of a prison again.

They'd spoken for many long hours about what they should do, what they shouldn't, and what was right. Dallas had offered to find someone to get Martha out and get her into a treatment facility. Ted had said they couldn't really trust anyone but the three of them.

The Warden wasn't going to get involved, and neither were any of Ted's still-practicing lawyer friends. Jesus knew a lot of people in the underground, and they'd gotten the most information from him—and the Internet.

Martha was not living with her mother, and Dallas had been most relieved about that. Her mom probably was giving her money, either knowingly or unknowingly. He'd been hoping and praying she wasn't stealing from her mother, but he'd known drug addicts in River Bay, and he'd heard Slate say once that he'd have done anything —*anything*—to get his next fix. If that meant he had to hack into his mother's bank account, he'd have done it.

They still hadn't gone up to River Bay to see their friends, but they had plans to go on the day after Christmas. The Warden had given them permission for the special visitation, and they'd been collecting gifts for Luke and Slate for the past couple of weeks.

Dallas really, really hoped he'd be in good enough

shape to attend the visit. Something sat in his gut that felt very much like a lead brick, and he hadn't been able to get rid of it for a week now.

They'd been ready to make this flight for that long, but they needed time to brainstorm and plan, strategize and agree on what they would and wouldn't do.

None of them were anonymous, Dallas knew that. Josh was a criminal, sure, but that didn't make him stupid. In fact, quite the opposite, and all three of them had agreed that they were walking into a dog fight.

He just wanted to get Martha somewhere safe, which would save him, Thomas, and Remmy in the process. Dallas took in a deep breath and focused on getting out of this airport. The thing was huge, and he still wasn't used to being around so many people.

Sweet Water Falls was a small town of maybe fifteen thousand. The ranch was even smaller, with less than fifty people there each day. The noise bothered him, distracted him, and made him question why he'd left his kids behind in Texas.

His heart squeezed for Thomas and Remmy, and the next person in his mind was Jess. She was far too good for him, and he didn't know how to make up the difference between them. He wanted to; he wanted to be the man she deserved. One who could make his own daughter's birthday cake and one who didn't have an ex-wife addicted to alcohol and speed, who'd left her children behind, and run away from an adult life.

Nate led the group, as Nate always had, and he'd flagged down a cab by the time Dallas wove through the crowd and made it outside. He slipped his backpack off his shoulder and got in the car last, setting his pack on the floor near his feet.

"Westside Drive," Nate said. "Near Pier 79, please."

The driver started tapping on his own phone, and Dallas's confidence took a dive. He didn't say anything as they pulled away from the curb, and no one in the back seat did either. Dallas just wanted to exist inside his own head until he had time and space to examine his true thoughts. He hated worrying about what hadn't happened yet, and he just wanted this whole ordeal to be over.

He'd never been to Miami, and he hoped he'd never come back. The blue water glistened beyond the pier when the cab came to a stop, and Dallas got out of the car first. Nate paid on his way out, and the three of them stood there in the weak, winter sunlight, looking back down the block.

They'd purposely designed their plan to have them dropped off a couple of blocks away from where Martha was reportedly staying. They'd split up; they each had a room in a different hotel. They'd watch the building for a day to see if they could catch sight of Martha or Josh.

Jesus had sent several pictures of other known associates of Josh and the gang, and Dallas had spent far too many evenings studying them after his children had gone to bed and before they'd come back in to sleep with him.

Part of him wanted to see them, and part of him didn't. He wanted to be in the right place, but he didn't want to deal with anyone. If Martha would only listen to him. He'd called her almost daily since Thanksgiving, and she'd answered her phone in the beginning.

After about a week, she'd told him to stop calling and to leave her alone. No amount of pleading, begging, or explaining had swayed her, and he wondered how she could've changed so completely from the woman he'd known and loved.

It's not really her, Nate had said. *Those are the drugs talking.*

Dallas couldn't help thinking that if she hadn't started drinking and using, she might have been the one to pick him up from River Bay. Her and the kids. They'd still be living in the sprawling house in Houston, and his life would be back to the one he'd left to serve his time.

In his quiet moments, he knew that wasn't what he wanted. Things happened that changed situations so completely that they simply couldn't be recreated. He'd forgiven her for abandoning him, but not for doing the same to Thomas and Remmy. He could handle disappointment; his children had already had more than enough.

"Let's meet for dinner," Nate said. "Seven, point one." With that, he was gone. Dallas watched him go, his step sure and his stride long. When he'd first met Nate, he'd wanted to be exactly like him. Certain and confident, contemplative and kind. He was smart as a whip too, and dedicated to always doing what was right.

Dallas looked at Ted, who looked up at the tall building next to them. "What do you think?"

"It's not my brain that's having the issues," Dallas said. "It's my gut, and it's saying we just need to get this over with."

"Maybe you just go in there, then," Ted said.

That brought a healthy dose of fear to Dallas's heart, stomach, and mind, and he couldn't comment again. His thoughts derailed, and he shook his head. "Let's stick to the plan for now."

"Okay," Ted said. "Just don't do anything stupid, okay? If you decide to go in, *call us.*"

Dallas nodded and said, "See you at seven." He went down the block toward the housing unit, his goal to find somewhere to sit where he could watch the proceedings. He crossed the street, keeping one eye on the building as if he expected a swarm of heavily armed men to come out and start firing shots.

No one did, and he made it to a bench that a mother and her son were sitting on. He flashed them the best smile he could under the circumstances and sat on the other end. He sighed and opened his backpack to take out the bottle of water he'd gotten on the plane.

He pulled his phone out of his pocket and pretended

to look at it. He watched and watched, seeing a couple of men he recognized from the pictures Jesus had sent. No one else seemed to be going in or out, and Dallas started to wonder if the residents were allowed to leave or not.

Once the work day ended, the streets got busier, and so did the revolving door at the building. Dallas sat, watching the world go by. He felt like he was the only one sitting still and everyone and everything else rushed by in a blur.

The crowds had started to thin when a man sat on the bench beside Dallas, not down on the other end. "Hello, Dallas," he said, and Dallas turned to look at him.

He had not been anyone in the pictures. He was no one Dallas had ever seen before. He wore a suit and tie and sighed as he set a briefcase between their feet. "What are you doing here?"

"Do I know you?" Dallas asked.

"No." The man kept looking straight ahead. "And you don't want to know me. I don't want to know you either. I just want to know why you're here."

"My ex-wife is in trouble," Dallas said.

"And you think you can save her."

"No," Dallas said. "I just want to be left alone."

The guy said nothing, and Dallas continued to study him. He had dark hair and dark eyes that didn't settle on anything. He radiated a coldness from his expression that kept people away, and Dallas wanted to get up and go meet his friends for dinner. He kept his hands folded in his lap, and Dallas noticed a triangular tattoo on the inside of his wrist. He wasn't sure what it meant, if anything. He knew he just wanted to leave.

He didn't dare move.

"What do we need to do to make that happen?" the man finally asked.

"Tell me who you are," Dallas said. "And where my wife is. I'm taking her home with me."

"What if she doesn't want to go?"

"It's not her choice at this point," Dallas said. "Her behavior is a threat to me and my children, and I simply cannot allow it to continue." Saying that so clearly, in such a strong voice, made him feel like he could bring a resolution to this conflict.

The man stood up and made no effort to pick up his briefcase. "Let's go talk to her then." He walked away, and Dallas stared after him.

"This is a once-in-a-lifetime opportunity, Dallas," the man said. "Bring that briefcase, would you?"

Dallas got to his feet and turned his back on the guy. He bent to pick up his backpack while he dialed Nate, and then he retrieved the briefcase too. He really hoped this thing didn't have a bomb inside and that he wasn't walking into the belly of the beast.

"Dallas?" Nate asked.

"What's your name?" Dallas asked, hurrying to catch up to him.

"Adam," he said.

"That's not your real name," Dallas said.

"You don't need to know my real name."

"You know mine."

"Yes, I do."

"Where are we going?"

"To see your wife," he said. "That's what you wanted, right?"

"Yes," Dallas said. "This is what? Hudson Street?" He tried to talk loud enough to get the message to Nate, and his friend didn't try to talk to him again.

The man stopped in front of the next building down to the one Dallas had been watching. He nodded to the doorman, as this building was much nicer than the one beside it. "She's in unit 2B," he said, opening the door for Dallas. "You'll need the briefcase."

Dallas looked into his eye. "What does she owe you?"

The man frowned, his glare intensifying. "I'm not sure."

"Don't treat me like I'm stupid," Dallas growled, getting right into the man's face. "I know she owes a bunch of money, because I've already worked off four grand of it while my children cried for their father. If you don't know what she owes, find out. I'm not going in there until I know and pay it off."

His fingers clenched tightly around the handle of the briefcase. "I'm not taking this, and I *am* leaving here with my wife, all of her debts settled."

"I'll need a moment," he said.

"Take it," Dallas said, his voice strong though he didn't feel quite as tough. "You can find a thousand other people to hook on your drugs. It's not going to be Martha anymore."

The man nodded and lifted his phone to his ear. He stepped away, and Dallas couldn't hear what he was saying. He quickly put his own phone in position and said, "Nate, I'm at 1155 Hudson Street. Martha's in Unit 2B. Sending you a picture of the guy now."

He hung up and snapped a picture of the man after he'd turned around, his phone still glued to his face. He did not look happy. Dallas did not care. Some of his attitude that he'd adopted in prison had returned, and his determination to get this situation settled had renewed.

He put the briefcase on the ground, sent the photo to Nate, who confirmed that he and Ted were on the way, and looked at Adam when he said, "Sixteen thousand."

Dallas nodded. "All I need is an account number, and I can have the money wired within three minutes."

"Your banks aren't closed?"

"No," Dallas said, because Nate had more money than Dallas had ever seen in his lifetime, and he had a banker in his pocket too. "Old family friend," he'd said, but Nate's voice and eyes hadn't displayed any friendship at the time.

"I've got my guy standing by," Dallas said. "You can confirm when you have the money, and I'll go get Martha."

Adam kept his frown in place, and it suited him so much more than the seemingly innocent businessman just walking home from work. He gave Dallas a bank account number, and Dallas dialed Sam Wiseman, the vice-president of the bank where Nate had all his money.

Dallas didn't turn away or look away from Adam as he said, "Yeah, hi, Sam. It's Dallas. I have that account number for you. I need sixteen thousand wired to it immediately."

Sam started talking, clicking happening in the brief stretches of silence. "From Mister Mulbury's account?"

"Yes, sir," Dallas said, knowing Nate had all of this set up already.

"I'm going to need the PIN," Sam said.

Dallas recited it to him, and Sam said, "This account has two-step authorization on it. Do you know the username?"

"WardenConnor4," Dallas said. When said quickly, one could hear, "Ward and Connor, four," and that was exactly why Nate had chosen it. He missed his brother terribly, and though he hadn't said much about it, the three of them were planning to take Connor to see his parents in White Lake after the family celebration at River Bay the day after Christmas.

Not only that, but they'd go by Ward's old house and see how it was doing. Nate had mentioned that he should probably think about selling it. He hadn't said why he hadn't done that yet; he hadn't had to put it so plainly into words.

"The account number where the money is going?" Sam asked, and Dallas gave that to him.

"It is after hours in Miami," Sam said. "This could take up to fifteen minutes to show as a pending deposit."

"Thank you," Dallas said as politely as he could without turning into a softie in front of Adam.

"Is that all?" Sam asked, his tone clipped and professional.

"Yes," Dallas said. "Thanks again." He ended the call and nodded to Adam's phone. "He said it could take up to fifteen minutes." Nate and Ted should be there by then, and Dallas was determined to wait for them. Something was screaming through his head that he should not enter this building alone.

Five minutes passed before Adam said, "It's here."

"I'm going to need something that says we're in the clear," Dallas said. "I don't want you or anyone who knows you, works for you, has ever seen me or Martha in their lifetime coming to Texas again. We're all off-limits. Is that clear?"

Adam snarled at Dallas, who didn't even flinch. He'd lived with the men who'd nearly killed him for three months after the beating. This guy was nothing. Less than nothing.

"We don't give receipts," Adam said.

"Make an exception." Dallas folded his arms and glared at Adam. He became aware of movement, and he'd never felt stronger than when Nate stepped to his left side and Ted to his right.

"Who's this guy?" Ted asked.

"No one," Dallas said. "He's going to give me confirmation in writing that the debt is settled, and then we're going to get Martha."

"In writing?"

"That's right," Nate said. "And if you try to say he owes you more at any time in the future, we know about fifty lawyers between us."

"And cops," Ted said, looking at Dallas and Nate. "I mean, the feds are always looking to make a big drug bust, aren't they?"

The three of them glared at Adam, who had the guts and confidence to stare right back. "Fine," he said. "Who has something I can write on?"

Nate swung his backpack off his shoulder and produced a small notebook with a black pen. Adam scrawled a note on it, signed his name with a flourish, and handed everything back. "You really will need to take the briefcase," he said. "It's the signal that you're safe."

"Fine," Dallas said, and Nate stooped to retrieve it.

"Pleasure doing business with you." Adam smiled then—actually had the audacity to smile—and saluted as he walked away.

Dallas finally got enough air in his lungs. He looked at Ted and then Nate. "Unit 2B," he said. "Let's go."

CHAPTER EIGHTEEN

"No, it is not okay, Martha," Dallas said as Jess entered his house, both of his kids behind her. She stopped instantly and turned back to them.

"Thomas," she said as Dallas started to say something else. "Will you please take Remmy back out to the mailbox? I think your dad was expecting something today."

Thomas had already heard his father's frustrated voice, and he looked behind Jess, who had blocked the door. "All right," he said.

"Thanks." Jess held his eye and tried to give him a reassuring smile. "And Tommy, maybe run next door and ask Mrs. Clyde if she'll let you two have some ice cream."

His face brightened then, and as he walked back down the sidewalk they'd already come up, Jess quickly texted Mrs. Clyde that they needed a few minutes to sort something out. She responded with, *I'll get the cookies and cream out now* and a smiley face.

Jess had met her only a few days ago, when Dallas had left for Miami. She'd been the emergency contact on the sheet of paper he'd left for her. The kids knew her, and they liked her. She loved them, and she'd brought Jess dinner on Saturday night.

Dallas had returned on Sunday evening, Martha in tow. She did not look good, and she'd been mean and crying when Jess had met her.

That was just yesterday, and Jess had left the children at the ranch while she'd come to see what they were dealing with. It hadn't been pretty, and Jess had cried the whole way back to the ranch. She'd kept the children at the ranch with her that morning, where they all fed and watered horses, rode horses, ate hot dogs and potato chips, and kept trying to guess what was in the packages under the tree in the West Wing.

She'd thought Dallas would admit Martha to a treatment center today, as they'd discussed. She wasn't expecting Martha to be at Dallas's at all.

Jess turned back to the house, and it seethed with tension, pulsing it out into the atmosphere like a heartbeat. She took a deep breath and stepped inside, closing the door behind her. For good measure, she locked it. That way, Thomas and Remmy would have to ring the doorbell.

She found Dallas faced off with Martha in the dining room. She sat at the table, looking worse today than she had last night. He wore pure anger on his face, and Jess was actually afraid of him for the first time.

He hadn't been in Miami for very long, but he'd come back a different man.

"We're back." She looked between Dallas and Martha, her eyes wide with worry.

"Where are the kids?" Martha stood up, looking around wildly for them. Her hands shook, and she looked like she'd painted red circles around her eyelids.

The air held no oxygen, and Jess felt like she was suffocating one breath at a time. It was a slow, agonizing pain that spread through her whole chest.

"You can't see the children when you're like this," Dallas said quietly. He still hadn't looked at Jess. "Martha, you need help. If you go to the treatment center, I'll bring the kids to see you as soon as you're clean. It'll only take a few days."

Jess hated the soft, kind way he spoke to her. She wanted the anger and frustration she'd heard in his voice only a few minutes ago to reappear, because this woman deserved it. Those two emotions built inside Jess, and she clenched her fists so she wouldn't do something she'd regret later.

Martha screamed, and she flew toward Dallas. He flinched away from her but still managed to catch her along her forearms so she couldn't hit him. "Martha," he said, his voice hard. "Stop it. Stop it now."

Jess's emotions surged, and she had absolutely no idea

what to do. The level of helplessness inside her threatened to drown her, and tears filled her eyes. "Dallas," she said while he continued to grapple with Martha. There was no way for him to hear her above Martha's incoherent ranting, and Jess felt like she'd entered a horrible, terrible movie that certainly couldn't be real.

She blinked, and the situation didn't change. It absolutely was her reality.

"Stop it," Dallas said again, and he managed to get Martha back into one of the chairs at the table. "We're going right now. You've lost your ability to make rational decisions, and I'm doing this for your own good." He finally met Jess's eye and added, "There's a bag beside the couch. Will you get it, please?"

She scampered over to the couch and picked up the benign bag. She wondered what he'd packed for his ex-wife's visit to a drug treatment facility, but Jess wasted no time opening it to see. She quickly pulled out her phone and texted Mrs. Clyde.

We have to run an errand, she said. *Could you keep the kids? I'll call Nate and have him come get them.*

Before Mrs. Clyde could answer, she dialed Ginger. "How's it going there?" Ginger answered after only one ring.

"Not good," Jess whispered. "Can you and Nate come get the kids? They're at Mrs. Clyde's next door. The white house with the green door."

"We're leaving now," Ginger said, and relief and gratitude painted Jess's insides. She wanted to be the kind of person who dropped everything when those she loved needed help, and Ginger had always been such a great example of that.

Jess looked back at Dallas, who had crouched down and was pleading with Martha. Actually pleading with her.

Fury rose within her, and something snapped. "Let's go," she said. "Right now, Martha." She marched over to the woman. Jess had trained horses to do exactly what they didn't want to do. She could get this woman into the car and then a treatment facility.

Dallas looked at her with fear on his face, but Jess didn't care. "Now," she barked. "You're coming with us."

"I'm not," Martha said.

Jess grabbed onto her chair and turned her to face her. "Listen, Martha," she said, her voice colder than she'd heard it before. This woman represented everything keeping Jess from her future, and she wasn't going to take her insolence for another minute. "There are two choices here. You get up and come with us to the treatment facility. You'll stay there for the entirety of the program, or we'll have you arrested. You'll get clean. You'll get to see your kids—who you do not deserve to see ever again." She raised her eyebrows, silently challenging Martha to argue with her. She didn't.

"And once you're done with that, you'll find a way to reenter society as a functioning human being. Maybe you'll get a job. A place of your own. You'll get to see Thomas and Remmy if the judge allows it. All of that."

Martha glared at her, and Jess knew she'd be dead if the woman's eyes had been equipped with lasers.

"Your other choice is to sit there and continue to be ungrateful for all this man has done for you. That's fine. You can choose to do that. I'll call the police and have you arrested right now for child endangerment. You're so out of it that they'll keep you in jail until you're sober, and that transition isn't going to be pretty. No one in the county jail is going to care, and you're going to have to manage your withdrawals all by yourself, huddled up on a mattress against a concrete wall."

She straightened, the fire inside her burning too brightly. She needed to pull back a little bit. Martha was still Thomas and Remmy's mother, and Jess pictured those two amazing children as she studied Martha. "You won't see your kids if you choose this option," she said. "You'll get out in a few days, by which time Dallas will have petitioned the judge to make sure you never see those kids again. Ever."

She stepped back to Dallas's side. "Your choice."

"Who is this woman?" Martha asked, her tone as icy as Jess's. She stood too, and for one terrible moment, Jess thought she'd lunge at her and start swinging. Dallas even stepped in front of her to shield her from Martha.

"Go," he said. "Martha, go get in the car."

The three of them stared at one another, and Jess

reached a breaking point and then hung on for another minute. Finally, Martha turned and stomped toward the garage exit. The door slammed behind her, and Jess crumpled to the floor, sobbing.

"I'm sorry," Dallas said, kneeling in front of her and gathering her into his arms. "I'm sorry, Jess. I'm sorry."

She clung to him, needing the extra support for just a few minutes. Then she gathered herself together and stood up. She wiped her face while Dallas got Martha's bag. "I can take her."

"We'll go together," Jess said, because she wasn't sure Dallas had what it took to get Martha inside the treatment facility. They had way more history than Jess even knew, and she had no idea what he was going through.

They did go together. Jess had to threaten Martha one more time to get her inside the facility, where she wailed and screamed and begged Dallas not to do this to her. In the end, the nurse asked Dallas to leave, and he turned and stormed out of the building.

Jess finished the paperwork and took the packet out to Dallas in the SUV. "The kids are with Nate and Ginger," she said, her voice somewhat robotic.

"I just talked to him," Dallas said, and he sounded so exhausted. Jess felt it deep in her bones, and she didn't say anything as he drove them out to Hope Eternal Ranch.

As they passed the sign, Jess wondered if hope really was eternal. Could it really go on and on? Was she a fool if she continued to hope for that new normal Dallas had spoken of only a few days ago?

She didn't know. She did know she couldn't go in the West Wing and act like everything was okay. She didn't want to get out of the safety of this SUV and face anyone or explain anything.

He parked in front of the fence, and they sat in the car, silently.

"I'm going to go to Montana for Christmas," Jess said. She'd already decided to go. Her airfare had been booked for twenty-four hours. Her mother had cried when she'd called to tell her she'd be there. "You're going to River Bay, right?"

"Yes," he said.

She nodded, so many things pinching tightly inside her. "I'm sorry if I overstepped my bounds with Martha," she whispered. "I just couldn't take another moment of you begging her to get help."

"It's okay," he said.

Jess got the distinct impression it wasn't, and she felt so stupid for inserting herself into his business. She opened the car door and hesitated. "So I'll see you when I get back?"

"Yes," he said again, his voice just as reserved, his demeanor just as calm.

"Okay," she said. "Merry Christmas, Dallas." She got out, her feet crunching on the gravel, and closed the door behind her. This was not the holiday celebration she'd had in mind when she pictured Christmas with Dallas as her boyfriend.

She'd taken a few steps toward the opening in the gate before he said, "Jess?"

She turned back to him and ran her hands up her arms, because the night had grown late, and a chill rode in the air. He came toward her in that strong, sure gait he had and wrapped her up in his arms.

Her emotions surged again, but she bit back the tears. She'd already dissolved in front of him once tonight. She would not do it again. He kept her tightly against his body, and she needed the strength of his arms to hold herself together.

"I'll go get the kids," she said, her voice nasally. She stepped out of his arms and walked toward the house. Inside, the scent of cinnamon and chocolate met her nose, and she suspected that Emma had made oatmeal chocolate chip cookies with the kids.

Sure enough, a wire rack held at least a dozen, and Remmy poked her head up from the other side of the couch. "Jess," she said. Both she and Thomas got up and came toward her, wrapping their arms around her simultaneously.

"Hey, guys," she said, enveloping them into a hug too. She stroked their hair, thinking Thomas might not like it. But he just clung to her too, saying nothing. He really didn't talk much, and Jess often wondered what was going on inside his mind. He'd gone to therapy that day, but he'd literally not said one word about it.

"Your daddy's outside," she whispered. "Let's go see him, okay?"

Thomas led the way, and he ran to Dallas, who scooped him up and hugged him tight. Remmy called, "Daddy!" in her cute drawl and ran toward Dallas too. He laughed as he picked her up in his other arm. They hugged him as he closed his eyes and smiled into the night sky.

Jess watched from the corner of the house, a sense of love and admiration for Dallas filling her. She'd never felt like this before, and she honestly didn't know what to do with the feelings.

He turned and helped his kids get settled in the SUV, and then he looked back at her. He started toward her, but Jess didn't want to have another hard conversation. She just wanted him to go be with his kids. They were why he'd gone to Miami. They were why he'd done everything he'd done in the past three months.

"Thank you, Jess," he said when he reached her. He took her face in both of his hands and dipped his head to kiss her. All the tension in Jess's muscles bled out, and she kissed him back, the sure knowledge that she was falling more in love with him right there in the forefront of her mind.

"There she is," a female voice said. "Jess!"

She turned right and found her sister, Abi, waving vigorously through a crowd of people. Jess's tears appeared again, and she was so tired of them. Who cried like this?

She swiped at them as she maneuvered her carryon through the crowds of people obviously trying to get to loved ones for the holidays. She finally reached Abi, and they hugged, Abi laughing and hopping up and down a little bit. "You're here. Oh, you're here."

She exhaled and stepped back, holding Jess at arm's length. "You look so good, too. How are you?"

"Good," Jess said, only a touch of a lie in the word. "Where is everyone else?"

"Dad wouldn't park and come in," Abi said with a frown. "He hasn't changed in that regard. Mom convinced him to go down to the gas station and get a couple of candy bars. Nia's back at the ranch, cooking up something for dinner. Huey's going to meet us there."

Jess nodded, and together, they walked over to the baggage claim area. Jess had decided to visit for ten days, but as she walked outside, she'd forgotten she wasn't in Texas anymore. She sucked in a breath, which froze her lungs together.

"Holy cow," she said as her teeth started chattering. "I need my coat."

"Dad's right there," Abi said, but she flipped up her furry hood and cinched it tight to keep the wind out. Jess thought she might freeze to death before their father's enormous black truck pulled to a stop at the curb.

Her mom spilled from the front seat, half-laughing and half-crying as she rushed Jess. They hugged, and Jess decided to just give up on holding back the tears. These were her parents, and she hadn't seen them in a long time.

"Dad," she said as he crushed her in a hug too.

"It's so good to see you, Jess," he said. "So good." He beamed down at her, and he was just as large as his truck. Square shoulders and big muscles though he'd cut back on his work around the ranch. "Let's get out of the cold."

"Yes, please," Jess said. "It's at least a hundred degrees warmer in Texas."

"I'll bet it is," her mom said. "It's been clear for a few days now, after a big storm. They're the coldest days of the year."

Jess could feel that chill sinking all the way into her bones. She got in the back seat with Abi and looked at her as their dad loaded Jess's bags into the back of the truck. She picked up Abi's left hand. "Still no ring?"

Abi heaved a big sigh and shook her head. "Honestly, I'm not sure it's going to happen."

"It is," their mother said from the front seat. She twisted all the way around, and Jess could only smile at her. She loved her mom, and she'd inherited the same crooked smile and the same dark complexion her mother had.

"Ready?" Dad asked as he climbed behind the wheel.

"Yep," Jess said, and she looked at Abi and then her mom again. "What?"

"Abi says you said you were seeing someone." Her mother looked so hopeful, and Jess once again thought about that elusive thing called hope.

Jess shot a look at her sister. She had mentioned Dallas in a text. A single text, and not by name. "Yes," she said, seeing no reason to deny it. "His name is Dallas Dreyer. He's the mechanical manager at the ranch."

"Dallas," her mother repeated. "Sounds very Texan."

"Okay, Mom," Jess said with a laugh. "It's just a name." She looked away, out the window, because she didn't want to talk about Dallas.

"That's all we get? His name and where he works?"

"Mom," Jess said.

"Come on," Abi said, and Jess suddenly felt ganged up on. Even her father met her eye in the rear-view mirror, and it was clear he wanted to know more. Jess supposed she hadn't told any of them very much about her relationship with Dallas, and she probably should. If only they weren't currently in the middle of something extremely trying.

"What else do you want to know?"

"How'd you meet him?" her mom asked.

"At Ginger's wedding," Jess said. "He'd just wiped up the floor, and I came running out in a new pair of boots. I slipped and fell, and there was Dallas."

"He can't have been working at the ranch for very long

then," her father said, and Jess sometimes wished he wasn't so quietly observant.

"No, just for a few months," Jess said. "He's smart, and good with his hands. He can practically see the schematics of an engine and seems to know right where every part goes."

"I'm surprised he's not a cowboy," Abi said.

"He wears the hat," Jess said. "Rides the horses. His kids love them."

Silence permeated everything, including the surprise on her mom's face.

"He has two kids," Jess said, backing up. "Thomas is ten, and Remmy will be seven in a couple of weeks." She still hadn't sketched out an idea for a princess cake, because she'd simply had too much going on.

"He's divorced then?" Abi asked.

"Yes," Jess said, and she definitely wasn't diving down into that pit of snakes. It really was too bad there was another one in front of it. "His wife, uh, filed for divorce and left the kids at her sister's house when he only had a few months left on his prison sentence."

"Is he—?" Her mother's voice muted as her brain caught up to her ears.

Jess looked out the window again, suddenly done talking about herself, her relationship with Dallas, or anything else really. "I'm tired, guys," she said, closing her eyes. She wished some of the painful situations she was dealing with would go dark as easily. "Can I tell you more later?"

"Leave her be," Dad said quietly as her mother pulled in a breath to surely ask another question, and Jess experienced a powerful sense of gratitude for her good father, and she kept her eyes closed the rest of the way to Bozeman and the ranch where she'd grown up.

CHAPTER NINETEEN

D allas wished the truck in front of him would step on the gas already. He'd left the ranch late, and he needed to stop and get the tacos for Remmy's birthday. Once this party was over, Dallas didn't have anything on his calendar until Martha's treatment program ended.

He'd survived Christmas with the kids, and they'd enjoyed a quiet morning at home with plenty of pretty, wrapped presents. He'd made blueberry pancakes and told them how his mother had made them every Christmas morning for him and his siblings growing up.

Dallas wanted to start some better traditions for his kids; memories they could take into their adulthood too. They'd gone out to the ranch in the afternoon, and Dallas had eaten Christmas dinner with everyone at Hope Eternal.

Emma, Jill, and Hannah had put together a feast for

anyone who didn't have family to go visit on Christmas—and anyone else who wanted to come. Dallas had felt like he belonged on that ranch, with those people, but there was one extremely important person missing.

Jess.

He'd called her, and she'd seemed upbeat and happy in Montana. She'd been back for over a week now, and Dallas still hadn't managed to take her out, just the two of them. There was so much going on with New Year's celebrations and then the planning for this party.

Martha hadn't shown up on his doorstep, and he called every other day to check on her. She couldn't talk to him, and in a lot of ways, her drug treatment program was worse than prison. He'd at least gotten phone calls in and out of River Bay.

He could ask if she was still there or if she'd left the program. So far, she was still there. Dallas prayed for her every day, and he hoped the worst of her withdrawals had come and gone. Now, it was about learning how to live a regular life without the drugs once she got released.

Dallas knew exactly how this felt, and he'd written her a long letter about his feelings surrounding getting out of prison after thirty months. He'd had no idea how to lead a normal life, but he'd figured it out.

She could too.

He'd told her he wanted her in their children's lives, and they'd sent her cards and drawings for Christmas.

The guy in front of him finally made a left turn, and

Dallas was able to speed up. He pulled through the drive-through of the taco joint where he'd ordered the food for Remmy's party and was given two long, covered trays.

The scent of seasoned meat and corn tortillas filled his nose, and his stomach roared. Before Christmas, he and Jess had usually spent their lunchtime together, but he hadn't seen her once since she'd come back from Montana.

Something was wrong.

As he pulled back onto the street, he tapped a button on the steering wheel of his SUV and said, "Call Jess."

The car dialed for him, and he listened to her phone ring and ring. She hadn't answered his calls for a solid week now, and pure irritation rose within him. "What did I do?" he muttered to himself.

In his opinion, they'd had a sweet interchange before she'd left for the holidays. "Something must've happened with her family."

He hated it when she went silent, and he ended the call without leaving a message. He immediately called her again, and when she still didn't answer, he said, "Jess, I'm just double-checking that you're still bringing the cake to Remmy's party. She's excited to see you."

He paused, wondering if he should bubble-wrap his heart so it didn't get shattered by this woman. "I am too," he said anyway. "I feel like we've lost touch, and I'm hoping everything is okay with you."

He turned to get to the street where he lived, only a couple of minutes late now. "Will you at least text me so I know if I need to go buy a cake for my daughter's birthday?" His voice carried some of the frustration boiling in him, and he quickly ended the call before he said something else that gave away too much.

Sighing, he pulled into his driveway, which didn't have anyone waiting for him. He still had a bit of fear every time he turned the corner, as if Josh or Adam would be waiting for him on the front porch. He hadn't seen either of them in weeks, and every day that passed added a little more comfort to Dallas's mind.

He got out of the truck and went around to the other side to get the tacos. "Daddy!" Remmy's voice filled the air, and he turned around to find her running across the neighbor's lawn. He grinned at her and raised his hand to Mrs. Clyde, who'd taken the kids after school today.

Thomas approached much slower, carrying both his backpack and Remmy's. He smiled at Dallas too, and he balanced the big trays in one hand and forearm as he gave his daughter a side-hug and then tousled his son's hair. "How was school?"

"Good," Thomas said.

"Daddy, we got to watch this video on polar bears." Remmy said. "They have paws as big as your head."

"Is that right?"

Remmy continued to chatter about literally everything that had happened at school that day as they went inside the house.

Dallas noted the fresh scent of flowers and pine, glad

he'd hired a one-time maid service to make sure the house would be clean for this party. He should've told them to come tomorrow too, because he had a feeling this princess party was going to be the death of him.

"You better go get changed," he said to Remmy, sliding the tacos on the counter. "Thomas, Nate will be here in a few minutes to take you to the ranch. Make sure you have your backpack and everything for school tomorrow."

"Yes, sir." He went down the hall after Remmy.

Dallas listened to his daughter singing at the top of her lungs, and he couldn't help smiling. He needed to shower and change, so he hurried into his bathroom, checked his phone to see if Jess had texted—she hadn't—and got the job done.

He'd just stepped into a clean pair of jeans when Nate called, "Hello? We're here."

"Coming," Dallas said, reaching for the T-shirt he'd just gotten out of his closet. He heard Thomas start to talk to Nate, so at least he wasn't standing awkwardly in the living room. Dallas skipped putting on shoes or socks and padded into the main living area of the house.

Nate, Ginger, and Connor had all come, and Ginger carried a box that had been wrapped in bright pink paper, complete with a purple and white frilly bow.

"Wow," Dallas said. "You didn't have to get her anything."

"Yes, we did," Ginger said, smiling.

"Let me get her," Dallas said, turning to go back down

the hall. He was surprised Remmy hadn't come out yet, actually. He found her in her room, a tube of bright red lipstick in her hand. "Whoa, whoa," he said. "Where did you get that?"

He hadn't bought it, that was for dang sure. She'd done a terrible job of getting it right on her lips too, and she looked more like the Joker than Belle from *Beauty and the Beast.*

Dallas gently took the lipstick from her as she looked up at him. "Where did you get this makeup?" She wore bright blue eyeshadow too, but it extended over most of her nose and way too far past her eyelids too.

When she didn't answer, Dallas grew uneasy. "Remmy," he said sternly, sitting down on the bed with her. She had changed into the yellow princess dress, her bony shoulders barely holding it in place. "Tell me where you got all this stuff."

"Julia got it from her mom's bag," Remmy said, dropping her eyes to her bedspread.

"Is Julia coming to the party tonight?"

"Yes," Remmy said. "I said if she'd let me take it home, I could get my makeup done, and then we could do hers at the party."

"Okay." Dallas stood up and gathered up the eyeshadow palette too. "That's not happening, okay? We have to give this back to her mother." That wasn't a conversation he wanted to have tonight, but Dallas did a lot of things he didn't want to do.

"Okay," Remmy said miserably.

"You don't need the makeup," Dallas said. "You're seven. I'm going to get Ginger to come help you take it off." He didn't even know if water would do the job. "Ginger, could you come help me?" he called over his shoulder, and her strong, sure steps came toward him.

"Yeah?" she asked, taking in the scene in a couple of seconds. "Oh, okay. Come on, sweetie. Let's go get you cleaned up." She extended her hand toward Remmy, who slid off the bed, still looking like a scary version of a miserable clown.

Dallas took the makeup into the kitchen and put it all in a zipper bag. He really needed to know if he should send Nate for a birthday cake or not. There was still time, because the girls were eating first, and then doing a couple of games before cake and ice cream. The whole thing would take ninety minutes, and Dallas hoped he could endure it.

Ginger had put the gift on the dining room table, and Dallas moved it so the kids would have somewhere to eat.

"What's goin' on back there?" Nate asked, nodding down the hall.

"Oh, Remmy got her hands on some makeup," he said, lifting the lid on the tray of tacos. "Ginger is helping her clean up."

"Mm." Nate reached for a taco, and so did Dallas. He handed his to Thomas, and the three of them crunched through the delicious shell while standing there in the kitchen.

The doorbell rang, and Dallas's eyes flew to the clock on the stove. Six-twenty-five. "Could be Jess," he said. Perhaps she'd been driving while he'd called and texted her, and she hadn't wanted to answer.

He pulled open the door to find a woman standing there with a little girl wearing a pink dress. It had a picture in a button on the front, but Dallas wasn't sure who it was. He hadn't had time to watch Disney movies in prison.

The woman smiled at him as if they'd be best friends. "Hello, I'm Melissa, Ingrid's mother." She held out her hand, and Dallas shook it.

"Dallas. Remmy's dad." He stepped back and let them inside. He hadn't specified on the party invitations that parents could just drop off their kids, and it looked like Melissa was here to stay. "This is Nate," he said, introducing his friend. "He's taking my son for the night."

"So there's no Mrs. Dreyer?" Melissa asked, and as Dallas turned back toward her, time seemed to slow to a stop.

He didn't know what to say. She wore a look of interest in her eyes, and shock cascaded through Dallas like a waterfall.

"No," Nate said, barely smothering a laugh as he met Dallas's eyes. "Well, there's an ex-Mrs. Dreyer."

"And you have custody?" Melissa asked, ignoring Nate.

"Yes," Dallas answered, because that one was easy. He really didn't want to air his family gossip right now, and thankfully, the doorbell rang again, and Ginger brought Remmy down the hall.

The little girls squealed and laughed as Dallas let in another mother and her daughter. *Oh, boy*, he thought.

"We'll get out of your hair," Nate said with a smile. He thanked Ginger and held the door for them as they left.

"Be good, Tommy," he called after his son.

"I will, Dad."

Dallas didn't close the door, because another woman was walking down the sidewalk, this time with two little girls. He put on his happiest smile and welcomed them to his home.

"Oh, this is nicer than I thought," the woman said, and Dallas did his best not to roll his eyes.

"Moms," he said. "You really don't have to stay. My girlfriend will be here any second, and you can come get your girls at eight." He made sure to enunciate the word *girlfriend*, and Melissa apparently got the hint. She left, taking both of the other moms with her.

Jess did not arrive in the next second, but two more girls did. The count was up to six, and Dallas's ears were already paying a hefty price. They'd only invited nine girls, so there couldn't be too many more coming.

He really just needed Jess to come.

Remmy started answering the door, and Dallas's eyes

never left it. He pulled out his phone when the eighth girl arrived and texted Jess. Again.

Are you coming? Should I call Nate to go get me a cake? He watched the text to make sure it went though. It did, but he had no way of knowing if Jess had read it or not. What he knew was that his time was running out.

The last girl arrived, and Dallas lifted both hands above his head. "All right, princesses," he said in a loud voice. They all giggled and looked at him. "It's time to eat. And do you know what princesses eat?"

"Tacos!" Remmy said, clapping her hands and jumping up and down.

"That's right," he said. He put the tray in the middle of the table, and opened the second one as he said. "Tacos. There are tons of tacos, and black beans and rice." He put that in the middle of the table too. "I can help anyone get what they want. Come sit down, all proper and perfect like princesses."

They clamored to do that, and Dallas thought seven-year-olds were the perfect age. Thomas had been seven when Dallas had gone into prison, and he still sometimes thought of his son as that little boy who was still losing his front teeth.

He wasn't that boy anymore, and he'd be eleven in March. Dallas wasn't sure where the time had gone, but he knew it had a funny way of passing.

He dished up tacos and beans and rice onto paper plates—pink, with all the faces of the princesses—and let the girls eat. His stomach twisted, and he ate a taco to try to soothe it.

Just as he put the last bite in his mouth, the doorbell rang again. It had to be Jess. It just *had* to be.

He crossed the room quickly and opened the door. Relief flooded him when he saw Jess standing there, a three-tiered cake in her hands. "You made it," he said, almost breathless at the sight of her.

She flashed him a tight smile—the kind he'd seen before when she was annoyed with him. He still had no idea what he'd done wrong, and he didn't want to have a serious, adult conversation with her during his daughter's birthday party.

"Come in." He got out of the way so she and the cake could come inside, and an uproar of tiny, female voices filled the air as he closed the door behind her. She'd gone straight to the table and put the cake down in front of everyone.

Dallas hung back, watching. The cake had been decorated in pale purple frosting on the bottom, and it circled up into white, and then pink on the top. Little figurines of the Disney princesses had been stuck into the tiers, and they were all waving.

Some of the little girls started waving back, and Dallas envied their innocence. He went back into the kitchen to be with everyone, and he said, "There's plenty to eat, Jess. Do you want any?"

"No, thank you," she said, the formality of it increasing

his worry. *Just get through the party*, he told himself. Hopefully he could talk to her in private later.

He did make it through the party, and by the time the last princess left with her queen-mother, Dallas was silently vowing to never have another child's birthday party again. He sagged against the closed door and looked at the mess in his house.

"Go get your pj's on," he said to Remmy. "Then come help me clean up all the tissues, okay?"

"Okay, Daddy." Remmy skipped down the hall, leaving him and Jess alone. She started stooping to pick up the tissues he was going to leave for Remmy.

"You don't need to clean up," he said.

"I don't mind."

He glanced down the hall. Remmy would probably be a few minutes at least. "Jess?"

She hadn't looked at him fully once during the party. She'd been all smiles and loads of fun for the girls as she led the party games and painted nails and lit candles. He'd done a couple of the girls' hair, and cut the cake and dished ice cream. They'd worked well together, and Dallas really wanted her in his life without all the awkwardness and frustration.

"Yeah?" She still didn't look at him.

"Did something happen in Montana?" he asked. "You've been...*we've* been different since."

"Not really," she said, stuffing more unused tissues into a recyclable shopping bag. "It's about a hundred degrees below freezing there. We went ice skating once, and I dang near froze."

He chuckled though she didn't add her laughter to the conversation. He didn't know what else to say, and Remmy returned to help Jess. She started telling her about the crown she'd gotten to wear that day, and how she got to be line leader even though it was Christopher's week.

Jess giggled and conversed with Remmy easily, and there was no awkwardness there at all. So it really was just him.

The three of them worked together and got the house cleaned up in only twenty minutes. "Bedtime, bug," he said to Remmy, scooping her up and into his arms. She squealed and laughed, and Dallas tickled her as he took her down the hall to her bedroom. He got her all tucked in and leaned down to hug her. "Did you have a good birthday, Remmy?"

"Yeah," she said with a sigh. "I think seven is going to be such a great year for me, Daddy." She looked so earnest about it too.

Dallas laughed and clicked off her lamp. "I'm sure it will be, bug. Go to sleep, okay?"

She didn't answer, and Dallas paused in the doorway. "I love you, Rems."

"Love you too, Daddy."

His heart melted as he pulled the door closed. Back down the hall, he found Jess shrugging into her jacket. "You're leaving?"

"I have a meeting for the horse show at six a.m. in the morning." She zipped her jacket closed, and Dallas felt her running from him. He quickly crossed the room to the front door and blocked her escape.

She collected the cake platter her concoction had come on, and she didn't see him until she was on her way toward him. She stopped, her dark eyes blazing now.

"Something's wrong with us," he said. "I think we need to figure out what it is, so I can fix it."

"I don't need you to fix it," she said.

"What did I do?"

Jess sighed and looked away. The motion almost made it look like she was rolling her eyes, and Dallas's exhaustion morphed into further irritation.

"It's nothing," Jess said. "Can I just go?"

Dallas didn't want to make her life harder. He really didn't. Lord knew he didn't need more complications in his life right now either. He stepped to the side and opened the door. "If you'd just tell me," he said quietly. "I could make it right."

Jess took a couple of steps toward him, and she hesitated close enough to him now that he could smell the sugar on her. The scent of fresh air and horses. Their eyes finally met, and the same powerful pulsing that had always run through Dallas when he was faced with Jess still existed.

"I don't think you're ready for there to be a real us," she said.

"We've talked about this already," Dallas said. Frankly, he was tired of talking about it. Tired of defending himself.

She nodded, absolute misery on her face. His heart started to pound. "I know," she said. "I just...maybe *I'm* not ready to be with who you are now."

"What do you mean?"

"I mean, I started to fall in love with the strong, sexy cowboy mechanic who knew exactly what he was doing out on that ranch. The man who was regaining his confidence one tractor at a time, one day at a time as he figured out how to be a single dad. How to juggle parenthood with his job. How to win over a woman." She shook her head. "I know I'm not making sense."

She wasn't, at least not much.

"But, Dallas, that's not who you are anymore."

"Who am I?" he asked softly.

"You're this strong, sexy cowboy mechanic who's trying to save everyone but himself."

He blinked, unsure of how to respond.

"You need help, Dallas," she said. "*You* do. You can't singlehandedly save Martha. Or Thomas. Or me, even."

He wasn't even aware she needed to be saved, or how he would do it.

"I can go see a counselor," he said, because he'd already considered that possibility. "We could go together."

She shook her head. "You could, if you think that would help you get back to who you really are."

"I know who I really am." Prison provided a man with a lot of time to contemplate that exact topic.

"Then you need to find him again," Jess said. "I want him. I want the man I started to fall for."

"I'm still that man," he said, desperation rising through him.

"No." She shook her head. "He got lost in Miami, Dallas, and I haven't seen him since." She started walking again. "I'm sorry. I should've texted you about the cake, so you weren't worried." She kept her back to him, half in his house and half out. "If not for that precious little girl, I wouldn't have come tonight."

"Jess." Dallas stepped over to her, reaching out as if to touch her. He didn't, because he didn't think he should. "Is this it, then?"

She turned and looked at him. "Maybe when you're ready, we can try again."

"I'm ready," he insisted.

She shook her head and said, "No, Dallas, you're not." With that, she gave him a small, sad smile. Added, "I wish you were, but you're not, and I deserve someone whose main focus is going to be on me, not their ex." She turned and left, the winter darkness beyond his front porch swallowing her whole.

He didn't know what else to do, so he simply closed and locked the front door behind her. He turned and stared around at the furniture in the house. He went down the hall to his bedroom, put on his pajamas, and got in bed.

He lay there, eyes closed, mind racing. Yes, he'd been focused on Martha, but he'd had to do that. He couldn't have drug dealers showing up at his house or the ranch, putting everyone in danger. Putting *Jess* in danger. Why didn't she get that?

His confusion turned to anger, which morphed into misery. He'd seen it on her face too, but right now, he was powerless to change the emotion for either one of them.

"Daddy?" Remmy's tiny voice asked. "Can I sleep with you?"

"Of course, baby," he whispered. "Come on."

She hurried over to the bed, and he peeled the covers back for her. She settled on the pillows next to him, and with her tiny lungs breathing in and out, his thoughts evened too.

They now rang with only one item: *Jess, Jess, Jess.*

How could he fix himself, get ready for a relationship where she was the focus, and then get her back?

CHAPTER TWENTY

"I don't know, Abi," Jess said, done with this conversation and it had just started. "It just happened. He's not ready, like you said, and Nia's right too. I deserve someone who's going to put me first in his life. Well, maybe second behind his kids, but not a distant last after his ex-wife."

Bitterness filled her, and it made the stables far colder than they really were. A bitter kind of cold that never seemed to leave Jess's soul.

"How long has it been?" Abi asked. "You didn't say anything last week."

"It's been a while," Jess said. "I'm not even sure what day it is."

"Okay, Jess, you're a mess," Abi said. "You always know what day it is. Day of the week. Date, even. You have training schedules for those horses that you make, remake, redo, and then do all over again for a fifth time."

Jess laughed, because that was true. Without Dallas in her life, she felt adrift. Purposeless. "I know what day it is," she said. "It's Friday, January twenty-second."

Dallas had been out of her life for fifteen days. She knew every minute of every one of them too. She just didn't want to hash it all out with Abi, her now-engaged sister.

She could still see Huey down on both knees in the foyer of the farmhouse. He'd been waiting there for Abi when they'd gotten home from the airport. He'd put Abi's favorite flower—the calla lily—everywhere in the house, and he'd set up his phone to record the whole thing.

He was sweet and romantic—and utterly focused on Jess's sister. As she watched Abi and Huey, and her mom and dad, and Nia and her serious boyfriend Walt, Jess had seen so many things lacking in her relationship with Dallas.

All of it boiled down to the fact that he simply had too much on his plate. She didn't want to be a spoonful of potato salad crammed in among the other things he'd taken on, and she'd spent a lot of time talking to her parents about the relationship, about him, about why he'd gone to prison.

She'd shown them pictures, and her heart had filled and warmed as she looked at her and Dallas beaming at the camera in one of their selfies. He'd taken it outside the stable one day, and Jess's hair was a mess, the wind was blowing, and Dallas had his other hand flat on his head to keep his hat in place.

But that didn't matter. They looked so happy, and Jess realized the picture had been taken very early in their relationship. The man who'd come home from Miami was not that smiling cowboy in the selfie.

She had pictures of her and the kids too, usually with one of them on a horse while she walked beside it. Remmy had both hands up, her fingers in peace signs, and Jess's chest constricted every time she thought about the little girl.

"Okay," Abi said. "But Jess, we're here for you. Dad is really worried about you."

"I know." Jess didn't know how to make him stop worrying. She paced back to her bed and sat down on it. "I'll call him. It's been a few days." She sighed and rolled her neck, ready to eat dinner, put something on her tablet that would wipe her mind, and go to bed. "I just don't want to hear his relief when I tell him I broke up with Dallas."

"He won't be relieved."

"Yes, he will," Jess said. "He didn't like that Dallas had been to prison. He looked up everything about it online. He also didn't like that he has kids or has been married before." She loved her father; she did. He was right to be worried, she supposed.

He'd said, "Marriage is already really hard, Jess." He'd

cut a look at her mom when he said it. "You're adding two kids to that, plus an ex-wife, plus a man who's restricted by being a felon."

His words looped through her head over and over, and she really wished they wouldn't. Didn't everyone deserve another chance? People made mistakes, and Dallas had paid for his according to the legal system.

Everyone got to make their own choices, too, and he couldn't control what Martha had done. He'd given her a second chance at life too—and that was what scared Jess the most. Once Martha got clean, would Dallas prefer to see if they could make their marriage work again? They had two children together, and Jess knew it was better for families to be together rather than split up.

No matter what, she'd have to share those kids with Martha for the rest of her life. Did she really want that?

Jess didn't know. She knew she wasn't going to break up with Dallas because of his prison term. She knew better than that; she'd seen so many men get their lives back together and find a new, better, and correct path to be on.

Everyone makes mistakes, she'd told her father. She wondered if she'd made one by breaking up with Dallas without giving their new normal a chance to begin.

"I have to go," she said to Abi. "Tell everyone hi. Tell them about Dallas. Tell Dad I'll call him tomorrow." She didn't have the fortitude to make another phone call tonight.

"Okay," Abi said. "We all love you, Jess."

"I love you all too." The call ended, and Jess set her phone on her nightstand. She didn't have the energy or spirit to even go into the kitchen and get something to eat. She'd see Jill and Hannah, and she didn't want to talk about Dallas.

They were worried about her too, Jess knew. Hannah had brought her a box of Milk Duds yesterday, and Jess opened the top drawer of the nightstand and pulled them out. They'd do for dinner tonight.

She changed out of her work clothes and into something more comfortable. Curling up in bed, she smelled the fresh scent of the dryer sheets on her comforter and snuggled into the mountain of pillows behind her. She just needed an escape for a little while. She'd be fine, if she could just be alone for a while....

"Ho," she called to the big, black horse she'd just gotten from the horse show she'd attended by herself. Lael Miller, one of the best trainers in Texas, claimed the beast couldn't be tamed, but Jess had a different opinion. She also hadn't put herself in the ring with the stallion, because he was free-spirited and absolutely huge.

She'd had Midnight Madness for a few days now, and while she liked working with him, he also challenged her in new ways.

The horse whinnied, and she went up on the fence rails to get more to his height. "You have to stay connected," she said to him as Midnight ran by again. "Stop tossing your head, or I'm going to make it tighter."

Sometimes one of the other cowboys would tease her for talking to the horses as if they could understand English. Jess did it anyway, because she believed they could. They could *feel* her spirit, and they knew she just wanted to help them.

Midnight ducked his head as he trotted away from her, and Jess watched him try to spit the bit. She'd kept him on the second shortest setting for the past two days, and he didn't seem to be ready for more line at all.

"How's he doing today?" Rich asked as he climbed up on the bottom rung of the fence too. Midnight rounded the corner and saw him, tossed his head, and nickered. "Oh, all right," Rich said with a laugh. "You don't like the bit or the line. Too bad, bud."

Too bad, indeed. Jess said nothing, sensing that Midnight simply needed to get his frustration out, and then he'd do what she wanted him to. She simply had to out-wait him, and no one had ever done that before.

"Time him," she said to Rich. "We say nothing until he's calm."

Rich pressed a button on the side of his watch, and she and Rich stood side-by-side on the fence and watched Midnight Madness trot around and around and around. He'd toss his head every time he passed, and eventually, it was every other time. Then every third time. Then not at all.

He finally slowed to a walk, his head bobbing exactly where a horse's head should, his breathing though his nose steady and strong.

"Time?" Jess asked quietly.

"Twenty-one minutes," Rich said.

"Start it again," Jess said. "I'm going to lead him." She climbed the fence and got in the ring with Midnight. She stayed on the outer ring as he walked by, aware that he was watching her too. The second time around, she stepped in front of him and walked along his shoulder. He let her do that too, and Jess relaxed completely.

"There you go," she said to the dark horse. "See? You and I are going to get along just fine."

She kept him on the lead for several more times around, then she released it from the clasp that kept him on the circle she wanted him on, and she led him around the pen. Each time they went, she pulled him out another foot.

Eventually, they walked along the rail, Jess going whatever speed she wanted, and Midnight following her.

"Time?" she asked Rich, because it felt like a lot of it had passed. Jess was surprised she possessed the patience to work with a horse like Midnight, but then again, she'd always had more patience and love for horses than she did people.

Another flaw, she supposed.

"Forty-seven minutes," he said. He deserved credit for standing there and watching all that time.

Jess smiled at him as she went around again. "One more time, okay, Midnight? Then you get to eat and drink, and I'll even put you in the shady pasture."

"You're going to spoil him," Rich called with a smile. "Then he'll think he can act all fussy and then get the best grass." He laughed as he stepped off the bottom rung. "I have to go drive the bus. See you tomorrow, Jess."

"Bye," she called to him, pausing at the gate that would leave the walking circle. Midnight did everything she asked of him, and she led him down the aisle in the row house to his stall, where he got brushed down for a good long while.

She gave him fresh water, and fresh hay, and a bowl full of cut up apples and carrots from one of the fridges they kept in the stable. "Don't go tellin' the others," she said to him as she stroked his neck. "These treats are for the best horses, and they all want them."

Jess made sure they all got them from time to time, too, because she wanted all her horses to think they were the best horse on the ranch. She stayed with Midnight Madness for a while longer than necessary, because she felt so much like him.

Too loud, and too impatient. Too big, and too rash with her decisions. She regretted cutting Dallas from her life, but she didn't know how to let him back in. He hadn't tried to come back into her life, and that kept her inside her own space too.

She took Midnight out to the pasture and walked back to the stables about the same time the kids started arriving for riding lessons.

"Jess!" a little girl called, and Jess turned to find Remmy running toward her.

A smile filled her face and her soul, and she crouched down to receive the girl into a hug. "Hey," she said into Remmy's neck. "How are you? What's seven been like so far?"

Remmy straightened and looked right into Jess's eyes. "So good, Jess. Dad got me a new bike, and I've been practicing on it every night. I can ride it so far now, and I never tip."

"That's great," Jess said. "I bet it's like riding a horse."

"Yeah." Remmy reached up and touched Jess's cowgirl hat. "Why don't you come for dinner anymore?"

"Oh, I've been real busy," Jess said, keeping her smile in place. "We got this new horse, and he is so big and so wild."

"Like a wild stallion?" Remmy's eyes rounded, and Jess giggled with her.

"Yes," she said. "Just like that."

"Remmy."

Jess looked up into Dallas's face, lightning striking right behind her ribs. She straightened and nudged Remmy to go to her father. He nodded at her, ducked his head so the brim of his hat hid his face, and he walked his daughter over to her horseback riding lessons.

Jess fell back out of the way, hiding in the shadows near the stable door to watch him with his daughter. It didn't matter what her father was worried about. Dallas was a good man, and a great father, and Jess loved his kids.

Go say something to him, she told herself. *Don't just let him walk away.*

He helped Remmy into the saddle and waved to her as the lesson began. He didn't turn to look for Jess. He simply walked away in the direction of the mechanical shed.

Jess released the breath she'd been holding. *Twenty-nine days,* she thought. It had been twenty-nine days since Remmy's birthday party when they'd broken up.

She couldn't dwell on all that she and Dallas could've been doing during those twenty-nine days. She'd told Remmy the truth—she was very busy right now. Dallas surely was too. Jess had to believe that, because she didn't want to think that he had time to make things right between them and had simply chosen not to.

CHAPTER TWENTY-ONE

D allas wasn't sure what had happened in January. The month passed in a blur of mechanical grease, math homework his ten-year-old didn't understand, and therapy sessions for everyone in his house.

Himself included. He'd also decided to get Remmy in to see someone too. Out of the three of them, she was the bubbliest, and she definitely talked the most. But Dallas knew she'd experienced trauma too, and he wanted her to get the help she needed.

He'd seen his son re-emerge from the shell he'd been in when Dallas had picked him up in September, and that made his heart heavy with happiness.

He paused at the far corner of the stable, having just taken Remmy to her riding lesson. He'd finally seen Jess around the ranch. It was amazing to him that they both worked there full-time and yet never saw one another.

Today, though, he'd seen her, and she was just as radiant and just as attractive to him as she'd always been.

His voice had fled, and all he'd been able to do was nod.

"You can't have her right now," he told himself sternly, and that was enough to get his feet moving again.

She'd been right, and he hadn't been ready for a serious relationship with a woman. He did have a lot going on in his life, and he hadn't been putting her first. His kids came first. His job came second. Providing some stability for all of them was extremely important to him. Making sure he could keep his children safe also sat very high on his priority list, as did making sure Thomas and Remmy could have a real relationship with their mother.

All of that had come out in therapy, and as Dallas had prioritized his life, he'd realized just how right Jess was.

He disliked it, but right now, there wasn't much he could do about it.

"Ten days," he muttered to himself. "Ten more days."

Martha's eight-week treatment program ended in ten days. He had not spoken to her since taking her to the facility before Christmas, but he'd be there on February fifteenth to take her away from that place too.

What happened after that, he didn't know. He could see how unfair he'd been to Jess—and to himself. While he wanted Jess in his life, he simply hadn't been ready.

He really wanted to be ready.

As he walked back to the equipment shed, he let his

mind cast forward, something his therapist had asked him to do in their last session. "What do you see?" she'd asked. "Tell me where you are. Where you live. What your house is like. What you're doing with your time. Who's with you."

He'd talked through where he was, and that was in a big house with a lot of land surrounding it. Trees and bushes and wild grass, with a nice, cultivated yard too. The house was old, and he'd told Dr. Wood that he liked spending his time fixing it up. "I'm good with my hands," he'd said. "Thomas helps me."

"So Thomas is there," Dr. Wood had said.

"Of course," Dallas said. "He and Remmy are always with me."

"Is Martha there?" Dr. Wood asked.

"No," Dallas said, and his eyes had shot open at that moment. He looked at Dr. Wood. "She's not there. What does that mean?"

"It means you don't want a future with your ex-wife," Dr. Wood had said, and they'd moved on to talking more about Martha and how Dallas could deal with the termination of his marriage, something he hadn't truly done.

As he walked now, the ranch breeze trying to steal his cowboy hat, he saw who was in the house with him.

Jess.

It was always Jess when he thought about who would walk in through the back door and say, "Well, I got that silly horse to listen to me."

Jess.

Dallas would smile at her and kiss her hello, his hand easy and comfortable along her waist. He'd tell her he'd made scrambled eggs and sausage for dinner, and she'd smile up at him and say breakfast for dinner was one of her favorite things.

The fantasy faded after that, because Dallas had arrived back at the equipment shed, and he needed to focus on getting the last tractor serviced for the day. Then it would be the weekend, and maybe he could figure out the next steps he needed to take to get himself into a place where he and Jess could be together.

"You're sure?" he asked Amy the next day. Martha's sister had kept in touch with him and his kids since he'd gotten out of prison, and Dallas sure was grateful for her.

"Absolutely," Amy said. "She'll hate it here, and it'll be exactly what she needs."

"But what about what you need?" he asked. "Martha won't be easy, Amy."

"I'm well-aware of what she'll be like, Dallas," Amy said, a crispness to her voice that Dallas had heard before. "I'm not trying to raise two children and run a household," she added in a much kinder tone. "I've thought a lot about it. Brent and I have talked about it extensively. We believe she should be here with us—that it's the right thing to do."

Dallas looked out the front window to make sure Remmy got to Mrs. Clyde's okay. He caught the last second before his daughter walked inside, and he turned back to the house. "She won't be able to see the kids."

Amy and Brent lived in Louisiana, and that wasn't a simple drive away. It was an all-day drive of just over eleven hours.

"She shouldn't see them anyway," Amy said.

"I want to be there with you when you pick her up."

"I'm going to ask her about it," Amy said. "Do I have your permission to call the treatment facility and have them send me the discharge items?"

Dallas took in the dirty breakfast dishes, the blankets that usually went on the back of the couch neatly, and the backpacks and shoes just discarded by the front door. The whole house needed to be cleaned, and he didn't want to do it.

"I want her to know she can see her kids whenever she wants to," Dallas said. "Thomas told me that he's been doing really great in therapy, and he's not mad at her anymore."

Amy allowed a pause to go by. "Perhaps you should bring the kids too," she said. "Maybe she could see them for a few minutes, and then we'll take her home."

Dallas nodded, emotion clogging his throat. "Thank

you, Amy," he said. "I don't know what I'd do with her here."

"She shouldn't be there," Amy said. "I don't know why I feel like that, only that I do. Here, she'll have me and Brent to help her. Daddy's willing to help out too. She'll be surrounded by familiar things and people, and there won't be any stress."

"Okay," Dallas said, because he couldn't argue with a woman's feelings. He'd been praying for a solution for Martha, and perhaps this was it.

"Thank you, Dallas," Amy said, as if he had any say in Martha's life anymore. "I'll call the center and let you know what they say."

"I'd appreciate that."

He set his phone on the kitchen counter and took a deep breath. The dishes wouldn't do themselves, and if he just got started, he'd find his rhythm. He did, and soon enough, the dishwasher was loaded and the bigger pans and bowls dried on the towel next to the sink.

He picked up backpacks and shoes and took them into the kids' rooms. He folded blankets and straightened pillows. He paid the bills he hadn't paid two weeks ago, and he showered so he was ready for whatever that day brought.

"Dad," Thomas said before Dallas could sit down on the couch and find something sporty to watch. His son came in through the front door, his blue Scout shirt untucked and too big.

"What's up?" Dallas asked. "Did you get all the flags in place?" The Scouts put up flags for major holidays and events, and Sweet Water Falls had been founded in February, so they put flags up for the first full week of the month.

"Yeah," he said. "And Milo asked if I could go to his house today."

"Okay," Dallas said, trying to remember which one was Milo. "He's the kid with the lizards, right?"

"No, that's Malcolm," Thomas said. "Milo's the one with all the telescopes and space stuff."

"Oh, right," Dallas said, smiling, because his son loved anything to do with astronauts too. "He just lives a couple of blocks over."

"Yeah." Thomas looked so hopeful, and Dallas couldn't remember the last time they'd said so many words to each other. He really had come alive in the past few months since starting therapy. "So can I ride my bike over there?"

"Right now?"

"Yeah, right now. I'm just going to change my shirt."

"Oh, sure," Dallas said as Thomas walked through the living room. A minute later, he returned, and Dallas handed him a twenty-dollar bill. "In case you guys need food or want to go do anything." He nodded toward the big back windows. "And it looks like it might rain. You should take a jacket."

"I'm fine," Thomas said, pocketing the money.

"Thanks, Dad." He left through the garage door before Dallas could insist he take a jacket. He remembered being a pre-teen and never wanting to be perceived as uncool because he had a jacket on when no one else did.

With Remmy gone to Mrs. Clyde's for a baking class, Dallas found himself with a decently clean house and nothing to do. He once again stepped toward the couch, thinking there had to be something on the sports channels that would steal time from him, but the doorbell rang before he could sit down.

Someone knocked too, and then the door opened. "Hey," Nate said as he entered with Connor and Missy. Ted followed them, and everything in Dallas's life got a little brighter.

"What are you guys doing here?" He clapped Nate on the back and did the same to Ted.

"The kids wanted their A-doughnuts," Ted said. "So we brought 'em to town to get those." He lifted up a brown box. "And some extras for you."

"Thanks." Dallas grinned and took the box.

"Connor has a birthday party in forty minutes or so," Nate said. "So I didn't want to drive back to the ranch. Can we crash with you for a minute?"

"Of course."

"Where's Remmy?" Connor asked, peering down the hallway.

"She's next door at a baking thing," he said. "I bet you guys could go."

Missy's face lit up, and she looked at Ted. He gestured for the kids to go with him. "Let's go ask." He looked at Dallas. "At Mrs. Clyde's?"

"Yep."

Ted took the kids, and Dallas took a doughnut from the box. He finally got to the couch and sighed as he sat down.

"How's the back?" Nate asked, and Dallas wondered what he'd heard in the sound to indicate that he was in pain.

"It's okay," Dallas said. "I shouldn't have gotten under that truck last night, that's all."

"You've got guys to do that," Nate said, frowning.

"They couldn't see what I needed them to see," he said. "As soon as I got under there, everything came together." He couldn't explain how he just knew where things were on the ranch vehicles. He'd been working on them and with his crew for months now, and they had everything running like the well-oiled machine it should be.

In fact, Ginger had just given him a pretty big bonus for getting them all caught up, and she'd offered him more money to stay on as the ranch equipment manager, with the official title. He'd accepted, because he loved working at Hope Eternal Ranch, and he saw no point in trying to find another job. This way, he wouldn't have to explain why he'd been in prison or see the doubt on an employer's face.

Nate leaned back and closed his eyes. It was nice to see the man a little run down, just as a reminder that he wasn't superhuman.

"How's married life?" Dallas asked, and Nate's eyes popped back open.

A smile crossed his face. "Great."

"Are you and Ginger gonna have kids?"

"Probably," Nate said. "She's not in a hurry, and neither am I."

Dallas nodded as Ted came back inside, sans kids. "The wedding is still on?" he asked Ted.

Ted glanced at Nate and back to Dallas. "We're doing relationship updates?"

"I guess," Nate said. "Mine was that married life is great, and we'll have kids when we're ready."

Ted gathered a doughnut from the box and sat in the recliner. "The wedding is still on."

"When is that happening again?" Nate asked.

"March tenth," Ted said. "About a month now." He stuffed a big bite of doughnut in his mouth and looked at Dallas.

Nate did too, and Dallas realized what he'd started. He wished he'd put his cowboy hat on the way the other two men had, but he hadn't.

"What's going on with you and Jess?" Nate finally asked.

"Nothing," Dallas said, and that was the absolute truth.

"Come on," Nate said, sitting up and leaning his elbows on his knees.

"Literally nothing," Dallas said. "She broke up with me a while ago. I wasn't ready, so she was right, and I don't know. I'm trying to get ready, and I need a plan to get her back when I am ready." He looked from Ted to Nate. "Any ideas for that?"

"When does Martha get out?" Ted asked.

"Nine days," Dallas said. "Her sister is taking over." Relief like he'd never known flowed through him, and he wondered why he'd thought he had to deal with Martha alone. She had other family to help, and he wasn't even her family anymore.

"That's a good idea," Nate said.

"I agree," Ted said. He polished off his doughnut and looked around the house. "Are you going to buy your own place?"

"Yes," Dallas said. "I just haven't had the gumption to start looking."

"Maybe you should," Nate said. "Get your own place for you and the kids. Somewhere Jess would really like. Then, you just go to her, Dallas. It isn't complicated. You just go to her, and you tell her you love her, and you're sorry for not being ready, but you're ready now, and you see what she says."

Dallas hung his head, though the brim of his hat wasn't there to hide his face. "It can't be that easy."

"It is," Nate said. "Right, Ted? Isn't that what you did?"

"Actually, I figured out all of Emma's favorite things, and I gathered those all together before I went to apologize."

"She's not perfect either," Dallas said. "Not that I need her to apologize to me. It's just...she seemed to go to Montana and listen to people who've never met me and make decisions based on what they told her."

"Did she do that?" Nate asked, his eyebrows up.

"I don't actually know," Dallas said. "It just feels that way to me." He looked up at his very best friends in the whole world. "How am I supposed to be with her now? Her family obviously doesn't like me. Maybe it's too hard." He shook his head and reached for the remote control.

He flipped on the TV and turned the sound down so they could still talk. "Then I see her, and all these kinds of doubts and fears just go away." He could picture her perfectly in his head from yesterday, and from the dozens of other times they'd spent time together.

"It's not too hard," Ted said.

"Not everyone gets their second chance," Dallas said. "I have kids to consider. I'll always have to deal with Martha. It's a lot for me to handle, and for someone like Jess? She doesn't even know what viper nest she's crawling into."

Misery ran through his veins, power-washing them out. "No wonder she broke up with me. Life would be much simpler for her if she found someone who'd never been married, never had kids, and never been to prison." He held up three fingers, still staring at the TV screen so he didn't have to face his friends. "Three strikes. I'm out, guys."

"That's just not true," Nate said.

"It is," Dallas said. "It could be, at least." He finally tore his eyes from the screen and looked at Nate first, and Ted second. "You guys got your second chance, but you don't have to deal with Connor's mom. It's easy."

Nate's jaw clenched, but he didn't argue.

"Same for you, Ted. Missy's dad isn't going to try to come get her. The dude's in prison now, and you and Emma are free to raise your family together. It will never be like that for me." If Martha stayed clean, she'd want to see the kids, and Dallas would let her. She'd be involved in his life, and his children's lives, and that meant Jess's life, if she chose to be with him.

"Maybe this *is* my second chance," Dallas said. "That's all I'm saying. I've got my kids. I have a great job that I like. I can get a house that's my own, and Thomas wants a dog, and I don't know." He shrugged and went back to flipping channels. "Maybe I don't get the happily-ever-after too."

Ted and Nate didn't argue. They didn't say anything, and Dallas found an NBA game and turned up the volume slightly. The three of them sat together, and it was comforting and serene.

An alarm on Nate's phone went off, and he groaned as he stood. "I have to get Connor to that birthday party."

Ted got up too. He took the box of doughnuts into the kitchen and turned to follow Nate. They both paused at the front door, where Dallas had waited to say goodbye to them.

"Slate's out in a couple of months," Dallas said. "He asked me to come pick him up. I think we should all go."

"When?" Ted asked. "He got his release date?"

"April sixth," Dallas said.

Nate and Ted both started swiping on their phones, and Ted answered first with, "Everything should be done and over for the wedding and the honeymoon."

"I can go," Nate said. "I'm going to have Ginger call about getting Luke to the ranch too. He's within six months, and maybe he can do the same program Teddy and I did."

"That's a great idea," Dallas said.

Nate clapped him on the shoulder and smiled. He took a step and then stopped. "Dallas, *everyone* has the chance for their happily-ever-after. The only way you're not going to get yours is if you don't take a chance and go after it."

Dallas didn't know what to say. Nate nodded and left, leaving Dallas to face Ted. "Is he right?"

"I have no idea," Ted said. "But Nate usually is. I got Emma a teacup piglet and M&M cookies. It wasn't fancy, but it meant something to her. All I had to do was show her I knew her, and I loved her. Everything else you can work on together."

Dallas nodded and held the door while Ted left too. He watched them go next door and get their kids—neither one of which actually came from their blood—and get loaded up in Nate's truck. He watched them back out of the driveway, and he waved to Connor through the back window.

"Daddy, look," Remmy said in her girlish drawl. "Mrs. Clyde showed me how to make banana bread today." She skipped toward him with two loaves, one in each hand, and pure joy on her face.

He blinked and saw the love on Jess's face while she'd interacted with Remmy yesterday. He'd seen it in Jess's eyes when she spoke with Thomas too.

"That's great, baby," he said, reaching for her as she came up the steps. "Bug, what's one of Jess's all-time favorite things?"

"Horses," Remmy said without even looking at him.

"Horses," Dallas echoed, wondering what in the world he could do with that to win her back. It certainly wasn't as easy as baking some cookies and buying a piglet.

CHAPTER TWENTY-TWO

Jess made sure she didn't cross through the riding pavilion in the afternoons again. She didn't need a repeat of the encounter with Dallas or Remmy. She held them both close to her heart, because she didn't know how to make them go away.

They simply wouldn't go away, and Jess knew she'd have to address that sooner or later.

She also knew what day she and Dallas had taken Martha to the treatment facility, and she should've been released by now. Jess's curiosity crept up a little bit more every day, but she didn't ask anyone.

Not Ted or Nate. Not Ginger or Emma. No one volunteered any information about Dallas, and Jess kept her mouth shut and her head down and did her job. The end.

A few days after Valentine's Day—where she'd worked

in the stables until night started to fall and then she'd gone to the West Wing and eaten steak sandwiches Hannah had brought back from town—Jess woke with the sun, as usual.

She thought about Hannah, and how Bill had been gone to his mother's for Valentine's Day, as she'd recently fallen and needed help until her hip surgery. Hannah had still gotten a card and a huge heart-shaped box of chocolates from the cowboy, and Jess had received nothing.

She showered and got dressed, as usual. She lingered on her cowgirl boots, as they were the pair she'd worn when she'd first met Dallas. They were almost to the point where she needed to throw them away and get new ones, but she'd kept holding onto them for some reason.

She poured herself a cup of coffee that Jill had likely made, and she buttered a single slice of toast before heading out the door. The ranch was beautiful in the morning, with a golden glow that Jess was convinced could only be seen in Texas. Everything in Montana was blue, but here, this close to the Gulf of Mexico, the sun turned everything to gold.

She breathed in the crisp air, as February and March were her favorite months in Texas. She felt her lungs expand and her spirits lift. Today was going to be a good day.

Midnight Madness had made amazing progress since he'd been delivered to Hope Eternal Ranch, and when she looked at the magnificent creature, she understood the meaning of hope. When she looked at herself, she wasn't sure she had anything left to hope for.

Pushing away the negative thoughts, she finished her coffee and tossed the paper cup into the recycling bin outside the stable. She almost always arrived first in the morning, and today was no different. She loved the stables when they only held the soft snufflings of dozens of horses and her own footsteps against the concrete.

Only a few steps inside today, though, and Jess paused. There was something wrong here. She first thought the air conditioner had gone on the fritz again, because everything was too quiet and too still.

But the cool kiss of air against her skin told her that the air conditioner was functioning. She cocked her head, listening.

The silence was absolute. There were no horse's hooves shuffling along in their stalls. No huffs or nickers. Not even any breathing.

Her heartbeat started to sprint, and that was all Jess could hear now. She hurried past the place where they kept the tack and feed to the first row of stalls.

All of the horses were gone.

She sucked in a breath as a scream built in her chest. Running now, she hurried to the next row over. No horses.

She ran through the whole stable, and she didn't find a single horse anywhere. Tears gathered in her eyes as she fumbled to get her phone out of her pocket. She didn't see Ginger in the West Wing anymore, as she and Nate lived in their own cabin now, but Jess knew she'd be awake.

She dropped her phone, her fingers trembling as the first tears streaked down her face. She'd never heard of a ranch getting robbed so completely, and all she could think about were the horses she'd befriended and trained over the years.

Diamond Valley.

Midnight Madness.

Marshmallow Crème.

Texas Tyrant.

Weeping Willow.

Noah's Ark—and that blasted horse had finally learned to leave his bandages alone.

Her chest pinched as Ginger's phone rang, and once again, Jess cocked her head. She could hear the line ringing in her ear...and nearby. Outside.

She strode that way, hearing someone say something on the other side of the door just before the call to Ginger disconnected. Jess paused, her heart pounding *and* sprinting now.

"What's going on?" she whispered to herself. Nothing else about this morning had been different or odd. "One way to find out."

She squared her shoulders and pushed through the doors that led west, out to the pastures and paddocks, the training circles and the arenas.

She didn't have to take more than two steps to find

what was going on, and she only took those because of her momentum.

Every single horse the ranch owned stood there, forming half of a box, all of them facing her. Instant relief painted her insides, and she quickly wiped her face clean of the evidence of her tears. She saw Spencer, Jack, Bill, Nick, Rich, Nate, Ted, and a few other cowboys. They were spaced every three or four horses. Hannah stood next to Noah's Ark, and Ginger had her hand on Midnight's neck. He nickered as if saying good morning to Jess, and through her confusion, she managed to smile.

"Why are all the horses out here?" Jess asked, but no one attempted to answer her. And not all the horses were out there. Diamond Valley was missing, as was Marshmallow Crème and one named Scalloped Potato.

She realized that almost every horse had been dressed up too. They wore ribbons and flowers in their manes, and a few even had neckties hanging from their necks.

The soft beating of horse's hooves met her ears, and Jess turned away from her horsed-off left and looked right, toward the sound.

More than one horse and rider were approaching, and if Jess had to guess, she'd land on the number three. Sure enough, Diamond Valley came into view, and her rider immediately pulled her to a stop.

Dallas sat in the saddle, wearing jeans, a bright blue shirt, and that delicious cowboy hat. Marshmallow Crème carried Remmy, and Scalloped Potato held Thomas.

Jess's throat closed, and she lifted her hand to it, as if she could knead it back into working order.

"Jessica Morales," Dallas said from atop that magnificent black and white horse. He'd somehow braided yellow and pink ribbons through the horse's mane, and Jess loved it. Marshmallow bore red roses, and they looked amazing with her creamy coat.

"I'm in love with you," he said next, and Jess sucked in a breath while several people standing by all the other horses sighed in happiness.

"You were right, you know. I wasn't ready for our new normal before. But I am now. I've been going to therapy and getting my priorities in line. My ex-wife is with her sister in another state." He glanced at Remmy first and then Thomas. They both looked at him, and then all three of them focused on Jess again.

"I don't have a whole lot to offer you," he said. "Just me and my kids. We found a really nice house, but we're afraid to buy it, because we want you to be happy in it." He swallowed, and his nerves struck her straight in the chest. "I'm hoping that you'll be like these amazing horses you tend to, and forgive me. Give me another shot. Let's try for *our* brand of normal. I promise you, Remmy, and Tommy will always be at the top of my list, and I promise you I'm ready for this."

He looked at Thomas, and the boy raised his hand. Jess watched as all the men and women Dallas had persuaded to go along with his plan reached into their pockets and pulled out hard candy. They crinkled the wrappers for the horses, and that really set some of them to talking.

They huffed and nickered, creating an applause of sorts that made Jess start to laugh. They got their rewards too, and Remmy called out, "Show 'er what you've got, horses."

The few she'd trained to go down on their front knee did, while others stood still while their humans slid signs from their backs to hang down from their necks. Each one had a letter on it, and together, the horses had made a sentence.

I'm sorry. We love you. Let's all try again and see if we can build a fam—

Jess had started on her far left and turned as her brain put the letters into words. She could fill in the last few letters, but then as she faced Thomas, Dallas, and Remmy, she didn't have to.

They each held up the last three letters, Remmy grinning like she'd just won a trip to Disneyland.

Thomas smiled too, but Dallas looked one second away from throwing up.

Jess sobbed, unable to keep her emotions in check for another second.

"Get to her," someone said, and the next thing she knew, Dallas gathered her into his arms and held her tight. He was strong when she was weak, and she'd been strong when he'd been weak. They complimented each other, and she didn't want a life without him.

She'd been living that life, and it was miserable, constrained to stables and a single bedroom. She wanted to *live*, and be out in the world, and experience everything with him at her side.

"I'm sorry," he whispered. "I'm sure you were panicked when you didn't find any horses inside."

She just shook her head and looked up at him. His light eyes searched hers, the hope burning in them so bright and so wonderful. "I really am ready," he said.

Jess nodded, tipping up onto her toes. She just needed to kiss him right now. Thankfully, he let her, and all the humans in the area started to cheer and clap. Jess laughed, so she didn't really get her kiss, and she tucked herself back into Dallas's chest.

He kept her close, his hands so big and so warm on her hip and shoulder. "All right, guys," he called. "I think it worked." The men in the crowd whooped again, and Dallas laughed. "Let's get the horses back where Jess wants them, okay? Thanks, everyone."

Jess looked at him again, marveling at his good heart. "You don't really play fair," she said.

"Don't I?" he asked innocently.

"No," she said as Ginger grinned at her and led Midnight Madness into the stable. "Using my horses against me. And your kids. Your kids *on* horses. That's so not fair."

"I miss you," he said, not seeming to care that other people could overhear him. "Do you really think we have a shot at a second chance?"

"Yes," she said without any hesitation. "I absolutely do, because I kinda fell in love with you too."

He blinked a couple of times before a smile filled his whole face. "Well, that's great news." He laughed, and so did Jess. He gestured for his kids to come over, and both Thomas and Remmy ran toward Jess.

She received them into a double-hug, telling them how much she missed them and loved them.

"So you'll come see the house, right?" Remmy asked, peering up at her. "It's so nice, Jess, and I think you're going to like it. Dad says there's this—"

"Remmy," Dallas said only a couple of feet away. "You agreed not to tell her."

"Oh, right." Remmy grinned at Jess. "You *have* to come see it though. Thomas is getting a dog, and it's got this huge yard, and they're going to build a big run back there for it. It's so big that Dad says I can get a cat too, and the dog won't even be able to find it."

"Wow," Jess said, grinning because so much hope and joy had filled her, and that made not smiling impossible to do. She met Dallas's eyes, and he shook his head.

"We're still working on how much Remmy talks," he said, drawing his daughter away from Jess. But Jess loved that Remmy loved to talk. She always had something interesting to say, and she found joy and cheer in the simplest of things.

"You two go take our horses to Rich," he said, going with them over to Diamond, Marshmallow, and Scalloped Potato. He gave two pairs of reins to Thomas and plucked a few roses from Marshmallow's mane.

With the kids gone and everyone else scattering with their horses, the world narrowed to just Jess and Dallas in the golden glow of the Texas sun. He fiddled with the roses in his hands, his head ducked down so the brim of his hat concealed his face.

"Everything I said was one-hundred percent true," he said. "I'm in love with you, and I'm ready to build a family with you." He looked up, the sincerity in his expression matching that in his voice. He handed her the small bouquet of red roses.

Jess took them, delicately smelling their sweet scent. "What I said was true too."

"The *kinda* fell in love part, or the part where you nodded and tried to kiss me." He smiled at her. "You didn't do a great job at that, by the way."

Jess smiled back at him. "I better fix it." She stretched up to kiss him, thrilled when he met her halfway. She took her time and really tried to tell him that there was no *kinda* involved in how she felt about him.

She pulled away several seconds later and said, "I love you, Dallas. I love your kids. I want to see the house, and I want to build a family and a future with you."

There was no *kinda* about that.

"Great," he murmured just before he kissed her again.

Jess realized as she kissed him back that she'd been right—today was a really great day.

When they parted this time, she asked, "How long did it take you to dress those horses up?"

"Hours," he said with a yawn. "So whether it was fair or not, it was definitely worth it."

CHAPTER TWENTY-THREE

Dallas herded his kids up the steps that went into the Annex, saying, "Don't do that, Tommy. The wedding is in fifteen minutes, and then you can take the tie off." His son had been tugging on his collar for the past thirty minutes since Dallas had helped him with it.

The noise inside the Annex hit Dallas like he'd run into a brick wall. All the men participating in Ted and Emma's wedding were gathering here, and cowboys weren't known for being terribly quiet when they got together. Because of that, no one paid much attention to Dallas as he entered the kitchen.

Thomas stayed right by his side, but Remmy went right into the fray, catching the attention of Nick, who scooped her up and handed her a baby carrot. She smiled at him, and he her, and Dallas was so glad he'd landed at Hope Eternal Ranch. Everyone here treated him like family, and they'd accepted him and his kids into their fold, no questions asked.

"Hiding out at the back of the room?" Nate asked, settling against the wall next to Dallas.

"Mm, yep." Dallas looked around at the other men in the kitchen, and he was surprised they'd been left alone with so much tasty-looking food on the trays littering the counter. No one tried to take any of the desserts though, and a roar rose up when Ted walked into the room, wearing a handsome tuxedo—and a cowboy hat.

Dallas grinned at him, and he waited his turn to hug Ted and wish him well. Once he'd gone around the room, he lifted both hands above his head. "All right, all right. Settle down, you lot. Are we ready?"

Another cheer went up, and Dallas took his son's hand and wove through the bodies to the back door. Nate and Connor joined him, as they'd be the first two to walk out behind Ted. They weren't having a very traditional wedding, just as Nate hadn't. At least they were having their meal after the nuptials had been completed.

Ted squeezed past Dallas and Nate and opened the back door. He went out onto the deck and looked left, toward the West Wing. The men continued to line up behind Dallas, and while the kitchen here was fairly big, he was starting to feel claustrophobic.

"Here we go, boys," Ted said over his shoulder. They quieted down, and Ted moved forward, freeing up some space for Nate to move into. Dallas followed him, still holding onto his son's hand.

"Remmy," he said over his shoulder, and the little girl skipped toward him. He took her hand too, just before they stepped onto the deck.

Ted kept his pace even and strong, and Dallas watched as a line of women walked across the cement and toward the Annex from the West Wing. Emma led them, carrying a massive bouquet of flowers in pale pink, coral, and yellow.

Ted met her at the bottom of the steps, and they linked arms. Right behind them walked Missy, along with the man and woman that had been raising her while Emma kept her hidden from her crime lord father.

Ginger was third in line, and she met Nate with a grin and a high five for Connor. They linked arms too, not breaking the processional as they continued across the grass toward the cabin where Emma lived.

A beautiful carved altar waited for them, half of the wood cleared of bark, polished, and gleaming in the spring sunlight. The other parts were still wild, with craggly bark where someone had stuck in a few more flowers that matched the ones in Emma's bouquet.

The pastor stood there, and empty rows of chairs waited for all the guests to arrive.

Dallas reached the bottom of the steps and looked at Jess. His beautiful, patient Jess. He was nowhere near ready to propose to her, but they'd been getting along really well in the past few weeks since he'd dressed up all her horses and used them to make up with her.

They'd gone to see the house he and the children had found, and she liked it as much as they did. Dallas had put in an offer on the house, and it had been accepted. He'd close in another ten days, and then, finally, he felt like a new brand of normal could begin.

Even as he thought it, he resisted. There was no normal. No set date for when it should begin. No event that would mark the end of abnormal and the beginning of something new. He just had to keep living each and every day to the best of his ability.

A wedding and marriage had been implied when they'd walked through the house with Jess, but he hadn't bought a ring yet. He was still getting to know Jess and all the things she liked and didn't like.

Ted and Emma reached the altar, and the rest of the crowd flowed around them, offering congratulations and shoulder pats as they did. They took their seats on the other side of the altar, and then the pastor and Ted and Emma switched places.

Dallas tried to imagine himself standing up in front of everyone and pledging himself to Jess. He'd been married before, and he knew what it took to get ready for a wedding. He knew what it felt like to have hundreds of eyes on him—heck, he'd endured that with the horse show he'd staged. He knew what it felt like to be so helplessly in love and to believe that the future held only rays of sunshine and magical unicorns.

He knew now that reality was very different than the wedding day. Yet, he still wanted to be standing at an altar like the one where Ted and Emma stood. He wanted to smile at Jess and find her the most beautiful woman in the world. He wanted to proclaim to everyone who could hear that he loved her.

He kept her hand secure in his, even when Remmy climbed on her lap and started whispering.

"Shh, baby," Jess said. "Ted and Emma are getting married." She pointed toward where they stood, only a few feet away. Last time Dallas had sat beside her at a wedding, she'd been texting. He'd sniped at her, but she'd been getting him a job at the ranch. The rest was history.

He leaned over to her as Ted started reciting his vows. "Could we maybe elope? Or have the wedding in Montana with just your family? I don't want a big to-do."

She tilted her head toward him, and she slid him a look out of the corner of her eye. "I've never been married, Dallas."

"You want a big wedding?"

"Not particularly, no," she said. "Now can you stop? This is *so* distracting."

He straightened as laughter built inside him. He held it back though his shoulders started to shake. He wasn't sure he'd make it through the ceremony, and he told himself not to ruin one of his best friend's wedding.

Finally, the pastor pronounced Ted and Emma husband and wife, and he clapped and cheered and laughed with everyone else.

Ted and Emma faced the crowd and raised their joined hands, both of them beaming for all they were worth. Ted's loud laughter filled the sky, and it filled Dallas's soul, the same way his infectious personality had while they'd served together in River Bay.

He faced her, and they shared a kiss. Dallas felt the love they had for one another, and when he looked at Jess and found her admiring them too, he felt the same adoration for her that he saw in Ted's face.

"What?" Jess asked, finally tearing her eyes from the happy bride and groom.

"You want to marry me, right?" he asked.

Her eyes widened. "Dallas, I—right now?"

"No," he said quickly. "I was just checking."

She put her arm around his waist and leaned into him. "I hope that wasn't the proposal," she said. "I really don't want to call my sister and say we got engaged while you were *just checking* to see if I'd marry you."

Dallas chuckled, but his throat felt a little too narrow. A proposal. That was obviously very important to Jess, and he couldn't mess that up.

He had some more research to do, and this time, he wasn't going to ask his seven-year-old for ideas.

"WHAT'S TAKING SO LONG?" DALLAS ASKED, PEERING through the windshield of Nate's truck. "Does it always take this long?"

"It's the BOP," Nate said without opening his eyes. "It's a hurry up and wait game."

Ted didn't even look up from his phone. Dallas had been back to River Bay a couple of times since the wedding, and he'd talked with Slate's lawyer, as well as Luke's. He'd signed to be the one to pick them up today, and they'd been waiting for half an hour after he'd checked in with the secretary so she'd know Slate and Luke had a ride.

"Could I just show her a diamond and ask her?" Dallas asked.

"No," Ted said in a deadpan, his attention still on his phone.

"I need help," Dallas said.

"No, you don't," Nate said.

He looked toward the doors, praying for any distraction he could. The only time he wasn't thinking about how to propose to Jess was when he was too busy. So he stayed as busy as he could, and he still didn't have a good idea for a proposal.

The doors opened, throwing sunlight into his eyes, and he opened the car door. "There they are." He practically jogged toward the two men walking toward him, and behind him, he heard Nate and Ted getting out of the truck too.

"Hey, hey," Slate said, plenty of swagger in his step. He laughed, and Dallas reached him first. They embraced, and Ted came up behind them and grabbed Luke in a hug.

Nate arrived, and everyone was laughing about their little band of brothers being back together again.

"I am so hungry," Luke said, and Dallas wasn't surprised at all. The man was always hungry. Jess liked everything but seafood, and Dallas thought maybe he could just ask her to dinner and present her with the ring.

He hadn't realized how much pressure he was under to produce the perfect proposal.

"Let's go to breakfast," Nate said, leading the group back to the truck.

"I have to be on the ranch by five o'clock," Luke said, and Dallas remembered that he wasn't quite a free man yet.

"How long?" Dallas asked.

"Three months," Luke said with a sigh. A smile followed, and he looked up into the sky. "Would you look at that? It's amazing how many clouds you can see when there aren't any fences in the way."

Dallas knew exactly how that felt. Everyone there did, and a sense of camaraderie descended upon them.

"Somewhere nice," Ted said. "I don't want fast food."

"That's what I got when Ginger picked me up," Nate said.

"And I'm sure it was just amazing," Ted said dryly.

"Somewhere nice. Let's try that Grits and Grub we passed on the way in."

"Your wish is my command," Nate said, and he got the truck moving.

"Okay, I need some fresh ideas," Dallas said, twisting in his seat to look at Luke and Slate in the back. They were both clean-shaven, as required in prison, and Slate watched him with eyes the same color as his name. Luke had piercing blue eyes, and they both looked at him, clearly eager to help.

"Dallas, I'm going to ask her for you," Ted said. "Just to get you to stop."

"Shh," Dallas said. "Don't listen to him." He grinned at Slate and Luke. "Say you had this amazing woman you were in love with. How would you ask her to marry you?"

"I'm calling her right now," Ted said, and he actually lifted his phone to his ear.

"Don't you dare," Dallas said, knocking the phone from his hand. The truck erupted after that, and Dallas ended up laughing while Nate yelled at them all to knock it off or he was going to pull the truck over and they wouldn't get any breakfast.

ANOTHER MONTH PASSED, AND DALLAS HAD FINALLY come up with an idea he hoped would work. He paced in the new house, which required more steps than his rental had to get from the front door to the back, while the line rang.

Finally, a woman answered with, "Hello?"

"Is this Abi?" he asked, his nerves practically searing through his brain.

"Yes," she said.

"This is Dallas Dreyer," he said. "I'm in love with your sister, and I need a really great way to ask her to marry me. I was hoping we could brainstorm a little bit...."

CHAPTER TWENTY-FOUR

J ess didn't drive her truck very often, especially because it tended to break down on her in the worst places. If she went in to see Dallas, she used a ranch truck. Sometimes, he drove her in so they could spend the evening together, and then he brought her back to the ranch.

The new house he'd bought was only a few miles from the ranch, on the far eastern edge of Sweet Water Falls, where Hope Eternal was too.

Today, though, she had an eye appointment, and all the trucks were being used. The boar hunt was on, and the ranch was extraordinarily busy.

Dallas said he'd checked her truck, and that while he could continue to patch her up, she was likely going to die in the next several months. She'd nodded and accepted the truck's fate, but she hadn't bought a new car yet.

She found the truck parked outside the stables, just like Dallas had promised. Upon opening the door, she froze at the scent that hit her in the face.

Someone had filled the truck cab with flowers. Roses, sunflowers, tulips, bluebonnets, poppies. A smile filled her face, and she reached for one of the delicate purple-blue flowers that symbolized Texas.

This had Dallas written all over it.

She found a yellow sticky note on the steering wheel, with a tiny smudge of grease in the corner. Also Dallas, and tears gathered in her eyes. The note read, *Jess, come "see" me when you get a sec, okay?*

Cheesy, but Jess peeled it from her steering wheel and pressed it to her heartbeat. He'd been leaving little things for her around the ranch for a solid month now. When she went to get reins for Midnight, she'd find a mini candy bar tucked between the ropes and wonder how long it had been there.

Once, she'd gone back to the West Wing for lunch and found a yellow sticky note like the one she held on her left-over box from their dinner the night before. It had simply said, *I love you, J. ~D*

She liked that she was in his thoughts, and that she was so prevalent that those thoughts became actions.

She looked over her shoulder to see if he was walking toward her, but he wasn't. She didn't want all of these flowers to wilt in the heat, and they would if she simply drove them to her eye appointment. After scooping as many as she could into her arms, she bustled into the stable and put them in the sink they used to clean the bottles for the babies. She ran cold water over them and let them rest there. In the air conditioned building, they'd be fine until she could put them in vases.

After her appointment, she walked around the stables, picking up anything she could find that would hold a flower. She put the ones she'd rescued in calf bottles, empty water bottles, flower pots, an old boot she'd found, and even an empty and rinsed can of soup.

She set them around the stables on the shelves and the tops of fridges. That way, she'd be able to see them and think of Dallas every time she did. Not that she needed a reminder to think of Dallas. The man made her feel like a queen, and she was beginning to wonder if she should ask *him* to marry *her*.

He'd asked her little questions here and there over the past couple of months since they'd gotten back together. Things like, *What ring size are you?* or *Would you even wear a big diamond while you work with the horses?*

She knew he was thinking about marriage and proposing. She just wasn't sure when that might happen. She understood Abi on a completely new level now, and as she left the newly decorated stables, she texted her sister.

How were you so patient with Huey? I feel like asking Dallas to marry me instead of waiting for him to get around to it.

Abi sent back a laughing GIF and then the words, *You*

sound like Nia. She's about ready to rent a sky plane and write JUST ASK ME ALREADY WALT above his farm.

Jess laughed, the sound free and easy. She hadn't always felt that way, and she was grateful that today, she did.

She entered the equipment shed through the tunnel and headed for Dallas's office, still engrossed in her texting conversation with her sister. Had she not been, she might have noticed how quiet the shop was today.

She finally did notice when she looked up and found Dallas leaning in the doorway to his office as if the frame needed him to hold it up. "Who are you talkin' to?" he asked in a real Texas twang.

"My sister." She pushed her phone into her pocket and looked around. "Where is everyone?"

"It's Friday afternoon," he said. "Ginger gave me permission to let them all off early."

Jess gaped at him. "You're kidding."

"When you're as organized and as caught up as we are, sometimes you get perks," he said with a smile. He reached for her, and added, "Did you like the flowers?"

She twined her fingers through his. "Yes, they were beautiful. I spread them out in the stables."

"I got you something else," he said, nodding behind her.

She turned and saw a small truck sitting there. Jess pulled in a breath, because that was not an old, beat-up truck. It wasn't new either, and it wasn't huge. But the mid-size vehicle gleamed like ivory, as it was cream-colored and very clean.

"What do you mean, you got me something else?" She looked from the truck back to him, having to move in a hundred and eighty degree line to do it.

"Luke's brother bought that truck, but he hates it. He gave it to Luke, but Luke doesn't need it. He said I could have it if I had use for it, and I said I did."

"So it was free," Jess said.

"I acquired it for very little," Dallas amended, leading her toward the truck. It was a king cab, with four doors, so she could put Remmy and Thomas in the back. All four of them could easily fit inside, and she ran her free fingers along the bed as he led her to the driver's seat.

"Just get in and try it," he said, opening the door for her.

Jess met his eyes briefly before getting behind the wheel. She saw the yellow sticky note on the radio screen, but she planted her hands on the wheel in proper driving position before she truly let herself read the words.

Look in the back seat.

Smiling, she twisted to look behind her.

"Surprise!" Remmy said, popping up and almost hitting Jess in the mouth. She giggled and handed Jess another envelope.

"What's this?" Jess asked her.

"I'm not allowed to say." Remmy sat down and

watched as Jess flipped over the envelope and out dropped the key to the truck.

Dallas hadn't closed the door, but Jess couldn't see him either. She got out of the truck, the key in her hand. He stood down at the tailgate with Thomas, both of them holding deep, luxurious red roses.

Jess hadn't known that roses were her love language until Dallas had started giving them to her. She held up the key, and he held up his rose.

Thomas came forward and handed her the rose he held without saying anything. Remmy climbed out of the truck, and the two children stood there and watched as Dallas dropped to both knees, that rose in his hand getting overshadowed by the little black jewelry box he'd procured from somewhere.

Jess pulled in a breath and held it. Her heart hammered in her chest, and everything seemed to be moving so fast now.

"Jess," he said calmly. "I love you, and my kids love you, and we want you to come live with us and be part of us. Will you marry me?"

She'd started nodding about halfway through, tears filling her eyes.

"Yay, yay, yay!" Remmy yelled, jumping up and down.

Jess stopped to kiss the top of her head and run her hand down the side of Thomas's face before she hurried into Dallas's waiting arms. "Yes," she whispered in his ear as she clung to him. "Yes, I'll marry you."

Dallas set her down as the kids came over. The four of them huddled together, and Dallas asked, "Who wants to tell her?" He looked at Remmy and then Thomas. "Not you, Remmy."

"Daddy—"

"Thomas is going to," Dallas said, silencing his daughter. She loved to talk so much, and Jess actually felt a little bad for her as her expression fell.

She looked at Thomas, who looked steadily back at her. "We want you to come be part of us real soon, Jess," he said. "So we're proposing a really fast engage-gage-ment." He looked at Dallas as he stumbled over the word.

Dallas nodded that he'd gotten it right, and Jess looked between the two of them.

"How fast?"

"You tell us how fast you can do it," Dallas said quietly. "We'll be ready."

Jess had no idea. She needed to call her mother. And talk to Ginger. And figure out what she needed to buy. Food. Flowers. A venue. Her mind raced, and she simply stared.

Then she closed her eyes, and she quieted the racing thoughts with one simple statement. *Help me to see what I should do here.*

She'd been working on listening and watching more, instead of panicking. Thinking things through instead of jumping to conclusions.

She did not need food or flowers. She didn't need a

venue—she could get married here on this ranch, or in that huge back yard of Dallas's, or on her father's ranch where she'd grown up.

She didn't need much. She needed the three people she stood with and a dress.

"Would you be willing to fly to Montana for the wedding?" she asked.

The three of them looked at each other, and the kids started nodding.

"I'll do what you want, Jess," Dallas said quietly. "But Luke can't travel until he's officially out, and that's not for two more months."

She nodded; she knew how important Dallas's friends were to him.

"Let's do it in the back yard," she said. "As soon as I can get my parents and sisters here."

"Really?" Dallas asked.

"Yes," Jess said. "You need something nice to wear, my cowboy mechanic." She kissed him, not caring that his kids stood there watching. She broke the connection early and looked at Thomas and Remmy. "You'll both need something nice too."

"We can get clothes," Dallas said. "I'll ask Ted about an altar too. See how fast he can do it."

"I'll need a dress," Jess said. "And my family here. I'll go call them right now."

Dallas nodded, and he started to take his kids back toward his office while Jess dialed her mother. "Jessie," her mom said, her voice full of light and energy. "What's up?"

"Mom," she said. "I just got engaged, and Dallas and I want to get married quickly. How soon can y'all get to Texas?"

"Engaged?" her mom repeated, the word full of air. "Clint, Jess is engaged and we need to get to Texas!" She squealed, and more screaming happened in the background. The phone went to speaker, and Jess laughed as her whole family celebrated with her over the line.

Her father finally said, "Jess, just tell us when. We've got guys we can call to work the ranch for a bit."

Jess turned toward the office again to find Dallas watching her. She started toward him, putting her phone on speaker too. "Well, you should come a couple of days early to actually meet Dallas," she said. "So how about three weeks from now?"

"Three weeks?" her mom asked at the same time Dallas's eyebrows went up. "Jess, that sounds crazy."

"Does it?" Jess looked right into those light eyes of Dallas's as she said, "Well, I only need Dallas, Remmy, and Thomas there. I need a dress, which I can get tomorrow. And I need you guys there. Doesn't sound crazy."

"Three weeks," her mom said again.

"We'll be there," her dad said. "We love you, Jess." Choruses of the same came from her sisters, and Jess repeated them back. She hung up, still looking at Dallas.

"Three weeks," she said. "Too long?"

"Yes," he said, gathering her into his arms. "About three weeks too long." He chuckled and swayed with her, finally pulling back. "But seriously, it's great." He leaned down and kissed her, and Jess had never kissed a man she loved as much as Dallas. She'd never kissed a man who loved her as much as he did. She'd never kissed her fiancé before.

She enjoyed every second of it, and when he finally pulled away, she said, "I love you so much, Dallas."

"I know," he said. "That's what's crazy."

They laughed lightly together, and then he added, "I love you, too, Jess."

Read on for a sneak peek at Jess and Dallas's wedding, as told by Slate Sanders, your next cowboy hero in

CHRISTMAS COWBOY!

SNEAK PEEK! CHRISTMAS COWBOY
CHAPTER ONE

S late Sanders drove down the highway next to the Gulf of Mexico, the window down as the sun came up. The scent of the beach and seaweed touched his nose every so often, and he couldn't wipe the smile from his face.

He'd spent four years behind the fences and walls of River Bay Federal Correctional Facility. He hadn't had a girlfriend or a wife when he'd gone into prison, and he hadn't thought he wanted one now that he was out.

Images of Nate and Ginger walking hand-in-hand, their heads bent together, flowed through his mind. He then remembered the way Ted and Emma sat on the back porch of their cabin, the love between them real and infectious.

Maybe Slate had been bit. Maybe he wanted to meet someone who would make his heart feel less like a black stone and more like a vital human organ. Maybe he could if he didn't literally run away from every female he laid eyes on.

He'd been at Hope Eternal Ranch for almost two months, and he still hadn't said more than hello to any of the women who worked there. A few women lived next door in the West Wing, but Slate never went there. More women worked out on the ranch, with the horseback riding lessons, or with other chores. He kept his head down and hadn't spoken to any of them either.

He wasn't sure why, other than he wasn't sure Hope Eternal was his final landing place. He couldn't go back to banking, but he wasn't as keen to grab onto the cowboy lifestyle with both hands the way Nate, Ted, and Dallas had.

The three of them never went anywhere without their cowboy hats and boots, and they fit right in on this ranch. Slate hadn't fit in anywhere, except with the other junkies.

"Can't go back there," he told himself. He absolutely would not go back to Austin, where he could easily slip back into the businessmen underground, where professionals worked their day jobs and then partied all night.

His phone rang, and Slate reached for it. Nate's name sat on the screen, and Slate slowed down to pull over. The truck he'd been able to get wasn't new or fancy, like the one Nate drove, and he couldn't talk without holding the phone to his ear.

"Hey," he answered as he pulled to the side of the road.

"Where are you?"

"Just driving."

"You're not going north, are you?"

Slate rolled his eyes, glad this wasn't a video call. "No, Dad," he said.

Nate didn't laugh, sigh, or otherwise make any noise. He did say, "Ted worries about you when you leave before dawn."

"Ted does, huh?"

"We all do," Nate said.

"I'm clean," Slate said. "I haven't touched drugs in over four years, Nate."

"I know that," he said. "I also know, as does Dallas, how loud the call of addictive substances can be. We love you, and we want you to be happy."

"I'm just driving by the water," Slate said, looking over to it. "I like the water."

"Yeah," Nate said. Several moments of silence went by, and then he added, "It's Sunday, and that means we'll have breakfast at the West Wing."

"Yeah, I know about it," Slate said.

"You've never come."

"No, I haven't." Slate didn't explain further. He'd only been twenty-nine when he'd gone into prison, and he'd only had a couple of girlfriends in his life at all. Once the drugs had taken center stage in his life, Slate didn't care about anything or anyone else.

He needed something else to focus on, but Slate had never felt so lost.

"I'll let you go," Nate said. "Just...call one of us if you need us, okay?"

"Okay," Slate said. He stayed in the truck for another minute, and then he eased back onto the road and pulled over into a parking lot at a beach. One other car sat there, and Slate barely gave it a glance as he got out of his vehicle. The warmth of the sun never really went away in Texas, but the morning was definitely the best time to find a whisper of cool air.

He went down the wooden steps to the sand, trying to remember who he was. Thinking about who he was five years ago, before everything had gone down at the bank, was like trying to think about someone else. Trying to live someone else's life, with memories that didn't fit who he was now. There was nothing to remember about who he was, because he wasn't that man anymore.

The wind picked up, and Slate ran one hand through his hair, thinking he'd like to grow it out as long as he could stand it. Then, and only then, would he cut it. Since he'd been out for a couple of months now, his hair had grown quite a bit, but Slate still didn't feel the need to cut it.

He went all the way to the water's edge, the horizon made only of waves and sunshine. He bent down and touched the gulf, feeling the power of the earth and the water all at the same time. In that moment, he knew he should get a job where he got to work outside, and another heartbeat later, he realized he already had a job like that if he wanted to keep it.

A sense of peace and serenity washed over him, and while he didn't have all the answers for his future, he at least felt like he could start making new memories for the new man he was.

A woman screamed, startling him and breaking into his little bubble of reflection. He stood and looked left, toward the sound.

A woman ran toward the water dozens of yards down the beach, and another primal yell ripped from her throat as she threw something into the water.

Slate wasn't sure if he should go make sure she was okay or just walk away. He watched as she bent and picked up something else from the beach. She screamed as she hurled it into the ocean too.

Without thinking too hard about it, Slate started walking toward her. She seemed like she could use a friend—or at least someone to help her if she threw herself into the ocean next.

As he got closer, she started yelling, and while Slate couldn't catch all of the words, he got the general idea. Someone in her family was very sick, and she'd come to the beach to release her frustrations at the injustices of the world.

Slate slowed, suddenly not wanting to intrude. He

knew exactly how she felt, though he'd learned to control and contain the rage and irritation while behind bars. He could box up everything and keep it silent. He could stare at the bottom of a bunk bed and let his thoughts run until he fell asleep, never saying anything to anyone.

Only Nate knew what Slate really thought. Then when he'd left, Ted. Dallas. Luke.

He needed to get back to the ranch.

The woman turned toward him, and Slate froze. He knew her, and his stomach dropped to his shoes before it rebounded back to its proper place. "Jill?" he asked.

She sobbed and flew toward him so quickly that Slate barely had time to open his arms before she latched onto him. He wrapped her up tight, her anguish seeping right into the fleshy parts of his heart and making him close his eyes and pray for her relief.

Twenty minutes later, he helped Jill into the front seat of his truck with a, "There you go. Yep, you're good." He met her eye again and closed the door before going around to get behind the wheel.

"I'm sorry," she said, wiping her eyes again. "I was just on my way back to the ranch, and I started crying, and...." Her voice trailed off, and she shook her head.

"You don't owe me any explanations," he said quietly.

"What did you hear on the beach?"

"Nothing much," he said. "Combined with the waves, it was just noise."

Jill nodded, the longer front pieces of her hair flopping a little bit. She sniffed as she pushed it off her forehead and tucked her hair behind her ears. "My mother is very sick," she said. "I am very angry at God about it."

Pure surprise flowed through Slate, and his eyebrows went up as their eyes met. "I can imagine," he said. "In fact, I don't have to imagine." He looked back out the windshield. "I have been very angry at God about things before." By the time he finished speaking, his voice was at whisper level. "Very angry at myself too."

Jill nodded and wiped her face again.

"I think there are some napkins in the glove box," he said.

She opened it and pulled out a couple of the scratchy, brown napkins Slate had gotten at some fast food restaurant. "Thanks." She wiped her nose and eyes and drew in a long, deep breath. She held it for so long that Slate thought he might have to perform some sort of rescue procedure this morning after all.

She finally released it and said, "I think I can drive back now."

"Okay," he said, flipping the truck into reverse.

"No, I meant I can drive myself."

"That's not happening," he said. "I've been precisely where you are, and you're just on the top of the roller coaster right now. There's another dip coming, unfortunately." He glanced at her as he pulled up to the highway. "How long have you known about your mother?"

"I just found out this weekend," she said, her voice pitching up on the last word. "She's a fighter. She's going to be okay."

Slate liked the optimism, but he also knew that sometimes things were not okay. He said nothing, though, because Jill deserved to cling to that hope and positivity if she chose to.

After a couple of minutes, he said, "I can bring someone to get your car any time."

"Thank you, Slate," she said, and he did like the way his name rolled out of her mouth.

"How long have you worked at the ranch?" he asked.

"Seven or eight years," she said. "Are you going to stay? Ginger has mentioned that you're up in the air."

"Yeah," Slate said. "That about sums up my whole life right now." It had all gotten tossed up into the air, and he had no idea where all the pieces would end up falling. He looked at her and found her with her head leaned back against the rest, turned toward him.

She had pretty blue eyes, even watery as they were, and her hair was a messy kind of short style she could muss up with her fingers and it would look better than before.

"Have you ever felt like that?" he asked, looking out the windshield again so he didn't drive them into the gulf.

"Like what?"

"Up in the air."

"No," she said quietly. "That's probably why I'm handling this diagnosis so badly." She half scoffed and half sobbed. "That's what my sister says, at least."

"How old is your sister?"

"The oldest one is forty, and she's, you know, perfect. Perfect husband, with the perfect job. Two perfect kids, perfectly balanced with a boy and a girl." She exhaled and wiped her face with the napkin again.

"I know the type," he said, seeing the family perfectly in his mind's eye. "That was my family growing up."

Jill sucked in a tight breath. "Oh."

"I'm not offended," Slate assured her quickly. "I just... know the type." He looked out his window at the gulf again, wishing he had the guts to call his parents and let them know he was out. The fact that they didn't know spoke volumes about their relationship, but Slate wondered if the new version of himself could try again to be the son they wanted.

The miles passed in silence after that, and after a few minutes, Slate looked over to find Jill leaning against the window, fast asleep. His heart went out to her, because he understood what it felt like to go through trauma and the sheer exhaustion that caused.

He wanted to protect her from the tumultuous times ahead, but he knew he couldn't. He'd learned to release the things he couldn't control in prison, and he couldn't control her mother's health.

When he turned onto the ranch and bumped from a smooth road to a dirt one, Jill jostled and woke.

"We're back," he said softly. "I'm sure they still have breakfast going in the West Wing if you want to eat."

Jill wiped her hair back again and glanced around. "I'm sorry I fell asleep."

"Don't be." He pulled into the gravel lot and parked. Neither of them got out of the truck. "You should probably eat something."

She looked at him, and Slate turned his head toward her. She was a beautiful woman, and his pulse performed a weird flip in his chest. He had no idea what it meant, only that he couldn't look away from Jill, almost like her gaze had become a tractor beam, and he'd gotten stuck in it.

"Will you come with me?" she asked. "I don't want to go in alone."

Slate didn't understand why. She'd lived here for years, and with one look at her, all of her friends would rally around her. They'd provide the support she needed, and Slate would disappear into the background.

He knew, because he'd seen the women here at Hope Eternal Ranch do that for each other several times in the short time he'd been there.

"Okay," he said anyway. "But I can't stay long. I have to get out to the...." He let his sentence die, because it was Sunday, and he didn't have to get out to the fields that day.

He had no reason why he couldn't accompany Jill to breakfast and then spend the rest of the day with her too.

No reason except the fear pounding through his bloodstream at the very thought of walking into the West Wing and eating breakfast with everyone on the ranch.

Jill Kyle shimmied into the pale blue bridesmaid dress, frustrated at herself for the extra few pounds she carried. A month ago, she wouldn't have the extra curve in her hip, but she'd had a very trying couple of weeks, and she'd been coping with her stress by eating.

Her kryptonite was ice cream and potato chips, and she'd been drinking a protein shake for lunch while carrying a bag of chips at the same time.

"You're stunning," Hannah said, and Jill turned toward her.

"You're joking," she said, taking in Hannah's much taller frame and much trimmer waistline. "I can't even zip this thing up."

"I can." Hannah stepped over to her, bringing the soft scent of a rosy perfume that Bill had given her. The zipper went right up, and Jill could still breathe. That was a win in her book, and she had something to put in her gratitude journal that night.

Jess and Dallas were getting married today, so she should probably put something like, *I got to watch one of my best friends marry the man she loves*, in her gratitude journal. She was grateful for that, and she decided to save the zipper for a day when she literally couldn't find anything to express her gratitude.

Hannah wrapped her in a hug, and Jill turned to return the embrace. "How are you today?" Hannah asked.

She searched her emotions, and thankfully, she'd found some stable ground. "I'm okay," Jill said honestly. She wasn't alone, and that helped immensely. She lived about twenty-five minutes away from where her parents did, and Ginger had been more than accommodating with Jill's requests to be there when her mom went to her doctor's appointments, and when she got home from the first round of chemotherapy.

Daddy was taking good care of her, and Jill's youngest sibling, McKenna, lived in Sugar Hill, so she'd been able to help a lot too. Haven, the oldest, lived thirty minutes in the opposite direction of Jill, and she'd been present at everything Jill was. Probably more, because Haven was the most perfect at everything.

Their brother had come to what he could, but he lived in Oklahoma now, and he had a wife and family there, along with an important job he couldn't just leave whenever he wanted.

"We better get going," Hannah said. "We don't want to be late." She slipped out of Jill's bedroom and down the hall to hers while Jill moved over to the closet to find her shoes.

Jess and Dallas were getting married in their backyard, and they were having the most traditional ceremony of anyone who'd been married in the past year. Jess was still going to ride her horse down the aisle, but then they'd have a traditional wedding dinner and dance following the nuptials.

Her parents had been in town for a week, and Jill already missed her sassy and strong presence around the ranch while she'd been off entertaining them and finalizing details for the wedding. She and her dad had come to the West Wing yesterday, and together, the two of them had cleaned out the bedroom where she'd lived for twice as long as Jill had been at the ranch.

Jess was still going to work at Hope Eternal Ranch, so Jill would get to see her. She knew it wouldn't be the same, because when change happened, things simply weren't the same anymore.

She put on her shoes, wishing it was as easy to slip on a smile. Stopping in front of the mirror mounted to the back of her closet door, Jill tried on her smile. It looked surprisingly real, and she paid attention to how it pulled, and how her muscles in her face felt. If she could just get through the next few hours with this smile in place, she could retreat to the safety of her bedroom and text her father to find out how Momma was doing.

She met Hannah and Michelle in the hallway, and the three of them walked into the kitchen one after the other. Jill remembered she couldn't go anywhere without Chapstick and detoured over to the drawer beneath the microwave, where they kept several tubes of the stuff. She slathered up her lips and tucked the tube into her bra before following the other girls out the door that led into the garage.

Michelle almost always parked in the garage, because she only lived at the homestead part-time. She came to the ranch about once a week to meet with Ginger, talk about the prisoners they had there, and offer other legal advice to keep the ranch in the clear. She had a bedroom here, because there was enough room—especially now that Emma, Ginger, and Jess had all vacated their rooms—and because she often came in the evenings after she finished her work in San Antonio, which was a two-hour drive from Sweet Water Falls.

She'd come on Thursday night and stayed until Sunday, and Jill had been crossing her path at odd hours as she did left the ranch when Michelle was arriving.

Her sleek, dark eggplant SUV sat just steps away from the entrance to the West Wing, and Jill rounded the hood to get in the passenger seat. She glanced to the back deck that extended off the Annex, and she found Slate leaning against the railing, looking out over the ranch.

He wore a dark suit that fit him like a glove, and coupled with that cowboy hat...Jill's pulse went crazy. She'd vowed not to date anyone for a while after her last boyfriend—a man she'd met at Nate and Ginger's wedding —had cited the reason for their break-up to be the distance between them.

Physical distance, he'd meant, and the drive was eighteen minutes.

Jill knew it was something else, but Mike had refused to say what. She'd decided she'd had enough of flirting and flitting from man to man. She was thirty-three years old now, and she was going to take her relationships more seriously. That way, maybe the men she dated would take her more seriously.

"Slate," she called, though she hadn't expressly told herself to speak. The faux cowboy turned toward her, his face a stoic mask until he recognized her. Then he lit up, and Jill wondered if that meant something.

It doesn't, she told herself.

He'd been extremely kind to her a couple of weeks ago, and Jill had not forgotten it. She'd been a complete mess, about to launch herself into the ocean waves and tell God to take her instead of her mother. Slate had been there, and he'd calmed her enough to get her into his truck. He'd spoken to her like her feelings and actions were normal, that she wasn't the only one who felt the way she did, and that she didn't need to apologize for the emotions raging through her.

Haven had scolded Jill about "falling apart" in front of their mother, and to "have more faith" to see them all through this crisis.

Jill wasn't even sure what that meant. All she knew was that she'd had plenty of faith about a lot of things in her life, and God did what He wanted to do anyway. What was the point of pouring her heart out to Him? Why should she kneel beside the bed and beg, plead, and cry, only to do it again the next night? And then the next. And the next.

She felt abandoned, and that morning at the beach had been the worst bout of abandonment of all.

Then Slate Sanders had been here, and while Jill had met him once and seen him around the ranch a couple of times, she didn't know him.

"Hey," he said easily, coming toward her though he remained on the deck. His smile was hitched in place too. Jill wondered if he'd looked in the mirror and memorized how it should feel on his face the way she had. "You ladies heading out for the wedding?"

"Yeah." Jill indicated the car. "Do you need a ride?"

"Nah," he said. "I'm waiting for Luke and Ted. We're going together."

Jill frowned, a conversation from last night's dinner tickling her memory. "You sure? Ted said he was going with Nate, I thought."

Slate frowned and looked toward the back door. "I guess I better find out."

"Do you want us to wait?" She knew the rules with the men who came to Hope Eternal Ranch in the Residential Reentry Program. Slate wasn't in that program; his sentence was complete. But Luke was, and that meant that he couldn't leave the ranch by himself. He had to be with a ranch employee, and Jill wondered if Slate counted.

He just likes to drive by the beach. Nate's words moved through her head. He'd been worried about Slate the past few weeks—worried that he'd get in his truck, start driving, and never come back.

"Maybe," Slate said. "Give me a minute, okay?" He strode away, and Jill could admit she liked the breadth of his shoulders in that suit coat. Wow, she thought. Tall, trim, tan Slate Sanders. A month ago, had she seen him like this, she'd have sidled up to him at the wedding and tried to get to know him better.

Now, her heart resisted what would come so naturally to her.

Jill loved people, and she'd always enjoyed talking to them, getting to know them, and spending time with them. She was no good alone, and she was usually the last one to go to bed, as she stayed up with whoever was willing to sit with her so she didn't have to be alone.

"Jill," Michelle said. "We don't want to be late."

"I'm not sure Slate and Luke have a ride," she said. "He said he needed a minute." She looked back to the deck, but Slate had gone inside the Annex, and he hadn't returned yet. "You guys can go. I can drive them in a ranch truck."

"Are you sure?" Hannah asked, getting out of the back seat. She looked at Michelle and then back to Jill.

"Yeah, sure," Jill said easily, and her pulse started an increased rhythm.

"They won't start without Luke and Slate," Hannah reasoned. "They're two of Dallas's best friends."

"We can wait," Michelle said. "Because she has a point."

"You can ride in the front," Jill said to Hannah.

"I'm fine." Their eyes met, and Jill had never had to spell out much for Hannah. She must've been able to say she had some sort of insane crush on Slate, because Hannah just nodded. "I do need to fix my mascara, and I can use the mirror in the front." She went around the back of the car and got in the front seat.

Slate came out onto the deck. "Can we ride with you guys? Ted left a while ago." He didn't look happy about it either, and Jill didn't blame him.

"Sure," she said. "We have room."

Luke came outside too, and Jill seriously doubted they'd fit in the back seat of Michelle's SUV. They had shoulders Jill had never seen, and she knew all the River Bay men met in the equipment shed at six-thirty to lift weights, something they'd apparently done together in prison.

Slate arrived at her side, and Jill smiled at him. "I'll

ride on the hump in the middle. You scoot on over, cowboy."

He grinned and reached up to touch his hat. "Do you really think I look like a cowboy?"

"You certainly do," she said. "I'm not sure if you are one, but you look the part."

"Good," he said, and he slid all the way over behind Michelle. Jill gathered up her skirt and got in the car too, sliding over into the middle spot. Luke managed to cram himself in next to her and close the door, and that alone was a miracle.

"All right," Michelle said. "Are we all in?"

"Yes," Luke said, and Jill looked at him. He was a handsome man too, and he'd started to grow a beard the same way Slate had. She smiled at him, and he smiled back at her before looking out his window.

Her pulse didn't react, and she knew he wasn't the one she'd spend her time with at this wedding. She didn't even dare look at Slate, because her hip was pressed into his, and her thigh too, and the entire left side of her body tingled with his touch.

He cleared his throat, and Jill glanced at him. "Do you have enough room?" he asked, moving his right leg over a little. "You can put your foot over here."

"Thanks," she said, and she did adjust her leg so it wasn't so tightly crammed into the back of the console between Hannah and Michelle. She smoothed down her skirt so her legs were properly covered and listened as

Hannah and Michelle started talking about the cooking show they'd watched last night.

With the radio playing, and conversations happening, Jill looked at Slate again. "Have you decided if you're going to stay at Hope Eternal?"

He shook his head, his slate-gray eyes still sparkling under that cowboy hat. "What do you think? Should I?"

"Do you hate it?"

"No."

"Do you like it?"

"You know what? I actually do."

Jill looked up at the charcoal-colored cowboy hat. "I mean, the hat fits, right?" She smiled, and it was easier than the one she'd practiced in the bedroom. The smile she could give him felt as easy as the flirty ones she'd doled out at the previous weddings she'd attended.

"So you're saying if the boot fits, wear it?"

"Sure," she said. "You have a nice room here. The Annex is big and air conditioned. You like the job. You look the part." She reached over and smoothed down his tie from where it had stuck on his lapel. Something hot and charged zinged through her, and her eyes immediately went back to Slate's.

He'd felt that, Jill could tell. She could no longer hear Hannah and Michelle talking, and if there was music playing, it wasn't reaching her ears.

"Okay," Slate said. "I'll stay." He shifted his shoulders so he could lean his head closer to hers. She actually leaned into him too, ducking her head so he could whisper in her ear. His hand landed on her knee, and Jill pulled in a breath as sparks shot up her leg and down to her toes.

"For you, Jill," he said. "I'll stay for you." He took her hand in his then, and his was so much bigger than hers. Warm, and large, and everything a cowboy's hand should be. Jill *loved* holding hands with a cowboy, and she smiled to herself as he settled their joined hands on his leg and looked out his window, the conversation obviously done.

The conversation her heart was pounding out to her brain wasn't done, but Jill didn't even listen to the two of them. She closed her eyes and leaned against Slate's shoulder, her fingers twined nice and tight with his.

Oooh, find out if staying at Hope Eternal Ranch for Jill is the right thing for Slate to do. **Read CHRISTMAS COWBOY today, it's available in paperback!**

BOOKS IN THE HOPE ETERNAL RANCH ROMANCE SERIES

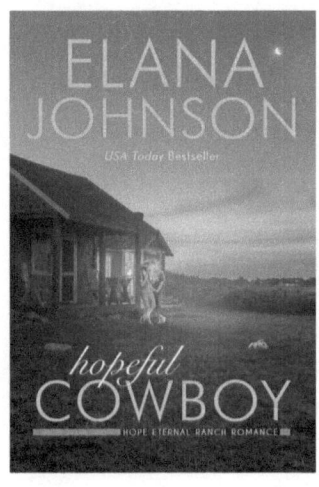

Hopeful Cowboy, Book 1: Can Ginger and Nate find their happily-ever-after, keep up their duties on the ranch, and build a family? Or will the risk be too great for them both?

Overprotective Cowboy, Book 2: Can Ted and Emma face their pasts so they can truly be ready to step into the future together? Or will everything between them fall apart once the truth comes out?

Rugged Cowboy, Book 3:
He's a cowboy mechanic with two kids and an ex-wife on the run. She connects better to horses than humans. Can Dallas and Jess find their way to each other at Hope Eternal Ranch?

Christmas Cowboy, Book 4: He needs to start a new story for his life. She's dealing with a lot of family issues. This Christmas, can Slate and Jill find solace in each other at Hope Eternal Ranch?

Wishful Cowboy, Book 5: He needs somewhere to belong. She has a heart as wide as the Texas sky. Can Luke and Hannah find their one true love in each other?

Risky Cowboy, Book 6: She's tired of making cheese and ice cream on her family's dairy farm, but when the cowboy hired to replace her turns out to be an ex-boyfriend, Clarissa suddenly isn't so sure about leaving town... Will Spencer risk it all to convince Clarissa to stay and give him a second chance?

Grumpy Cowboy, Book 2: He can find the negative in any situation. Like that time he got upset with the woman who brought him a free chocolate-and-caramel-covered apple because it had melted in his truck... Can William and Gretchen start over and make a healthy relationship after it's started to wilt?

Surly Cowboy, Book 3: He's got a reputation to uphold and he's not all that amused the way regular people are. Like that time he stood there straight-faced and silent while everyone else in the audience cheered and clapped for that educational demo... Can Lee and Rosalie let bygones be bygones and make a family filled with joy?

Salty Cowboy, Book 4: The last Cooper sibling is looking for love...she just wishes it wouldn't be in her hometown, or with the saltiest cowboy on the planet. But something about Jed Forrester has Cherry all a-flutter, and he'll be darned if he's going to let her get away. But Jed may have met his match when it comes to his quick tongue and salty attitude...

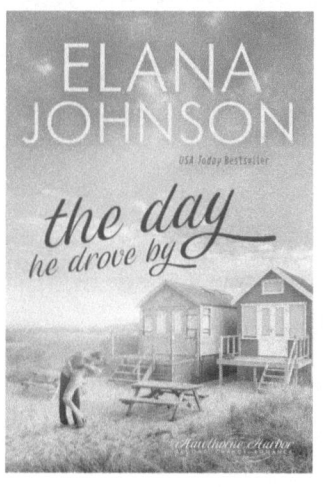

The Day He Drove By (Hawthorne Harbor Second Chance Romance, Book 1): A widowed florist, her ten-year-old daughter, and the paramedic who delivered the girl a decade earlier...

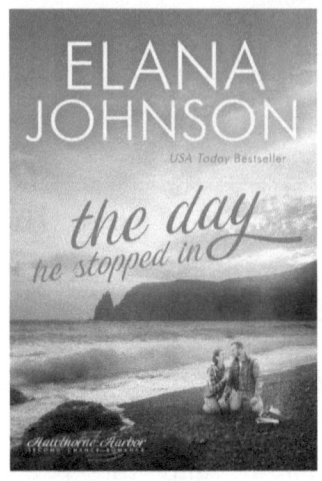

The Day He Stopped In (Hawthorne Harbor Second Chance Romance, Book 2): Janey Germaine is tired of entertaining tourists in Olympic National Park all day and trying to keep her twelve-year-old son occupied at night. When longtime friend and the Chief of Police, Adam Herrin, offers to take the boy on a ride-along one fall evening, Janey starts to see him in a different light. Do they have the courage to take their relationship out of the friend zone?

The Day He Said Hello (Hawthorne Harbor Second Chance Romance, Book 3): Bennett Patterson is content with his boring firefighting job and his big great dane...until he comes face-toface with his high school girlfriend, Jennie Zimmerman, who swore she'd never return to Hawthorne Harbor. Can they rekindle their old flame? Or will their opposite personalities keep them apart?

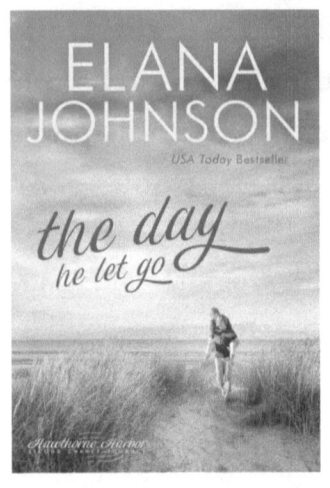

The Day He Let Go (Hawthorne Harbor Second Chance Romance, Book 4): Trent Baker is ready for another relationship, and he's hopeful he can find someone who wants him and to be a mother to his son. Lauren Michaels runs her own general contract company, and she's never thought she has a maternal bone in her body. But when she gets a second chance with the handsome K9 cop who blew her off when she first came to town, she can't say no... Can Trent and Lauren make their differences into strengths and build a family?

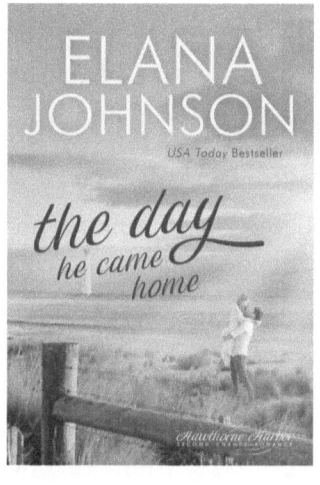

The Day He Came Home (Hawthorne Harbor Second Chance Romance, Book 5): A wounded Marine returns to Hawthorne Harbor years after the woman he was married to for exactly one week before she got an annulment...and then a baby nine months later. Can Hunter and Alice make a family out of past heartache?

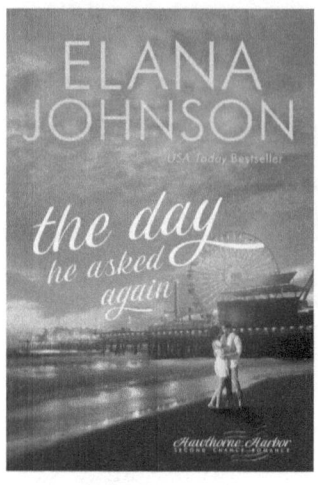

The Day He Asked Again (Hawthorne Harbor Second Chance Romance, Book 6): A Coast Guard captain would rather spend his time on the sea...unless he's with the woman he's been crushing on for months. Can Brooklynn and Dave make their second chance stick?

BOOKS IN THE CARTER'S COVE ROMANCE SERIES

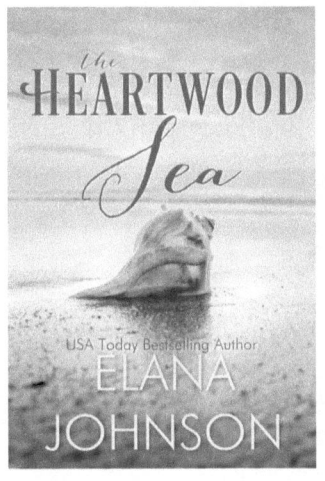

The Heartwood Sea (Book 1): She owns The Heartwood Inn. He needs the land the inn sits on to impress his boss. Neither one of them will give an inch. But will they give each other their hearts?

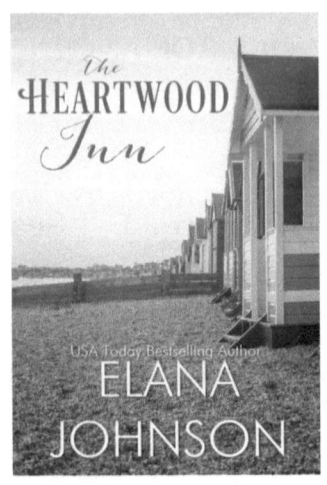

The Heartwood Inn (Book 2): She's excited to have a neighbor across the hall. He's got secrets he can never tell her. Will Olympia find a way to leave her past where it belongs so she can have a future with Chet?

The Heartwood Beach (Book 3): She's got a stalker. He's got a loud bark. Can Sheryl tame her bodyguard into a boyfriend?

The Heartwood Wedding (Book 4): He needs a reason not to go out with a journalist. She'd like a guaranteed date for the summer. They don't get along, so keeping Brad in the not-her-real-fiancé category should be easy for Celeste. Totally easy.

The Heartwood Chef (Book 5): They've been out before, and now they work in the same kitchen at The Heartwood Inn. Gwen isn't interested in getting anything filleted but fish, because Teagan's broken her heart before... Can Teagan and Gwen manage their professional relationship without letting feelings get in the way?

ABOUT ELANA

Elana Johnson is the USA Today bestselling author of dozens of clean and wholesome contemporary romance novels. She lives in Utah, where she mothers two fur babies, taxis her daughter to theater several times a week, and eats a lot of Ferrero Rocher while writing. Find her on her website at feelgoodfictionbooks.com